NEW BEGINNINGS AT ROSEFORD HALL

FAY KEENAN

Boldwood

First published in Great Britain in 2022 by Boldwood Books Ltd.

Cover Design by Alice Moore Design

Cover Photography: Shutterstock

A CIP catalogue record for this book is available from the British Library.

Paperback ISBN 978-1-83889-026-1

Large Print ISBN 978-1-83889-673-7

Hardback ISBN 978-1-80415-958-3

Ebook ISBN 978-1-83889-028-5

Kindle ISBN 978-1-83889-027-8

Audio CD ISBN 978-1-83889-024-7

MP3 CD ISBN 978-1-83889-670-6

Digital audio download ISBN 978-1-83889-025-4

Boldwood Books Ltd
23 Bowerdean Street
London SW6 3TN
www.boldwoodbooks.com

1

_____

As Stella Simpson pressed 'Send' on the covering email for yet another story for the online news and entertainment website AllFeed, she turned up the music in her noise-cancelling head-phones. The ungodly racket coming from the rooms below her was reduced to a dull whine as the far more soothing sounds of the Vitamin String Quartet reverberated through her tired mind.

One day, she thought irritably, my mother will realise that working from home is more than just an excuse to drink coffee and doomscroll Twitter all day.

Turning back to her spiral-bound notebook, where she'd jotted down a few ideas about how to tackle the next story on the enor-mous list, which, like the previous one, had a deadline of the end of the business day in California, where the main AllFeed offices were based, she pushed her thick dark-framed glasses further up the bridge of her nose and sighed.

When Stella had graduated from Oxford with a first in English, she'd entertained fanciful notions of writing novels for a living, but soon realised that she'd need a day job to indulge that passion, at least to begin with. Shortly after that, the job as a junior writer at

AllFeed had come up, and she'd jumped at the chance to learn her craft, hone her skills and hopefully make some connections in the publishing world. Alas, five years of writing opinion pieces on who wore what to where, and top ten lists of everything you never needed to know about the latest reality stars, and she was no closer to her dream. A couple of years back, she'd been switched to reporting on weightier matters, or so she'd thought, but although the subjects of those reports had changed from Z-list celebrities to politicians and the odd minor royal, the content had remained pretty much the same. And, let's face it, there were only so many ways to describe a mercy dash, an extramarital affair or a break-up, weren't there? Not to mention the problems that arose when the 'facts' of the stories were later disputed. That didn't happen often, but when it did...

Here, in her small office bedroom, in her mother's Regency house in a smart part of London, Fitz, the family collie dog, by her feet and her mother's recent interest in Grime music thudding upwards through the floorboards, Stella shook her head. Fitz, sensing her mood, raised his eyes hopefully.

'Oh, come on then.' Stella smiled down at him. 'It's about time we got some fresh air, anyway.' She stood up from her small but scrupulously tidy desk, shutting the lid of her MacBook as she did so. She might as well take Fitz out for his morning constitutional, since it sounded as though her mother was going to be busy for a little while longer. Grabbing her blazer from where it hung neatly on a padded coat hanger on the back of her bedroom door, and slipping her feet into a pair of comfy trainers, she pocketed her mobile, gave herself a cursory glance in the cheval mirror to make sure her curly brown hair, which was prone to unruliness, wasn't too wild, and then headed downstairs, Fitz at her heels.

'I'm taking Fitz out, Mum,' she called as she passed the large, airy living room. When no answer came, she paused and poked her head around the door. There, dressed in bright patterned leggings and an equally garish top, was her mother, doing an exercise video.

'I'm going to walk Fitz,' she yelled over the music. 'Do you want me to pick up anything on the way back?'

'No, darling, that's fine,' Morwenna replied, sweeping her hair off her face with a sweaty hand. 'I'm going out with Damon later, so I won't be in for dinner.' She paused the exercise class and turned round to face Stella.

'Okay,' Stella replied. 'Going anywhere nice?'

'There's a new Japanese place that's just opened up in Islington,' Morwenna replied. 'A mate of Damon's runs it, so he's treating me to dinner.'

Stella smiled. 'Sounds good.'

'I might pop over to his place a bit early, anyway,' Morwenna continued. 'So if I'm not here when you get back, don't worry about me.'

'I won't.' Stella leaned forward and kissed her mother's pink cheek. 'Enjoy. And say hi to Damon for me.'

'I will.' Morwenna smiled, then turned back to the television, where she unpaused the exercise video again.

Grinning, Stella walked back out of the living room as the glowing exercise instructor on-screen was exhorting her subscribers to 'push harder... feel the burn!'

As Stella left the house, she tried not to feel the growing sense of frustration about the fact that she was in her late twenties and *still* living with her mother. When she'd left university, she'd been convinced that, by this age, she'd have at least one novel under her belt, a place of her own, and a male in her life other than the shaggy black and white dog who was padding obediently beside her on the way to St James's Park. Putting down a hand to stroke his back, she took comfort in the sensation of his rough fur against her palm. Her mother had adopted the abandoned eight-week-old puppy on a whim a couple of years back, after seeing an advert on social media about a litter of collies left at Battersea Dogs' Home. And while Morwenna adored the dog almost as much as Stella did, the lion's share of the walking fell to Stella. She didn't mind; it got her out of the house and away from her desk a couple of times each day, but she couldn't help thinking that London was no place for a dog of Fitz's size and breed. However, neither she nor her mother would ever think of being parted from him, so he remained a city dog, with Stella taking him out into the park as much as she could, to give him a good run.

As they approached the park, Stella's phone vibrated in her pocket. Halting Fitz, she pulled it out and stared in confusion at the screen. The message, clipped on the Home screen, when revealed in its entirety was no more illuminating. It simply read:

Hi Stella, thank you for your application. We would like to arrange a Zoom meeting with you to discuss the job at your earliest convenience. Please could you let me know when you're available?

Job? She hadn't applied for any job! Surely there must be some mistake. But the text message had referred to her by name. Shaking her head, and thinking that there must be an AllFeed technology article to be written on the growing confidence of text scammers, she thrust the phone back into her pocket and continued her brisk walk towards the park. Fitz, in anticipation of his off-lead time, picked up the pace. London in the spring was a truly wonderful sight, and the budding catkins on the trees in the park, as well as the newest additions to the family of Canada geese bobbing along in the lake, lifted Stella's spirits. Who needed a change of scene, she thought, when she had parks like this on her doorstep?

2

An hour and a half later, after walking a broad loop around the perimeter of the park and then back to the house, Stella felt more than ready to tackle the next assignment on her list. As she let herself back into the house, she was grateful for the silence. As Stella walked into the kitchen at the back of the house, she could see the detritus of what had been a smoked salmon on rye toast breakfast spread all over the worktop, the empty salmon packet left on the counter, annoyingly just where the bin sat underneath, and crumbs strewn all about. She'd bypassed the kitchen on her way out with Fitz, and had eaten her breakfast a lot earlier, so hadn't seen the mess. Stella tried not to feel irritated, but she couldn't help feeling a bit jealous that her mother had been so excited to meet Damon she'd just left it for Stella to clear up.

Stella wasn't a neat freak by any stretch of the imagination, but tight deadlines for her job had forced a sense of order on her that she found comforting. There was a regularity to her life that some might have found dull, but to Stella it gave a sense of stability that, as Morwenna's daughter, she'd never really had as a child. Free-spirited to a fault, and with the means to be so when widowed at a young age, Morwenna wanted to 'kick the backside out of life'. Stella, cautious, sensible, bookish Stella, couldn't have been more different. Having been dragged along by her mother on many 'life-enhancing' experiences, leaving home to go to Oxford at age eighteen had been liberating, not because she wanted to try new things, but because she could regain a sense of order and routine that was her own. She could make her own decisions. That those decisions had involved a stack of books and seeing the inside of her college bedroom a lot more than many of her fellow students wasn't a worry for Stella. She'd spent so many of her earlier years flitting from Marrakech to Monaco and all places in between that the continuity of four walls in one place felt like heaven. She'd enjoyed the trips, and they'd brought her and her mother closer in the aftermath of her father's death, but university life had, ironically, allowed her some stability, and the opportunity to stay put for a while, which she'd been grateful for.

Now, though, after a few years working mostly from home, Stella had become, even by her own admission, something of a recluse. University friends had kept in touch, but were beginning to settle down themselves, and her established routine of writing on demand for AllFeed – stories that seemed ridiculous to her, but at least paid off her student loans and allowed her to pay rent to her mother – kept her on an even keel. And if her life seemed dull and routine to others, who cared?

Just as she was contemplating whether or not to throw together a quick macaroni cheese for tea, or order in from her favourite Korean place down the road, her phone began to ring. Unthinkingly, she swiped the green button. After all, it wasn't unheard of to get a tip-off about a news story by phone.

'Hello? This is Stella Simpson.'

'Stella? Good to finally hear your voice,' the man on the other end replied. Stella immediately noticed the broad West Country accent.

'I'm sorry?' she said. 'Who is this?'

'Sorry, love,' the man on the end of the phone replied. Stella didn't have time to bristle at the unasked-for endearment before he continued. 'It's John Handley, from the Roseford Hall Restoration Project, ringing about the Writer in Residence position.'

'Roseford Hall *what*?' Stella, all thoughts of early dinner forgotten, nearly dropped her phone.

'We've considered your application, and as you might imagine, there was a lot of competition, but we'd like to interview you for the post. How does next Thursday sound? We can do it over Zoom if you'd like. After all, it's a long way to come for you otherwise.'

'I'm sorry,' Stella stammered, clambering onto one of the kitchen barstools. 'There must be some mistake. I haven't applied for a Writer in Residence position. And I've no idea where Roseford is.'

'Oh,' John Handley replied, sounding confused and not a little put out. 'But you *are* Stella Simpson? The Stella Simpson who works as a content writer for AllFeed?'

'Yes, yes, that's me,' Stella replied. 'But I'm telling you, I haven't applied for a job. Honestly, there must be some mistake.'

'Well,' John Handley said after a heavy pause. 'That's a terrible shame, Stella. Between you and me, you seemed, on paper, to be just the kind of person we're looking for. But if you've changed your mind...'

'I haven't changed my mind!' Stella said quickly. 'I just didn't apply for the job. I'm not quite sure how you've got my details, and my CV. I'm sorry, Mr Handley, but clearly there's been a mix-up.'

'All right, then,' the man replied. 'Thank you for your time. Sorry to have bothered you.' And just like that, the line went dead.

Stella remained sitting on the bar stool in her mother's achingly trendy, cutting-edge kitchen for a long, long moment. What the hell had *that* been all about? Then, jolted out of her reverie by Fitz going into a paroxysm of ecstatic barking, she heard the front door open and then close as her mother wandered down the hallway and into the kitchen.

'Oh, hello, darling,' Morwenna said airily, heading straight to the fridge for her habitual evening glass of white wine. 'How was your walk?'

'Lovely, thanks,' Stella replied absently, her mind still very much on the weird phone call.

'Everything all right?' Morwenna's head appeared again as she closed the fridge, walked to the cupboard and got two glasses out of it. 'Fancy one?'

Morwenna asked her every night, Stella thought, and most nights she said no, but tonight she felt as though she needed a drink, if only a little one.

'Yes, please,' she said. If her mother was surprised at her response, she didn't show it.

'Good day?' Morwenna asked as she joined her daughter at the breakfast bar and handed over Stella's glass of white.

'Yeah,' Stella replied. 'Although I've just had the weirdest phone call.'

'Was it an obscene one?' Morwenna grinned. 'I thought all the heavy breathing of yesteryear had died along with the landline. Don't people just text photos of their genitals these days?'

'Not that kind of weird.' Despite herself, Stella laughed. 'Just... odd.'

'How so?' Morwenna took a sip of her wine.

'It was this guy,' Stella said. 'Asking me to an interview for a job I hadn't even applied for. In some place I've never heard of.'

The ensuing pause seemed to stretch on for hours. Morwenna had a habit of filling silences wherever they occurred, so when she didn't respond immediately with an 'I'm sure it was just a, what do you call it, fishy scam?' and Stella hadn't had to correct her mother's terms of reference to 'phishing', Stella's antennae immediately twitched.

'Mum...' she said softly but firmly. 'What did you do?'

Morwenna took another gulp of wine before she answered, looking more than a little sheepish.

'What makes you think I did anything?'

'Oh, I don't know... just that you're always on at me to stop prostituting myself to a, and I quote, *Silicon Valley word factory*, and get on with something worthwhile. I can't imagine why I might think you're behind this.'

Morwenna put her glass down. 'Okay. I'll admit it. I saw the Writer in Residence post advertised online and I applied for it for you. It's crap money, would barely cover your weekly shopping bill, but the accommodation's chucked in, and it's a year-long residency in one of the most gorgeous villages in Somerset. What's not to like?'

'And you didn't think to check this with me first?' Stella asked. 'Or, failing that, to let me know that you'd fraudulently applied for a job for me after you'd actually done it?'

'And what would you have said if I had?'

Stella looked squarely at her mother as she replied. 'I'd have told you to mind your own business, Mum.'

'Exactly.' Morwenna sighed. 'So do you blame me for not telling you?'

'But you've made me sound like a total idiot on the phone to the residency guy,' Stella retorted. 'I had to admit to him that I had absolutely no idea what he was talking about.'

'And what does that matter if you don't want the job?' Morwenna replied. 'You're never going to speak to him again, are you?'

'That's not the point, Mum!' Stella's voice was rising. 'You have no right to interfere in my life like that. I'm perfectly happy working for AllFeed and living here. Unless you want me to move out, of course?'

'Of course I don't,' Morwenna replied, although Stella noticed a slightly shifty look flit across her mother's face. 'Darling, this place is as much your home as it is mine. Daddy, God rest him, and I wanted you to always have a home to come back to. I just can't help thinking it's time you branched out a little.'

'By pushing me out into a part of the country I know nothing about, and expecting me to wax lyrical about it for a year, probably in some leaky old shed?' Stella snorted. 'I don't think so.'

'I'm sorry,' Morwenna said. 'I saw the ad, and thought it would be right up your street, give you a change, get you out of that study bedroom of yours, writing lists about celebrities and politicians, and back into the world. You're too isolated, too alone, day after day. You need people, a life that involves more than just putting your name to stories about other people living theirs.' She stood up from the table and moved round to where Stella was sitting, putting an arm around her shoulders as she did so. Despite her irritation, Stella leaned into the contact, enjoying the sensation of closeness.

'I live with you, don't I?' Stella murmured into her mother's shoulder. 'Sometimes, you're all the people I need.'

'Sweet as that is, apart from the odd coffee with Briony, who do you really see these days? You're losing touch with the real world, darling, with real people. You spend day after day in that room of yours, only emerging to give Fitz a run round the park. When was the last time you actually had a night out? Or a date?'

Stella shook her head. 'I see Briony enough. It's been less regular since her daughter was born, but we still keep in touch.' Briony was a close friend from university, who'd settled in London after graduation. 'And you know me... I'm not one for nights out.'

'Or relationships?' Morwenna said wryly.

Stella's face flushed. 'Not at the moment, Mum, no. Fitz is the only male I need in my life.'

'Will you just take a look at the job, darling?' Morwenna said gently, once she'd released Stella and gone back to her wine. 'What harm can it do?'

'Maybe,' Stella replied. 'I'm just not that keen on you trying to make decisions for me.'

'I know,' Morwenna said. 'But doing a few Googles can't do any harm, can it?'

Smiling inwardly at her mother's mangling of internet terminology, Stella shook her head. 'I'll see.'

A little later, having decided on a takeaway, and waiting for Uber Eats to deliver, Stella sat down at her desk. She checked a few emails, and sighed in exasperation at the jobs list, which seemed to be growing longer by the moment. Working for AllFeed was losing its charm, and she did need a change. Perhaps it was time to try something different. But on her terms, not because her mother told her to.

Despite her reservations, a few minutes later, she found herself putting 'Roseford' into Google. She was amazed at what she saw. Far from being a West Country backwater, it was a picturesque and rather beautiful place, made up of honey-coloured stone buildings and set amidst an expansive green valley, at the base of the Quantock Hills in Somerset. The village itself consisted of stunning cottages, interspersed with small terraced houses, with an expansive market square and a row of charming shops and businesses. The Writer in Residence post had been newly created to chronicle the events of a typical year in the parish, and had been part funded by the British Heritage Fund, an organisation similar to the National Trust, who were in the process of working with the owners of the large manor house in the village to turn it into a tourist

attraction. As her mother had mentioned, it also came with somewhere to live, although the details of that accommodation weren't
detailed. It could be a leaky shed, after all.

But it was too late, surely? She'd already told that bloke from
the project, John Handley, that he'd made a mistake when he called
her. It would be totally embarrassing to phone him back and tell
him that, actually, she *might* like to do an interview after all. Just as
she caught herself wondering if it was worth ringing him back, she
sagged in her chair. A move across the country, to a place she didn't
know, to a job that was merely temporary, on a salary that was
barely more than minimum wage? What the hell was she thinking?
No. She wouldn't be coerced into this mad scheme by her mother;
she'd had enough of those during her childhood. She liked her life,
she liked her job, and there was no way she was going to change
any of that, until it suited her.

Just as she was shutting down her laptop for the day, carefully
saving her work and waiting patiently for it to upload to AllFeed's
servers, her phone pinged with another message. It was from John
Handley.

Stella. Sorry to bother you, but we would really like you to interview for
the residency post. If you change your mind, you can reach me on this
number. We'll keep your name on the shortlist until the end of the
working day tomorrow, if you reconsider.

Well, he was nothing if not persistent, Stella thought, but she
held off from replying just a little longer. After all, agreeing to an
interview didn't mean she had to take the job, right? And it would
be good experience for her, since she hadn't had a job interview
since the sideways move a year ago. Perhaps she'd sleep on it.

As she drifted off that night, her dreams were textured with
warm stone, sunny days and a feeling she couldn't quite identify.

3

After initially sleeping well, but then waking at four o'clock with the birdsong, Stella couldn't get back to sleep. Morwenna had made herself scarce shortly after their discussion about the Writer in Residence job, and they hadn't spoken since. Perhaps her mother had been right to intervene this time? What if there really was a different life for her away from the pressures of online journalism and in the world outside her front door? Maybe it was about time she started to live that life instead of writing about it?

But here, home, with Morwenna, had been safety and stability since she returned from university. Of course, some might argue that she was old enough to make her own home now, but she just didn't feel quite ready yet. Could it be that the residency was her chance to make a change, just for a little while, on her own terms? University had been a liberating experience because she had made the choice to get away, rather than being her mother's travel partner. Was the Roseford residency a chance to do that again, or was it yet another idea influenced by her mother?

It couldn't hurt to do the interview, though, could it? After all, it was going to happen over Zoom, so she wouldn't even have to leave her room. She probably wouldn't get the job anyway. So it was that, at 4.30 a.m., Stella found herself reaching for her phone and, before she could change her mind, texting John Handley back to confirm that yes, she would like to interview for the post. What was the worst that could happen?

* * *

A few days later, Stella sat nervously in front of her MacBook, waiting for the interview to begin. She'd put on her smartest top and skirt, and swapped her glasses for contact lenses, which she usually only wore for nights out. Her foot tapped rhythmically as her right hand clenched her mouse, waiting to be let into the meeting. Zoom had become a way of life lately, as a way of reducing costs and carbon footprints, but she never really felt as if she came across well on it.

Morwenna had gone out for the afternoon, and for once had taken Fitz with her, so the house was quiet, and Stella could concentrate. As the meeting began, Stella took a deep breath.

'Hi, John,' she said, as a kindly looking older man with a shock of white hair appeared on her laptop.

'Stella!' John replied. 'So nice that you could make it.'

As they chatted idly about the weather, passing the time as if they were two friends in the local pub, Stella found herself feeling more and more at ease. Eventually, as if it was almost a by-product of the conversation, the subject turned to the residency.

'So why do you want to take on the job of Writer in Residence?' John asked.

Stella paused, mind blank, for a moment.

'Well,' she said eventually. 'My mum thought it would be a great idea.'

John, clearly amused, began to laugh. 'And do you agree?'

Did she? Oh, what the hell, she had nothing to lose.

'You know what, John? I think I do.' And she was off, waxing lyrical about opportunities to raise the profile of the village of Roseford, working closely with the British Heritage Fund and local residents to get a feel for the place, and trying, as best she could, to immortalise a year in the life of the village. As she paused for breath, John smiled down the line.

'Well, you've certainly given me a lot to think about,' he said. 'I'll have to discuss it with the other members of the committee, but we'll be in touch by the end of the day.'

Feeling the adrenaline rush of a job well done, Stella smiled. 'Thank you. I look forward to hearing from you.'

As she ended the Zoom call, she was shaking so much, she wondered if John had heard her panicky exhalations before hanging up. Now, all she could do was wait. Well, that wasn't strictly true, of course. She had another long list of articles to write. Perhaps, she thought, this would be the last long list she'd have to worry about.

4

For a few nail-biting hours, Stella waited for the call from John Handley. After everything she'd said to her mother about the job, and the worry about making this change to her life, she had suddenly realised that this might be what she really did want after all. As she sat down to eat the macaroni cheese she had eventually got around to making, purely for something to take her mind off the interview, her mother sailed in through the door, her partner, Damon, in tow behind.

'Hi, darling,' Morwenna said brightly, kissing the top of Stella's head as she moved past her to the kettle. 'Good day?'

'Not bad,' Stella said, glancing at Damon and giving him a brief smile.

'Tea or coffee, babe?' Morwenna asked.

'Coffee, thanks, babe,' Damon replied.

Stella tried not to cringe. Much as she liked Damon, she found the endearments a little hard to swallow at times.

'Any news?' Morwenna asked.

'Not yet,' Stella replied. 'John said I'd know by the end of the day.'

'Well, do you know what you're going to say if they do offer it to you?' Morwenna asked, dropping a spoonful of instant coffee in each mug before gesturing to Stella, who shook her head. Coffee, even instant, would give her more jitters than she already had.

Had Stella not been quite so preoccupied, she might have seen the glance that passed between Damon and Morwenna before they both sat at the table, one to her left, and one to her right.

'Darling,' Morwenna began, 'there's something Damon and I would like to discuss with you.'

Stella looked up quickly and saw that her mother had an uncharacteristically serious look on her face. 'Both of you?' she asked.

'Yes.' Morwenna gave another tense smile. 'You see, the thing is... I've asked Damon to move in. With me. Here. How do you feel about that?'

For a moment, Stella felt a fiery surge of irritation that her mother hadn't bothered to discuss this with her alone before springing it on her in front of Damon. Surely Morwenna should have raised this with her before bringing Damon in on the discussion? But then, this was Morwenna's house, and they were both adults. It wasn't like she was still a teenager, after all.

'Well,' she said eventually, after taking a restorative sip from the tumbler of water by her plate. 'Does it really matter what I think? I mean, since you're telling me this together, I assume it's a done deal.'

'Stella,' Morwenna began, reaching out for Stella's hand, which was still clutched around the water glass.

Stella drew a deep breath and tried to remember that she wasn't a vulnerable fifteen-year-old any longer. She had her own life, her own plans now. She raised her head and gave her mother the best smile she could muster. 'It's fine, Mum,' she said. Then, glancing towards Damon, who looked rather endearingly nervous, and definitely a bit uncomfortable about being there, she said, 'I'm happy for you. For you both.'

Standing up from the table, not really that hungry any more, she scraped her plate and then put it carefully in the dishwasher. 'Well, I'd better take Fitz for his evening walk,' she said as the dog came padding over in anticipation of leftovers.

'Are you sure you're okay with this?' Morwenna asked as Stella went to get Fitz's lead from the hook by the back door.

'Yes,' Stella said. This time, she tried a bit harder with the smile. 'And congratulations... to you both.'

A little while later, while Fitz was nosing out something stinky and interesting at the base of an ancient oak tree in the park, Stella felt her phone vibrating in her pocket with an incoming email. For a split second, she thought of what she would do if she didn't get the job; after all, there would be other opportunities. And what the hell did she *really* know about being a Writer in Residence, anyway? Many of her friends, like her closest friend, Briony, had opted to go into teaching once they'd finished their degrees, but she'd shied away from that option. If she took the post, she'd have to run workshops as well as be chronicler-in-chief of a place she knew nothing about.

Slipping the phone from her pocket, bracing herself for the news, whatever it was, she saw that John had asked her to call him as soon as she could. Well, she thought, this was it. Taking a deep breath, she made the call that could well change her life.

5

Six weeks later, having worked her notice with AllFeed, Stella packed up her room and piled all of her possessions into the back of the hired Transit van, ready to begin the trip to Roseford. Her mother was touchingly sad to see her leave, and hugged her warmly, but Stella could also tell she couldn't wait to 'officially' welcome Damon to the house, now that her daughter was finally moving out.

Not that they were going to actually be living there for the time being, Stella thought darkly. Shortly after she'd told her mother she'd got the job in Somerset, Morwenna had announced that she and Damon were off on an extended break to the south of France, to investigate the possibility of setting up a wellness retreat in one of the more affluent areas. Damon had bought a ramshackle farmhouse out there a few years ago, and was looking into the possibility of turning it into a business, rather than just letting it fall down.

'And what about Fitz?' Stella asked. 'Will he be going too?'

Morwenna looked a little sheepish. 'Well, since you're going to be out in the gorgeous Somerset countryside, I wondered if he might be better off with you.'

Stella sighed. She should have seen *that* one coming. But, to be honest, since she was the one who spent the most time with the dog, she was far happier to take him with her than see him off to a boarding kennels. 'Fine,' she said resignedly. Maybe having a dog in a new place would encourage her out from behind the desk a little more, and into the open air.

The month and a half between when she'd accepted the job to now had been both exciting and terrifying for Stella. At first, she'd thought that she could continue working for AllFeed in some form, while taking up the Writer in Residence post, but it soon became clear that the high-pressure nature of working for the online site was incompatible with the steadier but no less demanding role of the residency. She wouldn't be able to pull all-nighters and write the copy if she was expected to teach classes the day after or attend an event that she would have to write about. It wasn't until she'd phoned her friend, Briony, with the news that she'd realised how much of a change it was going to be. Briony, currently at home with a one-year-old, had told her to go for it.

'Imagine,' she'd said, when they'd met for coffee in the local branch of Costa a few days after Stella had accepted the post, 'a whole new set of people, a wonderful place, and the freedom to do what you've always wanted to do – write.' She smiled down at her tiny daughter, who was intent on snaffling a chocolate cookie from the pile on Briony's plate next to her coffee. 'I mean, it's about time you got out from your mum's place anyway, isn't it?'

'Yes, I suppose,' Stella replied. 'It just feels like such a leap, that's all.'

'This from someone who got dragged all over the world as a kid?'

'Yeah, but this time it's my choice, isn't it?' Stella took a sip of her coffee and sat back in her chair. 'But you're right, it'll be lovely to have a bit more control over what I write, and to explore some-where new.'

'And who knows who you might meet in the countryside?' Briony raised an eyebrow. 'You could be swept off your feet by a smooth-talking Somerset hottie!'

Stella laughed. 'Not likely,' she replied. 'Besides, I don't think I'm overly keen on the accent!'

Having passed her driving test at seventeen, but never having owned her own car, there were a few hairy moments as she navigated her way from London and then headed west. According to the satnav on her phone, the trip would take three hours, but since she was so nervous, she was keeping to the lower end of the speed limits on the roads, much to the irritation of the motorists behind her, she was sure.

Soon enough, though, Stella was out on the wide open winding roads of the English countryside, heading through the northern edge of Hampshire, through the chalky vistas of Wiltshire and then into Somerset, where the Quantock Hills, stingingly green against the mid-spring blue skies of a sunny morning, were a marked contrast to the high rises and frantic pace of the city she'd left. Fitz stared out of the window on the passenger's side of the van, tongue lolling out, looking faintly bemused at the change of scene. Stella got the feeling that he was pleased to be seeing somewhere new. The London house, with its tiny back garden, and a twice-daily run around the nearest park, wasn't really a substitute for the acres of trees and fields, with endless footpaths, that would welcome him in Roseford and the surrounding area.

Eventually, after several wrong turns when the GPS had cut out in the valley, she located the turning to the village. As she pulled off the main road and down onto a winding road not much wider than a single track, she kept an eye out for her new home. Rounding a sharp bend, intent on keeping the wing mirrors of the van intact, rather than catching them on the overhanging hedgerows, she didn't really take in when the road widened and the village of Roseford was revealed in all its glory.

'Wow, Fitz,' Stella breathed as she slowed to appreciate her first view of the place that was to be her home for the next year. As she rumbled over a small humpbacked bridge that led downhill to what she presumed was the main street, on either side of her, sandy coloured stone buildings lined the thoroughfare. To the left was the village pub, called the Treloar Arms, complete with a heraldic insignia painted on the sign that hung outside, and wooden tables out on the pavement. A few people, obviously taking the air on a beautiful Somerset afternoon, were sitting drinking at them. A little further on was a quaint-looking Post Office and next to it a general store, which still retained its independence, Stella was surprised to see. Not a corporate logo in sight, its dark blue sign with gold lettering proudly proclaimed that Southgate's Stores was open for business, and clearly buzzing with life.

The satnav directed her to carry straight on past the market square, and as she continued through the village, Stella caught sight of a village hall and a brown sign with the British Heritage Fund's logo pointing down an offshoot road to Roseford Hall. The village itself was often used as the backdrop for period dramas, which gave it an added edge. After all, who could fail to be excited at the prospect of the cream of British acting talent striding around the streets in breeches or crinolines? She wondered if there was anything due to be filmed here in the year that she was going to be in residence.

Driving through the village, she continued for another half a mile, before the turn that would, presumably, take her to her new home. She was glad, on reflection, to be a little out of the village itself. Thinking time was essential, she imagined, in this new job, and she liked the idea of a bolthole on the outskirts of the popular village, and, hopefully, fewer tourists and holidaymakers passing her front door.

Sure enough, she was soon approaching a driveway framed by iron gates, slightly rusty, and stone pillars on either side, with a mottled sign saying 'Halstead House' on one of them. As she swung the van carefully through the sharp turn, she saw, up the sweeping driveway, the imposing but seriously shabby-looking Victorian house at the top of the drive, and to her left, and she felt her heart thump at the sight of it, the small, cosy-looking gatehouse which would be her home for the duration of the Writer in Residence post. She couldn't help thinking that Halstead House looked very unloved, in contrast to the pictures she'd seen of the splendid opulence of Roseford Hall, which she couldn't wait to see close up, as soon as she'd settled herself into her new home.

Pulling up lopsidedly by the gate that led to a small front garden, mostly laid to gravel but with a border of roses already in bloom running down one side, Stella turned to Fitz, whose tail was wagging at the prospect of being freed from the seatbelt that clipped into his lead.

'Here we are, old chap,' Stella said, ruffling the fur on Fitz's neck. 'This is our new home.'

6

Unfortunately, Stella had forgotten that she was going to phone John Handley to let him know her estimated time of arrival at the gatehouse. She had been so preoccupied with getting everything packed into the van that morning and making sure that Fitz had everything he needed. So, as she stood on the doorstep of her new home, trying to remember where she'd filed all of John's emails about logistics, Fitz nosed around the garden, sniffing out the corners and lifting a leg on some of the bigger shrubs and rosebushes.

Just as she was navigating her way to what she thought was the correct email, a sharp blast on a car horn made her jump, and her phone clattered down onto the slabbed garden path. As she was picking it up, thankfully unbroken, the horn blared again. Fitz let out a bark, and belted over to the garden gate, tail wagging cautiously.

'It's all right, boy,' Stella soothed as she followed him to the gate. She pushed her glasses a little further up her nose and then glanced out into the driveway where she'd parked the van. Just behind it, a man was sitting in a grubby old Mitsubishi Warrior pickup truck, one elbow resting on the window frame, one hand just about to hit the horn again.

'Can I help you?' Stella asked, as she approached him. Drawing closer, she could see that his mouth was set in a grim line, he had a couple of days' growth of darkish stubble on his face and his dark brown hair looked as though it hadn't seen a brush in weeks. Mirrored sunglasses in a Matrix style shaded his eyes, which gave him an unnerving look, but she didn't need to see them to know he was clearly pissed off.

'I've told you delivery drivers to park more bloody considerately when you're dropping stuff off here,' he said. 'You're blocking the whole driveway with that thing.'

Stella, shocked at the rasp and aggression in his tone, took a step back. 'Sorry,' she said instinctively, although this guy clearly hadn't a clue that she was actually moving in today. But then, she thought, why would he?

'Well, can you move the thing, then?' he continued, not even bothering to turn his face towards where she stood.

At that moment, Fitz, who sensed his mistress wasn't involved in the happiest of conversations, took it upon himself to bound over the garden gate and fly to Stella's side, barking gamely.

'And keep that fucking dog out of my way, too,' the guy snarled.

'Don't take it out on my dog,' Stella, finding her wits at last, snapped back. 'He just doesn't like your tone of voice, that's all. And for that matter, neither do I.'

'Look,' the man lowered his voice and gave a sigh. 'Can you just move the van? Please? I've got a lot to do up at the house and I don't have time to keep waiting for other people's poxy deliveries.'

'Actually,' Stella said, feeling crosser by the moment, 'I'm not delivering anything. I'm trying to move in.' She paused, waiting for the man, whoever he was, to offer a word of apology, but not finding one forthcoming, she pressed on. 'But I'll happily move the van for you, if you'll give me a second.' Without waiting for a response, apologetic or otherwise, she wheeled around, whistled to Fitz, who looked a little confused to be getting back into the van so quickly after leaving it, thrust the key in the ignition and started the Transit.

She'd barely manoeuvred the van into a tighter position parallel to the gate and the garden wall before the man in the Mitsubishi gunned its engine and roared past her, kicking up a cloud of dust from the driveway and disappearing around the curve that led to the bigger house at the top.

'Twat,' Stella muttered. She wondered if he was a gardener or something, and thought, when she met the owner of the house, that she might have a word about the man's rudeness. After all, she hadn't parked *that* badly. It was only because he'd had one of those gas-guzzling trucks that he hadn't been able to get past. It was hardly her fault. Getting back out of the van, Stella gave Fitz's muzzle a quick rub, reassuring the dog that everything was fine, and then tried to find John's number, to get hold of the house key. She hoped he wouldn't keep her waiting long; she was dying for a cup of tea and to take a look at her new house.

Just as she was dialling the number, a woman's face, smiling, and with startlingly blue eyes, appeared around the side of the van. Stella smiled in acknowledgement, still waiting for the phone to connect, but annoyingly it went through to voicemail.

'Great,' she muttered. She knew it was partly her fault for not giving John her ETA, but it didn't help the fact that she was still stuck on the doorstep and unable to move into her new place. She had to drop the van back somewhere in Taunton later that evening, too, or she'd get stung for another day's hire.

The woman smiled and then dug around in her handbag, eventually producing a set of keys just as Stella had finished leaving her voicemail.

'Sorry,' she said as she held them up. 'I saw the van arriving and

I assumed it was you, but I was halfway through hanging out my washing and wanted to get it out – it's supposed to rain later. John dropped the keys with me yesterday and asked me to keep an eye out.'

'Thanks.' Stella smiled, reaching out and taking the keys. 'I was worried I was going to be stuck out here all afternoon!'

'I'm Helena Martin,' the woman continued. 'I live in the bungalow about halfway up the drive.'

Stella smiled back and introduced herself, although she still felt a bit weird about calling herself the Writer in Residence; it seemed such a pretentious title for someone as ordinary as her. But, she supposed, she had to get used to it sometime – it might as well be now.

'It's nice to meet you, Stella,' Helena replied. 'Now, I'll let you get settled in, and when you're ready, if you'd like to pop up the drive for a cuppa, please do feel free.'

'Thanks,' Stella replied, charmed by the easy friendliness of the woman, as opposed to the arrogance of the bloke in the Warrior. 'I will.'

'And bring this fella, too,' Helena added, stroking Fitz under the chin so that his brown eyes softened in appreciation. 'I do love dogs, and he looks like a character.'

'He is,' Stella said as Fitz turned his attention back to her.

'Well, I won't keep you,' Helena said. 'I'm sure you've got lots to sort out.'

Stella laughed. 'It's mad to think that basically my whole life is in the back of that Transit, waiting to be unpacked. I haven't felt this way since university!'

'Good luck,' Helena said, raising a hand as she turned back up the driveway.

'Thanks,' Stella said again. She felt the irritation of the encounter with Mitsubishi Warrior Twat, as she had now christened him in her head, ebbing away after the conversation with her really rather lovely new neighbour. Helena had kind eyes, and a gentle way of speaking that immediately soothed Stella. She hoped that she might be able to learn a little more about the place she'd moved to if she popped over to see her later.

But, for now, there was the van to unpack and a new home to explore. She felt more than a frisson of excitement as she headed back up the garden path to the front door, for the second time, and turned the key on her new life.

7

As Stella opened the door to the gatehouse that was to be her home for the next twelve months, she drew in a surprised breath of pleasure. The hallway was painted a wonderful shade of duck-egg blue, and to the right, on the wall, was a coat rack and shoe stand in wrought iron. 'Somewhere to hang your lead, Fitzy,' Stella said, smiling down at the dog, who promptly stuck his nose to the grey flagstones of the hall and started sniffing.

Progressing from the front hallway down the passage, Stella first noticed a small sitting room, furnished in a country cottage style, with a cosy light blue sofa and armchair, and a couple of rugs thrown over the flagstones to add a hint of colour and comfort. To the back of the property was a small but modern kitchen, with just enough room for a central island. There was a small conservatory beyond the back door, too, leading to the garden. Stella smiled as she threw open the kitchen window to let in some fresh air and found herself looking out onto a lovely, well-kept garden. It was bordered by a wall on either side and a thick conifer hedge at the back, with another garden gate out into the woodland that

surrounded the plot and rose in an incline to the top of a thickly
wooded hill.

Venturing upstairs, Stella found two bedrooms, one the master,
complete with a large wooden four-poster bed dominating the
room. She hadn't expected anything quite so opulent, given what
the residency was paying her. Two mullioned windows, one looking
out over the back garden and one over the side of the house, gave
plenty of light, and Stella again opened them to let in the warm
Somerset air. She could get used to the scent of trees, cut grass and
fresh air, she thought, breathing deeply.

Fitz, bored of Stella's dawdling pace, had dashed into the
second, smaller bedroom and was sniffing around in one corner
with great interest. Stella, noting the age of the house and the fact
that it hadn't been lived in for a while, hoped he wasn't sniffing out
mice or, worse, rats. Living in the lap of a large woodland, she
wouldn't have been surprised if some of them had found their way
into an empty house. Fortunately, there didn't appear to be any
evidence of them where Fitz was sniffing.

'Well, old chap, we can't spend the rest of the afternoon
wandering about. Let's get our stuff in, shall we?' Heading back
downstairs with Fitz once again at her heels, Stella went out to the
van and began to unload the first of many cardboard boxes, plastic
tubs and assorted bags that made up the contents of her current
life. Dumping the whole lot, for the moment, in the living room, she
was out of breath and red in the face by the time she'd finished, but
at least the van was empty and she could return it to the local
branch of the hire company on time. Thrusting the bag of chilled
food, including Fitz's raw dog food, into the fridge, she decided the
rest of the unpacking could wait.

She wondered if she should look into getting a car if she was
going to be doing a lot of travelling outside of Roseford, but figured
she'd cross that bridge if and when she came to it. If the bus routes

weren't up to much, it might have to be an option. Fortunately, she had quite a lot saved from living back at home so she could afford a small car if it turned out that she needed one.

'Sorry, darling,' she said to Fitz as she put his bed and a bowl of water down for him near the Aga in the kitchen, which it was entirely too hot to light right now, but she felt sure Fitz would appreciate in the colder winter months. 'I can't take you with me, but I'll be back in an hour or so. Be good.' Leaving him with one of his favourite chewy bones, she dropped a kiss on the top of his head and headed out.

Sometime later, having dropped off the van, Stella stepped out of the taxi that had brought her home and hurried back into the gate-house. Fitz, as was his usual way, had curled up in his bed, patiently waiting for her to return, and when she headed into the kitchen, he looked up briefly and wagged his tail. Grabbing his dinner from the fridge, she swiftly put some into his favourite bowl and watched him for the ten seconds or so it took him to demolish it. Rescued by Battersea Dogs' Home as a puppy from an owner who was farming collies for vast profits, he never hung about where food was concerned. Then, still unable to face the unpacking, she decided to head up the driveway to see if Helena's invitation for a cuppa still stood. Fitz needed his evening constitutional, too, so she went out of the kitchen door and through the back gate of the cottage to the woodland path, making sure to grab her waist belt with its pouch full of treats and poo bags on the way out. She assumed that the woodland belonged to the wider estate, and hoped that whoever owned the big house at the top wouldn't mind her walking Fitz in it for a few days until she got her bearings and could take him elsewhere.

Meandering through the cooler woodland, where the late-evening sunshine didn't quite permeate the canopy of leaves from the ancient oak and beech trees, Stella finally gave herself permission to unwind and relax a bit. She was here. She'd done it. Okay, so there was still the small matter of the unpacking to do, but she'd conquered the drive, got the keys to her new home and had even, possibly, made a new friend in her neighbour, Helena. Over the next few days, she'd be getting her bearings and meeting with various members of the Roseford Hall renovation team, as well as reps from the British Heritage Fund, who were currently working on restoring Roseford Hall to its former glory and who would need her input to chronicle the process, but this new chapter in her life had officially begun.

Disappointingly, as Stella approached the front door of Helena's bungalow, having walked Fitz around the woodland until he was tired out, Stella noticed that there was a note pinned to the door.

So sorry, Stella,
    Have had to dash out and collect my grandson from school.
Forgive me. Do pop in again sometime this week, if you have the time.
    Best, and welcome to Roseford!
    Helena

Oh well, Stella thought as she turned back down the neat path that led from Helena's front door to the wider driveway. There's always tomorrow. Besides, she really should at least sort out her workspace, and find where the heck she'd packed her toothbrush, if nothing else. Also, she was feeling a bit peckish. Thankfully, she'd packed a couple of ready meals, so one of those would do for tonight. As she turned right out of Helena's front garden, she chanced a glance up at the large, imposing but distinctly scruffy-looking house at the top of the driveway. Built in a high Victorian style, its red-tiled roof and imposing stone walls were still rather majestic, despite the fact it looked as though it had seen better days. There was a light on in one of the windows on the ground floor, but elsewhere the house was in darkness. Maybe the house belonged to a charming but penniless elderly eccentric, who couldn't afford to light and heat more than one room at a time?

Judging from the unkempt nature of the gardens to the front of the house, and the fact that, even from this distance, she could tell that a lot of the windows were smeary and had flaking paintwork on the frames, perhaps she was right. She couldn't help, whenever she saw something that piqued her interest, imagining what the story behind the scene was. Nine times of out of ten, she never got the chance to find out; glances were fleeting and her writer's brain was constantly making up stories, but as she was living so close to this big old neglected place for the next year, she might end up actually finding out if she'd been right, this time. Anyway, she thought, Helena would soon be able to fill her in, she was sure.

Heading back to the gatehouse, Stella suddenly realised how tired she was, and even Fitz was drooping by the time they trudged up the garden path and pushed open the front door. Unaccustomed to the silence of the countryside after the throbbing hum of London, the quiet rang in her ears and she wondered if she'd manage to get to sleep that night at all.

Tucking into her lasagne twenty minutes later, having discovered, mercifully, that the Aga had an electric oven option, she finally felt herself beginning to relax. She'd packed a bottle of red wine, too, so she poured herself a glass.

As she was eating, her thoughts wandered back to the inhabitants of the place she'd moved into. Helena seemed nice, and had certainly been a welcoming presence, especially when she'd handed Stella the keys to the gatehouse. She hoped she'd have time to pop over and see her tomorrow, and find out a little more about Roseford. Then there was the mysterious inhabitant of the big house at the top of the drive, whom she was sure she'd encounter at some point. The three houses did share the driveway, after all.

Again, idly, she found her mind wandering to the kind of person who might dwell inside that scruffy, rambling old house. She knew that Roseford Hall, at the other end of the village, had been taken over by the British Heritage Fund about twelve months ago, but the Victorian pile at the top of the drive probably was of lesser historical significance, although picturesque. Perhaps, she thought dreamily, it had originally belonged to some genteel woman, the mistress of the lord of Roseford Hall, who'd been set up in there on the outskirts of town for the sake of respectability. She imagined a tall, dark Victorian gentleman, in the mould of Richard Armitage from the BBC's adaptation of *North and South* some years ago, falling in love with someone deemed unsuitable by his family, and so keeping her as his mistress while he was pressured to 'do the right thing' and marry someone of his class. Unable to bear parting with her, he'd drop in from time to time and keep the fires burning.

Gosh, she thought, as she finished her meal and took another long gulp of the red wine, it didn't take her long to extrapolate a whole narrative from a glimpse of one light shining on the ground floor! Sometimes she had to admit that her mother was right when she'd accused her of having her head in the clouds too much, of failing to connect with the real world in favour of the wisps of fairy tales, and stories floating around in the ether. But then, her mother was fonder of trying to chase fairy tales in her actual life than Stella was, which must have been what made Stella so cautious in hers. Early experiences had taught her not to trust in fictions that presented themselves as facts; she hoped her mother wasn't falling foul of that again with Damon.

'Well, I think we'll call it a day, shall we, Fitzy?' Stella said as she got up from the kitchen table, a little before nine o'clock. Wandering over to the back door, she let the dog out for a last pee and a sniff around and then, worrying that he might feel lonely in a new house all by himself, she beckoned him upstairs. Just for tonight, she'd move his bed up to her room. She told herself if was for his sake but, actually, the silence in and around the cottage was unnerving her, and she felt as though she needed the company. As she drew the heavy sky-blue curtains across the latticed window that looked up the driveway, she could see the light on the ground floor of the big house was still on. Turning away from the window, and settling Fitz down in his bed, she was filled with a sense of excitement and trepidation about what the next few days would bring. Just before she turned in, she phoned her mother, who was pleased to hear she'd settled in okay, and texted Briony, to report that yes, Roseford was lovely, and no, she definitely hadn't been swept off her feet yet.

8

Chris Charlton staggered into the kitchen of the house that was slowly falling down around his ears and fought the urge to collapse into one of the rickety kitchen chairs that sat at a skewed angle at the scratched, scrubbed oak table that could have comfortably seated twelve people. Most of the time, these days, it only ever seated one. Two, at weekends, when his eleven-year-old son came home from boarding school, and very occasionally three, when his mother-in-law dropped in. More often, though, she preferred them to meet at her place. He knew it was less painful for her that way.

Throwing open the door of the large American-style fridge-freezer that lurked like some elderly elephant in the corner of the kitchen, he grabbed himself a beer and the remnants of last night's takeaway curry, chucking the latter into the microwave that perched on the cluttered worktop, which was a mess of paintbrushes, plastering tools and coffee mugs. He knew he should clear up before his son came home, but, as with so much these days, it all seemed like too much effort.

Taking a long pull of the beer, which he'd opened by cracking off the cap against the side of the kitchen table, probably denting and scratching it that little bit more in the process, he felt the cool liquid slaking his dry throat. It had been another long day, trying to get to grips with plastering the small living room on the upper floor. When he'd taken a plastering course a couple of years back, he'd been full of energy and hope, but now things were very, very different. Every day felt like an effort, and where there once had been a reward to be gained, a light at the end of the endless tunnel, now there seemed very little point in anything.

Deciding, eventually, to sit down while the microwave went to work, he closed eyes that felt grainy and sore, both from lack of sleep and from the plaster dust. He'd really wanted to be outside tackling the lawns today, but he hated leaving a job half done, so instead he'd been trying to finish the small living room, ready to repaint when it had dried, so that at least he and Gabe would have somewhere decent to sit of an evening. It had been his mother-in-law's idea, of course; she'd baulked at the idea that they were spending nights on the kitchen chairs, or sprawled on the floor watching TV. In her gentle but firm way she'd persuaded him that 'at least one room, darling' needed sorting out, even if the rest of the place could wait. Although, he often reflected, in his darker moments, what the place was waiting *for*, he no longer had any idea. It had been so different when he'd actually had a plan. But now...

The sharp ping of the microwave dragged him back from the familiar, well-worn mental road. Springing up from his seat, he grabbed a fork and a spoon from the cutlery drawer and, not even bothering with a plate, he dug in and shovelled the curry back. It wasn't quite as piping hot as it should have been, but he didn't really care. Food was most definitely fuel, nothing more.

Just as he was forcing down a fifth tepid mouthful, his phone beeped. Inclined to ignore it, but also mindful that it could be something important, he grabbed it off the kitchen table where he'd chucked it when he'd come in, and his stomach lurched.

'Shit,' he murmured as he scanned the message. 'But it's not Friday... is it?'

With a slightly shaky hand, he called the sender. 'Hi. Yes, I'm so sorry. I was mixing plaster in the basement for a fair bit of the afternoon and there's no reception down there, so I didn't get their call. You have? Thank you. Thank you so much. I'll be right over.'

Chris felt a combination of that brutal sense of guilt and utter uselessness at the reply from the other end of the call. 'Yes, well, if you're all right with that. Thank you. I'll see you tomorrow.'

He *should* drop everything and take action. But what could he say? It wasn't the first occasion he'd lost track of time in the past couple of years. Pieces had been picked up, and bridges rebuilt, but even so, he knew it was beyond unfair to those involved.

No longer hungry, he dropped the takeaway carton into the bin and the spoon into the sink, where it joined the detritus of almost a week's worth of cutlery. Tomorrow, he vowed, he'd make more of an effort. But then he always said that, and nothing much had changed.

Chris hadn't intended for things to turn out this way; two years ago, everything had been so different. Two years ago, he'd had a wife, a son who adored him and a dream to make this property the best business and family home it could possibly be. Then, in an instant, everything had changed. Even after all this time, he felt as though he was stuck in the mire, fighting just to stop from drowning. And the absolute worst of it? He knew that it was all, entirely, his fault.

9

The next morning, Stella woke feeling refreshed and calmer than she'd been in a very long time. Usually, she'd have set her alarm for 5 a.m., so she could check in on the late-night antics of whichever celebs she'd been asked to report on for AllFeed. However, she'd turned her phone completely off the previous night, not wanting to be woken by notifications, or her alarm, and as a result, she'd slept right through until just gone seven o'clock.

Fitz, who'd settled happily in her bedroom, raised his head from his paws as she stirred, and followed her to the window as she threw open the curtains to what looked to be another wonderful day of Somerset sunshine. As she opened the window and breathed in the morning air, the breeze whispering down from the woodland behind the house, she felt relaxation running through her, as if this was a holiday, rather than the beginning of a new life. She didn't 'officially' start her new job until Monday, so she had the whole weekend to unpack and get her bearings.

Once she'd set up a delivery from the nearest supermarket for later that day, she wanted to get out and explore her new village home. After all, she'd be writing about it soon. Although a lot of her work would be focused on the promotion of Roseford Hall for the British Heritage Fund, she was sure she'd also need to get to know the village and discover its quirks and eccentricities. Finding an 'angle' for a piece of writing was essential, and from what she'd seen of the village of Roseford on the way through yesterday, she was sure there would be plenty to catch her attention.

'Come on then, Fitz,' she said, once she'd had a bit of toast and he'd had his breakfast. The dog needed no second invitation, and dashed to where Stella had hung his lead by the front door after their walk last night.

The gatehouse was half a mile from the centre of Roseford. Whilst she was happy to immerse herself in the project, a little creative distance at the end of the day would work well. As with anything, the ability to wander off and close the door behind you could provide some clarity. For the past few years, working from home in London, she hadn't felt as though she'd had much of that.

Roseford couldn't have been more different, she reflected as she walked. Even the main road into the village seemed quiet on this sunny Saturday morning. So quiet, in fact, that she dropped Fitz's lead and let him sniff unencumbered through the undergrowth on the wide grass verge where they walked. He was, like most collies, excellent at walking to heel, and he didn't stray far from her in search of new scents. She called him closer when the odd car trundled past, but the verge was wide enough for her to feel safe.

As she approached the village, the road widened out into the market square, and she caught sight of some of the places she'd glimpsed on the way through yesterday. Southgate's Stores, on the way to the square, plum centre in the row of buildings that lined the road, was open for business, its vibrant red and white striped awning bright and cheerful in the already warm sunlight. Outside were racks of fresh seasonal produce, including strawberries and new potatoes, caked red with the West Somerset soil. Free range eggs sat in boxes, and leafy beetroot was stacked up alongside the potatoes. Stella hoped that the online supermarket orders might become a thing of the past, if the cost of shopping locally wasn't too prohibitive. She had to remember that she was on no more than a small salary this year.

'Morning!' a fair-haired man, who looked to be in his thirties, called out as she approached Southgate's Stores. He was wearing a red apron with the shop's logo emblazoned across the front, and was rearranging a bucket of flowers that sat alongside the vegetable rack.

'Hi,' Stella called back, pausing to admire a bouquet of Sweet Williams that were just crying out to be placed in a vintage milk jug on a sideboard in someone's farmhouse kitchen. Their vibrant red and purple flowers were as cheerful as the man's welcome.

'Gorgeous day,' he continued, as he straightened up. 'Can I help you with anything? I'm Niall Southgate, the manager of this place.'

'I'm Stella. Nice to meet you,' Stella replied. 'I'm just browsing at the moment, thanks, trying to get my bearings.'

'Tourist or new to living here?' Niall asked.

'Living here, at least for a bit,' Stella replied. 'I moved in yesterday.'

'Well, on behalf of Southgate's Stores, let me be the first to welcome you to Roseford,' Niall replied. He picked out a bunch of the Sweet Williams that Stella had been looking at a moment earlier, and handed them to her. 'For you. On the house.'

Stella smiled, for a moment unsure if she should accept a gift from a friendly stranger outside a shop, but then, he was the owner, after all. She tucked them into the bag she'd brought with her. 'Thank you. I feel very welcome now.' It was better than the 'welcome' she'd received yesterday from Mitsubishi Warrior Twat, she reflected.

'So are you working locally?' Niall asked. 'Or commuting further afield?'

'Oh, I'm going to be local.' Stella smiled. 'I'm, er, working for the British Heritage Fund.'

Niall rolled his eyes. 'Oh, our benevolent overlords since the lord of the manor handed the place to them. Well, at least the village will be safe from development in the future, if not an invasion of tourists in the summer.'

'I'd have thought that would be good for you,' Stella replied. 'Surely an independent store like yours welcomes the trade?'

'Oh, absolutely,' Niall replied, rearranging the remaining bouquets of flowers as he spoke. 'It's just that I'm worried the lovely, sleepy nature of the place might be, er, somewhat *diluted* if it gets put any more visibly on the tourist map.' He shook his head. 'Not that I get a say, of course. It's all a done deal now, evidently.' He regarded her again. 'What did you say you were doing for them?'

'I didn't,' Stella replied wryly. 'But, since you asked, I'm going to be their, er, Writer in Residence during the renovation and opening year.' She cursed inwardly at *still* not being able to say that without a self-conscious stumble. It somehow didn't sound like a proper job when she said it out loud.

'Oh, wow,' Niall said. 'Well, that's certainly going to be an interesting posting. I'd better watch what I say, just in case it finds its way into your work!'

'I wouldn't worry.' Stella grinned, feeling a whole lot less self-conscious as Niall grinned back. 'You've already made a good impression with the free flowers!'

'Glad to hear it!' Niall replied. 'And can I interest you in anything else from the store on this very fine day?'

Stella kept smiling. 'I'll pop back after Fitz and I have had a bit of a look around the rest of the village, if that's okay. We need to get to know our patch if I'm going to write about it.'

'Fair enough,' Niall replied. 'It was nice to meet you, Stella.'

'You too.' Still smiling as she wandered away from the cool, protective awning of the stores and back into the sunlight, Stella felt her mood growing lighter with every step.

10

Stella kept wandering along the main street, noticing a sweet-looking tea room a few doors down from the general store, a couple of independent shops that sold handmade gifts and treats, everything from wooden children's toys to chocolate, it seemed, and a small gallery with a selection of landscapes in the window that all felt pleasingly local and familiar. Sooner or later, a British Heritage Fund shop would join them, she ruminated, and hoped it would be in keeping with the rest of the village. From what she'd remembered of visiting the village of Lacock, in Wiltshire, a few years ago, which was mostly owned and managed by the National Trust, these organisations were good at working with the local features and blending in with what was already there. She hoped the restoration of Roseford would be as sympathetic.

The gorgeous stone of most of the buildings on the street looked as warm as freshly baked shortbread in the sunlit morning, and the lightest of breezes whispered past as she and Fitz continued their walk through the village, and Stella found herself heading towards the driveway of Roseford Hall.

And what a house it was. She drew a breath as, turning the wide corner through the wrought-iron and stone gates that led to the house, she caught sight of it, tall and imposing, at the top of the drive.

Stella had done some homework; she knew that Roseford Hall had been under extensive restoration since the British Heritage Fund had acquired it three years ago, and that it was very shortly due to open to the public, but nothing had prepared her for her first view of it. There was a lush sweep of manicured green lawn leading to the front terrace of the house, and serried ranks of flower beds that included delphiniums, rhododendrons and old English roses on the sidelines. An ancient oak tree held court at the bottom of the long lawn, and it didn't take a great stretch to imagine Regency ladies and their suitors on picnic rugs underneath it on a hot summer's day.

The romance of the place was sure to inspire her, she thought. It had remained in the hands of the same family since it was built in 1601, although the place had undergone many structural changes through the four centuries of its existence. Now, it was a pleasingly eccentric hotchpotch of old Elizabethan architecture, with chimneys and turrets springing out from all angles, a kind of bricks and mortar representation of the long line of Treloars who'd inhabited the place, and still did, albeit in somewhat reduced circumstances. Its warm stone front façade looked wonderfully inviting on a summer's day.

Fitz was straining to be let off the lead again to explore such a huge sweep of lawn, but Stella held him firmly. She knew he wouldn't be welcome on that particular front garden. She'd ensure he got some lead-free time again on the way back home. For the same reason, she didn't venture as far as the house on this morning's stroll. She'd be back here on Monday, anyway, to start her new job and get her bearings; this was just a bit of a recce so she knew exactly where she had to come.

Taking a long last look at the house, trying to consign it to memory, Stella felt a flutter of butterflies as she thought about coming back here on Monday. What if she wasn't up to the job? What if they'd chosen her because they couldn't afford anyone better? What if she couldn't do justice to the scale of this project, and the beauty of this house and its surroundings? All of the familiar feelings of being just-not-good-enough began to creep in, despite the warmth of the day and the prettiness of the place. Emotions she'd tried to suppress of a time when she hadn't been 'good enough' at her job threatened to creep back to the forefront of her consciousness; of a moment in her past career when her inexperience had led her into very hot water. Perhaps her new start hadn't banished them at all, just made them worse.

Don't be stupid, she told herself. You were offered this job. And no one is going to take that away, despite what happened in the past.

'We're not open yet, love,' a voice called to her, breaking her away from her suddenly gloomy thoughts as she was turning back towards the village.

'It's okay,' Stella called back. 'I'm, er, going to be working here on Monday. I thought I'd come and take a look so I knew where I was going.'

The voice had come from behind one of the mature plant beds that lined the driveway, and as Stella began to walk back the way she'd come, an elderly gardener appeared from behind an impressive bed of rhododendrons.

'Well, an extra pair of hands'll be welcome up at the house, I'm sure,' he said as he stuck his spade into the soft earth of the flower bed. 'And if you can send any of 'em down my way, too, I'd appreciate it!'

'I will,' Stella said. What a contrast this kindly old chap was to Mitsubishi Warrior Twat. She shook her head; the encounter with him had upset her more than she'd admitted to herself at the time. Not so much because he'd been rude to her, but because he'd also been abrupt to Fitz, who didn't know any better. Putting him firmly out of her mind, she headed back into the village centre, determined to enjoy this morning of leisure, where she could just soak up the atmosphere of the place she was now going to call home.

Having skipped breakfast in her eagerness to get out and about, she decided on an early stop at the quaint-looking tea room on the way back. As she tucked into a freshly baked scone with the most delectable raspberry jam, Stella idly listened in to the conversations around her. The tea room was doing good business, even at this time of the morning, and Stella smiled at the young woman who was busily putting together the orders as she passed her table to give an elderly couple sat nearby some scones, too. 'Thanks, Lucy,' the elderly gentleman said, and then spent a minute or two asking after Lucy's family. Stella felt a warm glow of pleasure that the Roseford community seemed to be very much alive and vibrant, despite the takeover of the Hall by the British Heritage Fund, and as she listened in, she learned that Lucy had a young daughter. Stella was reminded of Briony, and resolved to give her a call later.

Scones finished, Stella headed back up the main street, deciding to pop back into Southgate's Stores to grab one or two extras that she'd forgotten to add to her online food order. When she approached the shop again, she smiled to see that someone had propped a bike, complete with wicker basket and comfy leather saddle, against the wall of the shop, with a 'For Sale' sign against it. Painted a lovely shade of peppermint green, it looked perfectly in keeping with its surroundings. All it needed was a bunch of flowers in the basket and the scene would be complete. Immediately, Stella had a thought: she needed transport, and wouldn't a bike be a better option than a small car? It wasn't as if she had far to go to work, after all. Tying Fitz up outside to the metal ring that had been put into the wall for that purpose, she wandered into the shop, picking up a pint of local organic milk, a box of tea bags and a packet of plain chocolate digestives as she went.

'Hello, again!' Niall hailed her from behind the counter. 'Did you have a good walk?'

'I did, thanks,' Stella replied, handing over her purchases. 'I don't suppose you could tell me how much the bike outside is, could you?'

'Ah,' Niall replied. 'I told Shirley that it wouldn't be out there long before someone asked about it, and there you go, I was right.'

'Shirley?' Stella asked.

'Yup.' Niall grinned. 'She bought it last year when she was on a fitness kick, but on her first trip out she fell off and broke her right hip. It's been in her shed ever since. She came in this morning, determined to list the thing on Gumtree, but I persuaded her she might get a better result if she put it outside the shop. Seems I was right.'

'Literally one careful lady owner, then?' Stella laughed.

'Something like that. She wants seventy-five quid for it, if you're interested.'

'I am,' Stella said, before she could change her mind. 'Is there a cashpoint in the village?'

Niall laughed. 'Cash is so twentieth century! Shirley's left her PayPal address for anyone who showed an interest in buying Bertha. Wait a sec, I'll grab it for you.'

Bertha? Stella thought, but then, why not?

In a moment or two, Niall had found Shirley's details, and in a few more minutes, Stella was the proud owner of the bike.

'Just mind how you go on the routes out of the village,' Niall said. 'People tend to meander through the centre, and then put their foot down the minute they reach the boundary. It's only going to get worse once the big house is fully open, too.'

'Thanks for the warning,' Stella replied. 'I haven't got too far to go – I've moved into the gatekeeper's cottage at Halstead House, so hopefully I'll make it there and back unscathed.'

Niall looked thoughtful for a moment. 'Oh, yes,' he said, 'I know it. The guy who owns Halstead had such huge plans for the place when he moved in, but nothing seems to have come off since...'

'Since?' Stella's antennae were twitching at Niall's tantalising tone.

'Well, I don't want to be caught gossiping, of course, but something terribly tragic happened up there, and things have rather stood still ever since. No one really sees much of the guy who owns it; it's almost like he's become a bit of a recluse. You'll be lucky if you see him at all while you're living there.'

Stella's imagination got the better of her instantly. In no time, she was imagining some poor, tortured soul living at Halstead House, in the image of Maxim de Winter, brooding, tall, dark and unapproachable, or even just some lonely old man, white haired and bent over, living out his days in solitude in a crumbling house, with only his memories for comfort.

'I'll let you know if I do,' Stella replied, realising that a slightly strange pause had descended between herself and Niall while she'd been thinking about Halstead House's reclusive resident.

'Oh, he does come in from time to time,' Niall replied, 'but, as you can imagine, he's not the greatest conversationalist.'

'I'll bear that in mind,' Stella replied, smiling.

Snapping back to the moment, and pushing aside all thoughts of anything else but getting home, she thanked Niall and headed out of the shop. Her first thought was that she'd need a helmet to go with the bike. She hadn't ridden a bike since her university days, where it was practically a requirement, although her cycling career had come to an abrupt end halfway through her third year, when Cedric, her trusty third-hand bicycle from a graduate who'd passed it on to her as a first year, had been nicked and thrown into the river by a pissed-up group of hockey players the day finals had ended. Poor Cedric; she still regretted his untimely end.

Fitz looked quizzically at her as she folded up the 'For Sale' sign and popped it into the litter bin outside the shop. 'I know, I know,' she said, grinning down at him. 'This might not be one of my better ideas!'

Deciding against trying to ride the bike home without a helmet and with a dog on a lead to control as well, Stella looped Fitz's lead around her wrist, popped her shopping bag into the wicker basket on the front of the bike and flipped the bike's stand with her foot, before pushing it the half mile back to the gatehouse. She felt a frisson of excitement about making such an impulsive purchase, even though it was at heart a practical one, too. It would make getting to Roseford Hall a little quicker, and would save her the expense of a car. If she needed to go further afield, there was always the bus service or a taxi, after all.

As she arrived home to wait for her supermarket delivery, Stella busied herself with unpacking some of the boxes of books she'd brought with her. Thankfully, the living room of the gatehouse had tall mahogany bookshelves lining the entirety of one wall, so there was plenty of space. As she arranged her collection carefully, she felt as if the books represented the pieces of her life, all starting to fall into place. Now, if she could only tell people what she was doing for a living without the self-conscious pauses, she really would be making progress, she thought.

11

Waking later than he'd intended, Chris Charlton was not having the best start to the day. But then when was he ever, he thought, as he swung his feet out of the side of the bed, wincing as they slapped the rough wooden boards of the bedroom floor. The house, arctic in winter because of the bad windows, the patchy roof and the general lack of modern heating, was a whole lot more liveable in the summer months, the thick walls at least keeping the place cooler when the summer heatwaves occasionally kicked in, but the pleasure was always short-lived. With five large bedrooms and two bathrooms on the second floor, two on the first floor, and a vast dining space and small living room there, too, and a ground floor where the kitchen, further reception rooms and the main family bathroom were, it was a huge place to heat, and an even bigger renovation project.

Glancing at his phone, which he kept by the bed out of habit more than expectation, he saw that he hadn't received any messages. He'd better get dressed and pop over and collect Gabe from his mother-in-law's place, he thought. Guilt, that ever-present emotion, gnawed at him for not going to collect him the previous evening. He was the boy's father, for goodness' sake; he should have dropped everything and brought Gabe back home the minute she'd rung him. But exhaustion and emotional inertia, which were two states that had persisted for well over two years now, had once again taken over.

However, he knew well enough to ring his mother-in-law first. She hated being dropped in on unannounced, and it might well be that she'd taken Gabe out somewhere. She and Gabe had always been close, but had grown even closer over the past couple of years. On his good days, Chris was grateful for this bond. On bad days, it made him paranoid that he was being shut out of both of their lives; not that he could have blamed them if that had been the case, given what had happened.

'Oh, don't rush over,' his mother-in-law had said breezily when he called her after making a cup of instant coffee from the rapidly depleting jar in the cupboard. 'I've got to go to Waitrose and I thought Gabe and I could grab some lunch in Taunton on the way back. There's no hurry.'

Pressing the 'end call' button, Chris once again thought he should have just gone and got Gabe last night. Now, he would be subjected to his mother-in-law's scrutiny *yet again* when he went to pick him up. Not that she did it unkindly; she was, understandably, deeply concerned about him. Under the circumstances, he couldn't blame her. More importantly, he'd missed having Gabe around last night. Friday had become their pizza-and-a-bad-action-film night together; with the boy boarding at a school in Bruton all week, it was a pleasure Chris looked forward to, and he'd kicked himself for not realising what day it was until it was too late. Perhaps they could do it tonight instead.

Oh well, he thought, if Gabe was out and about, at least until the afternoon, he might as well get on with finishing the plastering in the small living room. If he could break the back of that today, he could paint it next week and have it looking a whole lot better for when Gabe came back the following weekend. There weren't that many weekends until school broke up for the summer now, and it would be nice to have somewhere to sit and relax together of an evening, when the work was done. It didn't escape Chris that his thoughts often swung like this; one minute he could feel a spark of optimism, see a future for himself and Gabe here at Halstead House, where they managed to crawl out of the dreadful hole of the past couple of years and make it a place they could both call their home. The next, he'd feel overwhelmed with the sheer amount he had to do to get the house halfway habitable, and remember that he was doing it all virtually single-handed. Then it would wash over him again, how futile it all felt. Mind you, he thought, at least he was starting to recognise that now. In the early days, he'd been in such inescapable agony that his whole life had vanished under a fug of horror, grief and guilt.

Was that progress, he wondered, as he headed back down to the basement to mix up the first bucket of plaster of the day? And if it was, was that a good thing? Did it mean he was finally moving on?

12

Mid-afternoon, with the supermarket delivery safely stowed away, and most of her books now lining the living room shelves, Stella decided that it was far too nice an afternoon to be cooped up in the house unpacking any more boxes. For a moment, she imagined what it would be like if the gatehouse was actually hers; that she wasn't just its tenant for the year, but that she was making it her forever home. She'd already started to like what she saw of Roseford, and the more research she did into the place, the more inspired she felt.

Fitz, too, was agitating to go out again, although the first flush of his near boundless energy had been expended on the walk to Roseford and back, so she decided to take him through the woods behind the house. He ambled at her heels so calmly that she unclipped his lead and let him have a good sniff about to his heart's content. They spent a wonderful hour exploring the woodland, and Stella smiled to see her dog so energised in the countryside around her new home. She snapped a couple of shots on her phone to send to her mother.

On the way back down the driveway, she drew closer to Helena's bungalow, and found herself mooching to the front door, which was ajar. Fitz, desirous of new, more exciting company, bounded ahead, and as Stella knocked at the half-open door, the dog pushed it fully open with a questing nose and padded into the hallway.

'Fitz! Come back here!' Stella hissed as he wandered further into the bungalow, turning sharp left into the kitchen and then disappearing. From the exclamation of not entirely undelighted surprise that Stella then heard, she surmised that Helena didn't mind the intrusion.

'Sorry!' she called as she stepped over the threshold. 'He's awfully nosy.'

'It's fine, come on in.' Helena's voice came from the direction of the kitchen. As Stella hovered in the kitchen doorway, Helena turned and smiled. 'I was just making a jug of iced tea. Would you like some?'

'That would be great,' Stella said. 'I'm sorry, I didn't mean to barge in.'

'You're not,' Helena said firmly. 'I did promise you a cup of tea and a natter, didn't I? Well, now's as good a time as any.'

'Gran? Who are you talking to? Is Dad here yet?' A boy of about eleven or twelve, but tall for his age, came through the back door of the kitchen that led, Stella guessed, to Helena's back garden. He was dressed in a dark blue T-shirt and jeans, and had a mop of brown hair that he kept pushing back out of his eyes.

'Not yet, sweetheart,' Helena replied patiently. 'This is Stella.'

'Hi,' the boy replied. 'I'm Gabe.'

When the boy thrust out a hand to shake, Stella immediately recognised the slightly formal body language and schooled polite-ness of a private education. She'd encountered enough students from independent schools when she was at Oxford to be able to recognise it almost straight away. She shook his hand and smiled. 'It's nice to meet you, Gabe.'

'You've moved into the gatehouse, haven't you?' Gabe said. 'Gran told me she was the first to meet you yesterday.'

'That's right,' she replied. 'I'm hoping to get to know this gorgeous place while I'm here. Maybe you can give me some ideas about where to explore?'

Gabe grinned. 'I'm not here during the week,' he said, 'but Gran knows all the best stuff. She's here *all* the time.'

'Thanks, Gabe.' Helena rolled her eyes. 'I do get out sometimes, you know.'

She turned to Stella. 'Gabe's been helping me to plant out some pansies in the pots. Shall we go into the garden and drink this, so you can admire his handiwork?'

'That would be lovely,' Stella replied. She followed them both out to the back garden, with Fitz close at her heels. Intrigued by yet another new place, the dog took off as soon as he could, trotting around the borders, which were stuffed with lavender, borage and other bee-friendly plants, and upon which Fitz had no hesitation in lifting a leg.

'Sorry,' Stella said, embarrassed, 'he likes to mark new territory.'

'No harm done,' said Helena, smiling. 'It's only natural. I miss having a dog myself. If you need a dog-sitter, I'd be more than happy to have him.'

'Thank you,' Stella replied. 'I'm not sure if I'll be allowed to take him with me on the days I'm at Roseford Hall, so I might just take you up on that.' She hoped she'd only be there for a couple of days a week; the rest of the time she should be able to work from home. She already knew from the conversations and emails she'd exchanged with John Handley that most of the workshops she'd be running would take place in one of the newly restored function rooms at the house, which would also cut down on the travelling she'd have to do.

'Dad won't let me have a dog,' Gabe said gloomily. 'He says it wouldn't be fair as I'm away all week, and he's so busy.' He rolled his eyes at Helena, who patted his hand consolingly.

'Now, Gabe, you know your dad's got a lot on at the moment, and on this one I do have to say I agree.' She glanced at Stella. 'Perhaps Stella would let you play with Fitz sometimes? A kind of doggy loan.'

Gabe's pale face lit up at the thought. 'That would be cool.'

'I'm sure Fitz would like the company.' Stella smiled at the boy. 'He gets awfully bored when I'm writing all day.'

As she admired the terracotta pots of pansies that Gabe had planted for his gran, Stella sipped her iced tea and felt a wave of contentment wash over her. She'd only been here twenty-four hours, but she already hoped that Helena was going to become a friend. She'd drifted away from her friends in London, apart from Briony, as the hours writing for AllFeed were often antisocial and the pace frenzied. If a story needed chasing, she'd had to cancel plans too often, and eventually it had been easier to communicate online than in person. She knew, as a twenty-something in the twenty-first century, that she wasn't unusual in this regard; many of her peer group were the same, and preferred the distance of online friendships to regular meetups. That wasn't to say that when she had met up with her friends that they hadn't all had a brilliant time; it was just that it tended to happen far less often these days. It would be nice to have a friend who was literally just up the road, who she could talk to face to face more regularly.

Gabe was looking at his phone, which he'd pulled out of his back pocket, and frowning. 'Dad said he'd text me when he was coming down.'

'I let him know we were stopping for lunch in Taunton after shopping,' Helena said. 'He's probably just allowing for us dawdling.'

'I suppose.' A shadow crossed the boy's face. 'Are you sure he didn't forget me yesterday, Gran?'

'Of course not.' Helena's reply was a little too quick, and delivered a little too heartily, to be convincing, even to Stella's untrained ears. She sensed that Gabe might have hit upon the truth, but then chided herself for reading too much into a three-word reply. What did she know about this family's dynamic, other than that it was clear that Gabe and Helena adored each other, and liked spending time together? Stella felt a shiver of wistfulness as she listened to them chatting, and saw how at ease they were. It reminded her of when she used to stay with her late father's parents when she was growing up and Morwenna had been off on one of her adventures. The ability to just *be* with someone else, with no expectation, and enjoy each other's company had been perfect for a growing girl, and gave her a lot of the security that was missing from her life with her mother.

Just as she was relaxing back into the cushion of the wooden garden chair that sat slightly in the shade on Helena's patio, Fitz let out a sharp bark, his gaze fixed on the back gate. Gabe, who up to this point had been chucking a ball for the dog, which Fitz had been having enormous fun retrieving and playing tug with, froze as the gate opened, dropping his hand from the ball that was wedged between Fitz's jaws.

'What is it, boy?' Stella asked, a beat too late. The dog was stockstill, and staring in the direction of the gate, obviously on the defensive. 'Come here, Fitz.'

For a moment the dog hesitated, but as Stella clicked her fingers, he reluctantly turned back towards her, glancing repeatedly back over his shoulder as the gate opened and the new visitor to the garden walked through, turned and latched it shut behind himself.

'Dad,' Gabe said, running towards the newcomer. 'I was wondering when you were going to come and pick me up.'

Stella, who'd been occupied getting a treat for Fitz out of her pocket and making him sit in front of her, to restore his equilibrium, took a moment before she looked up, and with a jolt of shock and recognition realised that the man Gabe had just called Dad was none other than Mitsubishi Warrior Twat himself.

For a moment, nobody spoke.

The man, who had been preoccupied with greeting Gabe, finally glanced up. He didn't seem to recognise Stella, but gave Helena a brief smile.

'Thanks for picking him up,' he said. 'I was up to my ears in plaster in the small living room last night, and if I'd left before it had dried, it would have been an absolute bloody nightmare to finish this morning.'

'No problem,' replied Helena. 'And have you finished?'

'Yup,' he smiled briefly. 'A couple of days to dry and it'll be ready to paint.' He looked down at Gabe and slung an arm around his shoulders. 'And then we'll actually have a decent place to sit and watch the football.'

To Stella, who was a keen observer of people, the man's excuse seemed a little too well rehearsed. She was reminded of Gabe's rather uncertain question to his grandmother, about the real reason his father hadn't picked him up from school last night.

'Well, we've had a nice time potting up some pansies, and Gabe's had a good lunch, so probably won't need much feeding tonight,' Helena said.

Stella remained seated in the garden chair, wondering what would happen when Mitsubishi Warrior Twat recognised her. He was still focused on Helena, who was regarding him with a searching gaze as if looking for signs of health or otherwise. Stella knew instantly that she was worried about him. Under the bright light of the afternoon sun, Stella could see why. The man looked pale, despite the summer sunshine, and although he'd brushed his hair and put on a cleaner shirt than the T-shirt and jeans he'd had on when she'd encountered him yesterday, his eyes, devoid of the sunglasses this time, looked shadowed. At least his expression was a lot softer than it had been when she'd first seen him, which she put down to being with the people he loved. He was clearly dotty about Gabe, and kept his arm around his shoulders protectively, and perhaps apologetically.

Finally, pleasantries exchanged, he turned his gaze to where Stella sat.

'Oh, hello,' he said guardedly. Then, a slight flush crept across his pale features. Was she imagining a pleading expression flitting momentarily across his gaze? As if he didn't want Helena to know about his awful behaviour the afternoon before? Seeming to confirm that, he continued. 'I, er, don't think we've met. I'm Chris. Chris Charlton.' He thrust out a hand to Stella, who shook it, playing along with the charade.

'Stella,' she said quickly. 'Stella Simpson. I've moved into the gatekeeper's house at the bottom of the drive.'

'It's so nice to have someone in that house again,' Helena enthused.

'I agree,' replied Chris. 'It's about time it was lived in again.' He turned back to Stella. 'Are you new to the area?'

'Yes,' said Stella, keeping up the pretence. 'I moved in yesterday. This is Fitz, my, er, *dog*.' She arched an eyebrow at her obvious, to her and Chris at least, omission of the word *fucking* from that description.

Chris put a hand down to stroke under Fitz's chin. The dog, still a little unsure about him after yesterday, tossed his head away, but didn't growl. Kneeling down, Stella heard Chris whispering in Fitz's ear. 'Sorry, boy.' She allowed herself a small smile.

'Well, if you need anything, please give me a shout,' Chris said.

'Oh, are you local?' Stella asked. She'd assumed so, when they'd 'met' yesterday, but it was better to keep up the charade in front of Gabe and Helena.

'You could say that,' Chris replied, standing back up and turning to face her with a still slightly sheepish smile. 'Literally just up the drive, in fact. I own Halstead House.'

Stella, jolted both by this sudden revelation and the fact that, up close and without the barrier of sunglasses, Chris's eyes were a really rather gorgeous grey blue, spoke without thinking. 'I thought that you were just a builder or something when I saw you... er... going up the drive.'

Chris, to his credit, jumped in to save her, although, she reflected later, perhaps he was saving himself from being outed as Mitsubishi Warrior Twat in front of his son and mother-in-law. 'Yes, I can see why you might have thought that.'

'Well, I'd better get back to the gatehouse,' Stella said, suddenly keen to escape this conversation in case she let something slip about the way Chris had spoken to her yesterday. And the way he was looking at her, part apologetically and part gentle pleading, was unnerving her a little as well. 'I've still got a fair bit to unpack, and then I start work on Monday.'

'Well, it was nice to meet you,' Chris said. 'And please do come and find me if you have any issues with the house.'

'I will. Thank you.' Still unsettled by the contrast in the man from yesterday, and all of the cross-currents she was feeling between the three other people in the garden, Stella popped her iced tea glass back on the tray on the garden table and turned back to Helena. 'Thank you again for the drink, and the company.'

'My pleasure, dear. Any time.' Helena smiled, but Stella couldn't help thinking she was missing something in the dynamic here. There was a piece of the puzzle still unturned, too far from her reach.

'I'll see you soon,' Stella said. 'Come on, Fitz, let's go home.'

As she walked towards the back gate and down the driveway to the gatehouse, some of it suddenly fell into place. Niall Southgate had mentioned something about there being a tragedy up at Halstead House, and the guy who owned it having been a virtual recluse ever since. Could it be Chris Charlton who'd had the tragedy? He must be the unsociable owner. She felt her face burning as she recalled her ideas about Halstead's owner being either Maxim de Winter or a little old man... neither seemed particularly apt now she'd actually met him.

Decidedly none the wiser, but relieved that Chris didn't seem to be the total tosser she'd assumed when she'd encountered him yesterday, she headed back home to dinner and more unpacking. She was determined to have the gatehouse organised by the time she had to go to Roseford Hall for her first day, and she had more than enough to think about after that garden conversation. She couldn't help her writer's curiosity, much as she tried to put it out of her mind. What had actually happened up at Halstead House to gain it that reputation? And when?

13

Chris, having got over his surprise and embarrassment at encountering the woman he'd been so rude to yesterday sitting having iced tea at his mother-in-law's place, was now chivvying Gabe along. 'Come on,' he said, keen to get back home and away from Helena's assessing gaze. 'You can choose the takeaway and the movie tonight if you want to, seeing as we didn't get to do it last night. Go and grab your stuff.'

'Cool!' Gabe shot off into the bungalow to gather his things, and left Helena and Chris alone in the garden.

'I've washed his uniform,' Helena said, after a pause. 'It's still on the line, but I'll drop it over tomorrow when I've ironed it.'

'Thanks,' Chris said, feeling a sudden, sharp stab of embarrassment again. He appreciated Helena picking up the slack, but felt abject shame that she should have to. It was yet another thing he was failing at. 'I appreciate it, Helena.'

'I know you do.' Helena smiled, and then, with a creak of bones, got up out of her garden chair. 'Look. Chris...'

'Not now,' Chris said, more sharply than he'd intended. It had been all he could do to brush up and make polite conversation with his mother-in-law, let alone that new woman in the gatehouse, and the last thing he needed now was a pep talk.

'I really do think we should discuss...'

'I said not now. Please.' The sun had suddenly vanished behind a cloud, and Chris felt the familiar weariness overtaking him again. Ashamed at his tone, he leaned forward and kissed Helena's cheek. 'I know you mean well, but I can't talk about... anything right now. I just need to focus on this weekend, and spending time with Gabe.' He smiled down at her. 'One day at a time, remember?'

Helena shook her head. 'I'm worried about you. And I'm worried about Gabe, too. He's growing up so fast. We need to be there for him – *both* of us.'

'I know.' Chris shook his head, feeling the weight of her words, and a deeper, darker sense of guilt about why she was having to say them. 'I appreciate everything you're doing. For us both.'

'Ready, Dad?' Gabe came back out into the garden. 'Oh, Fitz has left his ball. Can I go and drop it back to Stella before we go home?'

'Not at the moment,' Chris said, trying to make his voice sound brighter. 'We've got a couple of things to do before we can settle in with food and a film later. Maybe tomorrow.'

'I'm sure we'll be seeing a lot of Stella and Fitz,' Helena said to Gabe as she walked him and Chris to the back gate. 'He'll probably be along to collect it himself at some point.'

'I wish we had a dog,' Gabe muttered, then turned hopeful eyes on Chris, who, to his surprise, found himself grinning down at his son.

'One day, perhaps,' he replied. 'But not while the house is in such a state.'

'So never, then?' Gabe quipped back. 'I mean, it's going to take *ages* to get it all done, isn't it?'

Chris shook his head. 'Hopefully not,' he replied. But even as he said it, he felt a shifting cloud of gloom threaten to settle over his head again at the prospect. But then, he thought, it was difficult to feel enthusiastic about a building that had had its heart ripped out. He knew exactly how that felt.

Later that evening, pizza demolished (mostly by Gabe) and suitably unchallenging, but engrossing action movie selected from Netflix, Chris and Gabe were comfortably slumped next to each other on the worn but comfy sofa in the newly plastered small living room. Chris tended not to sit in there during the week, preferring to keep all of the decorating stuff out, ready to continue the job the next day, but, mindful that he'd dropped the ball by forgetting to pick Gabe up the previous evening, he wanted to make more of an effort. While packing away the plastering buckets and throwing the Hoover around wasn't exactly up there on the high-effort barometer, he wanted them to have somewhere slightly more comfortable to spend their Saturday evening together, for once. It was good to have tidier, more comfortable space to relax in.

'So, Toby's asked me if I want to go and stay with him for the first week of the summer holidays,' Gabe announced, apropos of nothing, about halfway through the film.

'Which one's Toby again?' Chris asked, eyes still trained on Liam Neeson's exploits on an icy road.

'You know, the one with the mum who fancies you.'

Chris genuinely laughed out loud. 'That narrows it down. I mean I'm clearly such a babe magnet!'

Gabe punched him playfully in the ribs. 'She does. Toby told me during prep last week. Anyway, I like him, whatever his mum thinks of you. So can I? Go and stay?'

Huge brown eyes – eyes that reminded him painfully of someone so dreadfully missing from their lives – turned on Chris, and before he knew it, he found himself agreeing to take Gabe up to Shropshire during the first weekend of the school holidays, which was looming alarmingly on the horizon. Gabe's school broke up in the second week of July, and he'd be at home until the beginning of September. Chris loved having him home, but it meant that the renovations on Halstead House would inevitably slow down. Not that he'd been pushing forward with much gusto over the past year or so, anyway. He'd been firefighting the serious issues: the leaking patches in the roof, the rising damp, the gradual replacement of the windows, one by one, but really, he should be far further ahead with it than he was. An extra week might be just what he needed to make some more headway, so that Gabe had more than just a redecorated living room to come home to.

'It would be cool to be able to invite my friends back here.' Gabe was thinking out loud, his head now lolling on Chris's shoulder. 'Do you think that maybe I might be able to do that in the summer holidays?'

Chris wrapped an arm around Gabe and buried his face briefly in the boy's hair, smelling the almond scent of his shampoo. 'Maybe,' he said, not wanting to commit to a firm 'no', which, after all, was probably the true answer.

'Thanks, Dad,' Gabe said sleepily, clearly shattered after a busy week at school and gardening with Helena.

As Chris pulled his son closer in a hug, he tried to concentrate on the plot of the film once again. Then, as regular as clockwork, the guilt started to whisper in his mind, and he realised that, as much as he wanted to escape it, that would never, ever be possible.

* * *

After a lazy Sunday spent putting the last of her books on the shelves of the gatehouse's living room, and touching base with

Morwenna, who'd settled in nicely with Damon in the farmhouse in the south of France, Stella decided an early night was best. After all, she needed to be bright-eyed and bushy-tailed for her meeting with John Handley at Roseford Hall on Monday.

Alas, when she needed it most, sleep eluded her, and she found herself staring wide-eyed at the dawn as it crept slowly through her bedroom curtains at around a quarter to four on Monday morning. Sighing, knowing that there was no way she was going to fall back to sleep before her alarm went off at six, Stella swung her feet out of bed and resolved on a cup of tea and a read-through of the notes she'd been making on possible ideas for pieces about the evolution of Roseford Hall. As she understood it, her job was to create a kind of 'year in the life' portfolio of the place, once its doors opened fully to the public. She'd be clearer after her meeting at the house, though.

At five o'clock, she decided to take Fitz out for an early walk through the woodland. It was handy that the back of the gatehouse had a small conservatory, which led out into the back garden, so she could lock up the rest of the house and move Fitz's bed into the conservatory, leaving the door to the back garden open for him while she was at work. She didn't know how long her days would be, and while she should be able to cycle back to the gatehouse to check on him in her lunch break, having some secure and easily accessible outside space for the dog was an unexpected bonus.

The air was humid, and Stella felt the drips from a sudden downpour an hour earlier dropping blearily from the leaves above her head as she ambled with Fitz through the woodland, her feet treading the well-worn path towards the rear of Halstead House. She felt drawn, inexplicably, to the place now she'd met its owner, and intrigued to know what the story was. The sudden rainstorm had only made the house look sadder, and shabbier, as if it was dying on its feet. She could see water spilling from the broken places in the guttering and splashing down to the terrace below. There were many cracked tiles on the roof, and Stella imagined the damp must be dreadful, especially in the winter months. The exterior walls needed a paint job, and many of the window frames looked flaked and rotten. It was a house that was crying out to be loved, to be saved. Stella wondered how it was possible to buy somewhere like this and then not make it better, but she felt sure there was some piece of the puzzle she was missing; something she just hadn't understood yet.

A movement from one of the first-floor windows caught her eye as the woodland path led parallel with the back of the house. The shrubby hedge that divided the garden from the wood had recently been chopped back, giving her a clear view onto the rear of the building, with its huge sash windows. The ground rose higher into the woods, putting her almost level with the first floor of the house from the pathway, and she found her gaze drawn to the one of the middle windows. There, standing in full view, wearing a grey T-shirt and black boxer shorts, looking as though he was lost in thoughts of a destination a million miles away, was Chris Charlton.

Without thinking, Stella raised a hand in greeting. Clearly, he'd had as much trouble sleeping last night as she had. Chris, startled out of his reverie, and surprised to see her in his line of vision, looked shocked, and Stella felt her face flush in embarrassment. What was she doing, waving like a kid at a man who'd insulted her the first time they'd met and she'd barely spoken to since, excepting the polite but somewhat strained conversation at Helena's yesterday? What a gauche idiot she must look!

In a moment, though, Chris's face had composed itself and the smile that fleetingly passed over his features transformed them into something much friendlier, and attractive. He raised a hand to her in greeting, and she found herself smiling back. Perhaps she hadn't made such an idiot of herself, after all. They stood, united briefly across the gap between the house and the woods as her eyes locked with his.

All too soon, though, the moment was over. Chris lowered his hand once more and turned away from the window. Stella looked down at Fitz, who was looking expectantly back at her.

'You're absolutely right, boy,' she said. 'It's definitely breakfast time.'

As they wound their way home through the woods, Stella tried to put the thought of Chris in his T-shirt and boxer shorts out of her mind. His T-shirt had been form-fitting enough to show the tantalising outline of a toned torso, despite the fact that he seemed a little gaunt, as though he could do with a decent meal or two. With sleep-ruffled hair and that faraway expression on his face, at least before he'd spotted her across the way, he was decidedly attractive. And when he'd smiled at her... Oh, for heaven's sake, she chided herself! The guy had been a total twat to her on first meeting, and had probably only been nice to her at Helena's because he didn't want to show himself up in front of his mother-in-law. Besides, she thought, if Helena was his mother-in-law, that meant that Chris had a wife somewhere, didn't it? She wondered where the woman was. No. Chris Charlton may have turned out to be less of a prat than she'd first thought, but there was no way she was going to occupy any more of her time thinking about him. Even if, she was embarrassed to admit to herself, he had looked nice in his pants.

At five to nine, exactly on time, Stella parked Bertha, the bicycle, in a newly created cycle shelter, took out her laptop from the pannier on the back of the bike and stowed her helmet, which had come via Amazon Prime the day before, in the basket. She was due to meet John Handley at nine o'clock, and he was going to give her a guided tour of Roseford Hall and show her where her on-site office and the potential teaching rooms were.

As she headed up the wide stone steps to the imposing front door of the property, which was ajar, various British Heritage Fund workers headed in and out for another day of preparing for the grand opening of the house, which would happen at the end of July. Stella already knew that a big party had been planned in the grounds of the house, to celebrate two years of hard work and to thank the staff and volunteers for their tireless efforts to get Roseford Hall ready to meet the public. That would be the first major event she'd have to write about, although she was sure that there would be plenty to inspire her, leading up to that.

And inspiration was upon her, pretty much from the moment she walked through the heavy oak door and into the entrance hall. Roseford Hall was clearly a very, very special house indeed. The long entrance hall branched off on either side, a library on the left and a little further down, a dining room, in the process of being dressed with furniture and crockery. Further on, and the space opened up and out into a central square, with a wide, sweeping staircase up to the first floor. Stella looked around for, and found, a grand piano tucked away under the rise of the stairs, and smiled. She hoped it would be left uncordoned, like the one at Tyntesfield House, just outside Bristol, for visitors to tinkle the ivories if they wanted to.

'Stella! You made it!' A booming voice that she recognised from the Zoom meeting hailed her from somewhere above. Glancing up to find its owner, John Handley, she smiled. John was dressed in a maroon British Heritage Fund sweatshirt and brown cords. He came bounding down the stairs, and took her hand, shaking it heartily.

'It's nice to meet you in person,' Stella said, finding her whole arm being shaken. He hadn't come across as quite that loud on Zoom.

'Likewise. Well, now that you're here, let's show you around. Don't worry, you've got A2AA.'

Stella looked momentarily mystified until John clarified. 'Sorry, it's acronyms galore at the moment.' He handed her a folder that he'd been holding in his other hand which, along with a mountain of forms and papers, contained a building pass on a maroon lanyard. 'Access to all areas,' he said as she slipped the lanyard round her neck. 'After all, you need to be able to see the place in its full glory, don't you?'

Without waiting for her to reply, he started to head back up the staircase, narrowly dodging a volunteer carrying a box full of bone china coming back down.

'I'll show you to your "official" office, and then the rest of the place,' John said.

Her guide must have been well over sixty, Stella observed, but he bounded up the steps like a gazelle. Clearly he was a man who loved his job. But then, working in this place, why wouldn't he? Stella was smitten with the house and she'd only been here five minutes. She felt the tingle of excitement, of inspiration starting to flow. She'd been right to say yes to this job.

Five minutes later, and she wasn't feeling quite so overjoyed. With a slightly apologetic air, John led her down a dimly lit corridor to the very last room on the left. Clearly not part of the building that would be open to the general public, it had been reached by a second staircase, which had been used mainly by servants, and must have been part of the old staff quarters. As John pushed the door open, Stella immediately caught the musty smell of damp in the walls. Someone had given the woodwork a quick squirt with furniture polish, as the cloying scent of Mr Sheen was evident, but the room obviously hadn't had any fresh air in a while. The small window suggested that it had once been a servant's bedroom, and the shabby wooden desk in one corner had clearly hastily been put there to create a makeshift workspace.

'Sorry about the slightly, er, compact and bijou accommodation,' John said. 'Believe it or not, we're pushed for space where you won't be disturbed, so this little room seemed to be the best bet. On the plus side, it's tucked right out of the way, so you won't be bothered by people in the wrong place.'

Stella smiled. 'It's fine, John. Thank you.' After all, she thought, she had plenty of workspace back at the gatehouse, and she was sure to be out and about getting a feel for what to write about most of the time, anyway.

'Well, it's a base if you need it,' John replied. 'Now, on to more important matters. Let me show you where the staff kitchen is, where you can, at least, get a decent cuppa and a biscuit most of the time.'

Closing the door gratefully on her so-called office, Stella gradually began to realise why she might have been offered this job, rather than a more established writer. She could imagine many people being pissed off about the room, but she was nothing if not adaptable. She was sure she could make it work.

Wandering back down the servants' stairs, Stella found herself in a busy, pleasant kitchen, where several people were sitting around the wooden table, working out logistics for the coming day.

'Everyone!' John called in that booming voice of his. 'This is Stella Simpson. She's a new member of the team, and Roseford Hall's Writer in Residence.'

Stella suppressed a smile as she saw the woman seated nearest to John wince at the volume of his voice. She wondered how many people who worked with him needed ear plugs.

'Nice to meet you,' 'Hi,' and 'Welcome to Roseford,' were all murmured in her direction before the group returned to their work.

'We're all up to our ears at the moment,' John said, by way of mitigation for the group's muted welcome. 'The Treloar family are away on holiday for the next week, so we're trying to get the really antisocial jobs done before they get back. Even in a house as large as this one, it's still not great for them having so many people on site, knocking it about and rearranging all of their things.'

'Fair enough,' Stella said, although, privately, she thought that anyone who lived in such a gorgeous place should just put up with the disruption. Perhaps she didn't quite understand yet, though.

As if on cue, a fair-haired man walked through the back entrance to the staff kitchen, and the atmosphere perceptibly changed.

'Simon!' John put down the coffee jar he'd been holding and rushed over to shake the man's hand. 'It's great to see you. Welcome back! I thought you and the family weren't due back until Sunday?'

'Ma got a bit fed up with all the rain in the Lake District, as beautiful as it is, and decided she'd come back early. I've got a few things to finish up so I thought I'd head back with her. Sarah and the kids are still up there, but they'll be back at the weekend.'

'Well, it's always good to have a member of the family around,' John said heartily. Suddenly remembering that Stella was there, he turned back to her. 'Stella Simpson, this is Simon Treloar, head of the family and the one who put this whole project in motion.'

'Steady on, John!' Simon grinned. 'Don't let Ma hear you talking like that. She's still in *real* charge, you know.' He extended a hand to Stella. 'Although he's right about me being the one who's managing this transition, from the family side, at least.'

'It's lovely to meet you,' Stella replied. 'I'm the new Writer in Residence for Roseford Hall.' She must be getting used to saying it as she didn't feel quite as self-conscious about the title this time.

'Great to meet you, too.' Simon smiled down at her. Stella, at only five feet four, felt dwarfed by Simon, who had to be nearly a foot taller. They breed them tall in the West Country, she thought unguardedly. She knew some of the history of the Treloar family from the research she'd done before the interview, but it was faintly unnerving to see a living, breathing representative of that family standing in front of her, looking startlingly like the ancestors she'd found online.

'John, I think Irving wants to talk over some of the plans for the Upper Gallery pictures.' Simon turned his attention from Stella for a moment. 'He asked me to come and grab you for a pow-wow when you're ready.'

The slightest flash of irritation on John's face wasn't hidden from Stella, fleeting though it was. 'Sure, sure,' John said. 'I was just going to give Stella the tour, but I'll see him after that.'

'I can show Stella around if you like,' Simon said, glancing back at her with an ill-disguised trace of amusement in his eyes. 'Irving was quite adamant that the pictures needed to be decided as soon as possible, so they could be taken to the restorers and returned in time for the grand opening.'

John, realising that he'd been ever so politely outranked, concurred. 'Of course.' He nodded at Stella briefly. 'I'll see you later, Stella?'

'Definitely.' Stella smiled back at John, sensing that he'd rather have liked to have given her the tour himself, but also slightly relieved that this less *full-on* character had now stepped in. She wondered again about buying some earplugs if she was going to be spending significant amounts of time with John.

'You can bring your coffee if you like, Stella,' Simon said, swiftly pouring himself one and topping it up from the milk bottle that had been left on the side. 'Ordinarily, we ban hot drinks from anywhere other than this kitchen, but since it's your first day, and you've got your own travel mug, I'll let you off.' He grinned conspiratorially at her. Stella wondered if anyone else would have got off so lightly, but with the head of the Treloar family giving his permission, she figured no one could argue.

'See you all later,' Simon said as he and Stella headed back out. She was slightly reassured to observe that the group's response to Simon had been as muted as it had been to her. Perhaps titles didn't count for much, round here.

14

Simon led Stella out of the kitchen and back through the main hall, nodding and exchanging hellos with people as he went. As soon as he knew he was out of earshot of anyone, he turned back to her with a grin. 'I hope you don't mind me muscling in on John's offer of a tour, but he can be a touch *overwhelming* when you first meet him.'

'In contrast to being guided by the owner of the house, you mean?' Stella said dryly, but grinned back.

She was unfazed by titles, having met a few people who possessed them at university, so she didn't feel particularly over-awed by Simon. Especially when he laughed down at her and replied, 'As you can probably imagine, the title's not worth the paper it's written on these days. That's why we're working with the British Heritage Fund!'

They were heading back upstairs, and as they reached the top, Simon led them into the first of four adjoining rooms, a suite comprising a bathroom, a dressing room, a large bedroom over-looking the long sweep of front lawn, and a smaller room, possibly another dressing room.

'These rooms are nearly ready,' Simon said. 'They were the master suite when the house was fully lived in, although they've not actually been slept in since before I was born. It's nice to have them all spruced up and looking as they should, again.'

'Doesn't it bother you?' Stella asked. 'That hundreds of people are going to be traipsing all over your family home very soon?'

Simon shook his head. 'You obviously didn't see the place before the restoration started! The damp alone meant that we were basically hiding out in the back part of the house. At least now it's all been fixed, and we get to stay living here, even if it's not ours any more.'

'You seem very philosophical about it,' Stella said as they wandered through the dressing room, which had been dressed with a beautiful Chinese silk privacy screen in pale yellow, decorated with vibrant blue-green peacocks, and also housed a chest, inside which were various dressing up garments for children to try on.

'It was work with the BHF or lose the house,' Simon replied. 'And no one wanted that. I mean, the rumours a few years ago that we were going to sell to a famous Australian pop star were enough to send the local media into a tailspin! If that had happened, no one would ever have been able to see the place again. This way, anyone who wants to can come to see it.'

'So long as they pay the entry fee,' Stella said wryly.

'Well, yes,' Simon agreed. 'But you, of course, have access to anything you want.' He paused as they made their way through to what Simon explained was the Queen Mary Room. 'This room has the best view in the house from the turret window,' he said, beckoning her over. The floorboards creaked warningly as Stella took a step forward, and then she drew breath as she turned a full 180 degrees, to be able to see the gardens from all sides.

'The Lady Treloar who had this room at the turn of the century fancied herself as a bit of a poet,' Simon said as Stella took in the view. 'She used to spend hours sitting on the window seat here, trying to draw inspiration from outside the window.'

'How wonderful!' Stella breathed. No one could fail to be inspired by the panorama set out in front of her. 'Do you have any of her work that I could see?'

'Unfortunately, yes.' Simon laughed. 'It's not exactly Christina Rossetti, I'm afraid, but the old thing wasn't exactly the most erudite of wordsmiths. She idolised Lord Tennyson, apparently, but didn't really have his gift for verse!'

'That gives me a great idea for a workshop,' Stella said, suddenly feeling a spark of excitement. 'Imagine being able to handle the primary sources of Lady Treloar's work, and then challenging students to write their own, inspired by the same view.' Eagerly, she grabbed her notebook from her bag and scribbled down the idea before she could forget it.

'I'm glad you're already feeling inspired,' Simon said. 'It can make you a bit jaded, seeing things happening so gradually, day in, day out. I kind of forget that there's all this history and heritage in the place, just waiting for people to discover. When you've lived with it your whole life, it's just… there, somehow.'

Stella shook her head, half thinking out loud. 'If I lived here, I'd revel in it.'

Simon looked at her quizzically. 'Sorry,' she said quickly. 'I tend to get carried away when I'm inspired. My mother always tells me I never live in the real world; I far prefer the one in my head.'

'Sometimes it's easier to deal with things that way,' Simon said, and he looked troubled for a moment. 'So, er, how are you finding the gatekeeper's house?'

'It's lovely,' Stella said. 'The perfect place for me and Fitz.'

'Fitz?'

'My dog,' Stella replied. 'He never really got on that well, living in London. He much prefers the countryside.'

'Well, by all means, do bring him in with you, if you can,' Simon said. 'He's more than welcome to explore the grounds, and I'll even turn a blind eye if you want to bring him into your office.'

'Thanks.' Stella smiled up at him, marvelling at how easy-going he seemed, given that his whole house had been ripped up and put back together over the past year. How different he was from the unfathomable Chris Charlton! Trying to push away any thoughts of the latter, she followed Simon back through to the upstairs hall, and along the other side of the staircase that crossed to the opposite wing of the house. She could see, immediately, how the British Heritage Fund was arranging the spaces so it was easy to flow from one room to another, to shepherd their visitors a logical way, and to stop them from veering off into places they shouldn't go.

As they were talking, a strange, high-pitched wail came from the direction of the gardens.

'What's that?' Stella asked, hurrying over to the study window. Just below, on the terrace, strutting their stuff in the most self-important way imaginable, were a pair of male peacocks.

'Oh, don't worry about *them*.' Simon joined her. 'They shout a good game, but they're largely decorative. The louder one is Bert and his partner in crime is, er, Ernie.'

Stella burst out laughing. 'Seriously?'

'Yup.' Simon looked momentarily embarrassed. 'What can I say? My sister Sarah's kids named them and they're *Sesame Street* fans.'

'And is there a Mrs Bert and a Mrs Ernie?' Stella found herself giggling.

Simon shook his head. 'They seem to prefer their own company. Their mother's a feisty one, and keeps them in line. My nieces are desperate for us to get a female so they can breed, but I think they might be a little long in the tooth for that now.'

'So do your nieces live locally?' Stella asked.

'You could say that,' Simon said, a shade ruefully. 'As of last year, they moved back into Roseford Hall with Sarah. It's been a bit of a squeeze.'

'Really?' Stella snorted. She found that difficult to believe, given the scale of the house.

'Well, okay, so it's not like we're all crammed into a one-bedroom flat, but the girls can't quite understand why they can't run around the place like they used to when they were younger. We're pretty much confined to a few rooms at the back of the house these days.'

'But they must love having the gardens to play in,' Stella replied. 'And the pet peacocks, of course.'

Simon nodded. 'Absolutely. They realise they're luckier than a lot of people, and so we're all adapting to living together again. With about fifty British Heritage Fund workers, of course!'

They'd circled back to the staircase again, and Simon gestured for Stella to go downstairs. 'I'll show you the ground floor and the outbuildings, too. It'll be good to get away from the nitty gritty for a while.'

As they crossed the hall, Simon returned to the subject of Stella's accommodation. 'So the gatehouse is okay for you, then?'

'Yes,' Stella replied. 'It's great for getting to the Hall and has everything I need.'

'That's good to know,' Simon replied. 'When the Fund came up with the Writer in Residence idea, I wanted to make sure whoever got the post had a decent roof over their head. The owner's an old mate of mine, too, who could really do with the rent money, even though he'd never admit it, so it was good to be able to sort that out for him.'

'Who owns it?' Stella asked. 'Are they local?'

'You could say that!' Simon smiled, although this time his expression was somewhat guarded. 'I presume you've been up the drive and discovered the wreck that is Halstead House at the top? Well, Chris, the owner, bought the gatehouse at the same time as he bought the main place. The plan was always to rent it out, and the residency came up at just the right time.'

Ah, Stella thought. So Chris wasn't just her neighbour, but also her landlord. That was worth keeping in mind, if anything came up. She was curious, though, how well Simon and Chris knew each other but, mindful of the tragedy Niall Southgate had alluded to, and not wanting to rock the boat on her first day, Stella was reluctant to ask.

'Yes,' Simon continued. 'Chris and I go back a way.' He paused. 'He can be a tricky character to get on with, though, so do let me know if I can help in that regard.'

'How do you know him?' Stella asked, figuring that Simon had said enough to allow her to ask.

'I knew his wife,' Simon said, slightly more quietly. 'We were at university together.'

'Oh,' Stella said, unsure quite what to say to that and still none the wiser, but something about the tone of Simon's voice said it all.

'Olivia died,' Simon said quietly. 'About two years ago. Chris hasn't... well, he hasn't really managed to come to terms with it yet.'

Stella's heart thumped painfully in her chest at this revelation. 'Oh, my goodness,' she said softly. 'How awful for him, and for Gabe.'

'Oh, you've met Gabe,' Simon said, his mood lifting slightly. 'He's a great kid. He's at boarding school most of the time, which should mean Chris is getting on with the renovations to Halstead House during the week, but it's not quite working out that way. Helena, Chris's mother-in-law, who if you haven't met yet, you definitely should, is trying her best to keep Chris on an even keel, but she can only do so much.'

'I had no idea,' Stella said softly. 'Was it, er, sudden?'

'You could say that,' Simon said. 'She had an aneurysm. Poor Chris saw it all. I'm amazed he didn't go off his head with the grief.' Simon, suddenly aware that he'd probably disclosed too much to someone who was, to all intents and purposes, just his friend's tenant, shook his head. 'I'm sorry,' he said quickly. 'I didn't mean to offload all of that onto you. It just still shocks me, sometimes, you know? Catches me out.'

'I can see why,' Stella said softly. 'Poor Helena, too. Losing her daughter so suddenly.'

'She's been an absolute rock for Chris,' Simon said. 'And Gabe, too, of course. But these things take time.'

'They do,' Stella replied, thoughts flickering in her mind, memories long suppressed, of the horrors of her own father's death, and how long it had taken her mother to come to terms with that. Grief left such scars on people and their lives.

'But enough of that,' Simon said, obviously deciding he'd revealed quite enough for one day. 'Let's think about the present. I'll take you to the site office, where you can sit down with the education officer and discuss your ideas for the workshops over the next year, and then I'll let you get settled in.' They walked back in the direction of the house, Simon trying to lighten the mood by introducing her to Bert and Ernie, who looked at her with ill-concealed disdain and indifference.

'Don't be surprised if you wake up one morning and they're outside your bedroom window.' Simon laughed, as Ernie ambled up to him, looking for treats. 'They have a habit of going rogue, especially in the mating season, even though they're devoted to each other. I'm always getting messages and calls to retrieve them from vegetable patches and back gardens.'

'I'm not sure what Fitz, my dog, would make of them!' Stella laughed, too. 'I don't think he's ever seen a bird that big before.'

'They're pretty fierce when provoked,' Simon continued, 'so I think they could hold their own. Although they are rather partial to marmalade on toast, if you need to distract them.'

'I'll bear that in mind!' Stella said as they headed back to the house. She felt a conflicting combination of emotions as she readied herself to meet the BHF's education team; she knew she should be concentrating on the job, but she couldn't stop thinking about what Simon had told her about poor Chris, Helena and Gabe. Losing a parent at such a young age was incredibly hard – losing a wife, and a daughter, equally so. She felt as though she was beginning to understand why things were the way they were at Halstead House, and her generous heart, touched by the sadness that she herself had once experienced, ached for all three of its residents.

15

That night, after a busy day talking through plans and ideas with the education team, Stella wearily pedalled Bertha back from Roseford Hall for the second time. She'd dashed home at lunchtime to check on Fitz, who seemed content to amble around the garden in her absence. He'd not been inclined to walk, so Stella had just grabbed a sandwich and sat in the garden with him until it was time to go back to work. An afternoon of intense discussions had followed, at the end of which Stella had a much clearer idea of what the British Heritage Fund expected from her for their money. She was going to be running workshops with local school parties once the Hall had fully opened, and also other local groups, including a group of writers from the nearest branch of the Romantic Novelists' Association. Stella looked forward to this meeting; she wanted to know if all of the things she'd heard about RNA members over the years were true. If so, she'd probably have to prepare herself for a riot.

In between the public-facing activities, she was expected to write a regular blog on Roseford Hall's website, about a theme or issue that was relevant, and also to produce a series of short stories inspired by artefacts in the house, which she could choose herself. All in all, it was a hefty workload, but one that was a welcome change from the 'Ten Things You Need to Know About Celebrity Z' puff articles that paid her bills in between the more investigative stuff she'd produced for AllFeed. Of course, there had been other reasons she was grateful for the change, too; as a young journalist, she'd made some errors that had impacted greatly on her own confidence and had taken a while for her to come to terms with. She was relieved to be away from those memories, too. One job in particular had nearly ended her career before it had truly begun. But now, four years on, she recognised it for what it had been; she'd been paid to do a hatchet job on a rising star, and she'd done it.

Stella still wondered what might have happened if the piece in question hadn't been debunked. It hadn't been entirely her fault; she'd been told the sources were cast-iron but had turned out to be anything but, and, to a certain extent, her career had been protected because she was so inexperienced, and she'd had support from an editor who had a great deal of influence at AllFeed. She'd weathered the storm, and carried on building her career, and the subject of the article had done the same; in fact, he'd succeeded brilliantly in his field. But she still carried the shame of it with her; of not checking her sources and facts *one last time* before she'd uploaded the article.

Now she'd left AllFeed, she hoped she'd finally find the closure she was looking for, but her inner perfectionist still nagged at her for making such rookie mistakes all those years ago. She'd expected the story to launch her career, but it had very nearly torpedoed it instead.

But this wasn't the time to be looking back. Roseford was a fresh start, and one that she was going to embrace. Besides, it was clear that her new neighbours had far more to deal with than one professional mistake a few years back. Chris, Helena and Gabe were living with their dreadful loss every day. Her mind kept drifting back to that first day she'd met Chris, when he'd shouted at her about her parking, and she found herself softening a little. His grief didn't excuse his poor behaviour, but it was certainly an explanation for it.

After a light dinner, because she was still too keyed up from the day to eat too much, Stella took Fitz for an evening walk. This time, she decided to head west from the gatehouse, across the fields that sprawled gently uphill and wrapped green arms around Halstead Hall and its woodland. Ever on the lookout for livestock, despite Fitz being incredibly well mannered around sheep and even cows, she tried to take in the lush, wide-open spaces, the way the fields undulated and then rolled away before her as she neared the top of the incline.

From her vantage point at the top of the hill, she could see Roseford like an idyllic model village below. She could make out the High Street, with its neatly arranged shops and stores, the sweeping driveway of Roseford Hall, leading up to the magnificent vanilla ice-cream-coloured stone building itself, and then, as she brought her gaze back to the other side of the village, the red-tiled roof of her own house, Helena's cosy bungalow halfway up the drive and then the austere, shabby-looking eaves of Halstead Hall. There is a place and a family that needs some more love, she thought, her mind drifting back again to all she had learned today.

But there *was* a family living there, she reminded herself. Chris and Gabe were the ones who had to make a go of the place despite their tragic loss. With a pang, she found her thoughts drifting towards Morwenna, out in the south of France. Perhaps she'd give her mother a call tonight, see how she was getting on with looking at the possibilities for the wellness retreat project. At the moment, she wouldn't be able to take time off to go and visit Morwenna and Damon, but perhaps in a few months' time she'd grab a week or so and fly out to see them. Funny, she thought, as she and Fitz went back to the gatehouse. All the time I was living with Mum, she irritated the hell out of me. Now she's hundreds of miles away, I actually miss her. Morwenna was, after all, the only family she had. Maybe she'd taken her mother for granted a little too much; after all, you never knew when things could change. Her own loss, as well as Chris and Gabe's, was definitely proof of that.

16

Chris sat down on Monday evening feeling marginally less guilty than he usually did after a weekend with Gabe. Perhaps it was the fact that he'd actually slept well on Sunday night, and that Gabe, rather than wanting to go back to school on Sunday afternoon, had asked to go back on Monday morning instead. They'd spent some time together clearing out one of the larger rooms on the second floor, which Gabe had earmarked as a new bedroom for himself, and by Sunday afternoon they'd moved his bed into the new room, even though it would eventually need decorating. Facing south-west across the valley, towards the Quantock Hills, it had a glorious view and the perfect amount of space for a growing boy. Of course, he might have to move out again if Halstead House ever became more than a family home and transformed into the business that he and Olivia had dreamed of creating, but for the moment, Gabe could have his pick of the rooms.

Driving Gabe back to his small, smart independent school on the edge of the county, Chris felt more than the usual pang in his gut. He missed Gabe during the week, although the stability of the boarding school had been essential during the structural side of the renovations, and also in the aftermath of Olivia's death. Chris had barely been in a state to look after himself, let alone his son, and the school had been incredibly supportive. He did wonder, though, whether it would be better to rethink now. After all, the place, while shabby, was liveable, if not comfortable. But perhaps a nice warm weekend in the summer wasn't the best time to make that decision. After all, the November winds in this part of Somerset came howling from the south-west, and Halstead House would soon be freezing again.

Nevertheless, it had been nice to spend some time with Gabe where he hadn't been stressed, trying to get a nasty job done or having to worry about money. Despite forgetting the boy on Friday night, their Saturday and Sunday had been lovely.

As if on cue, his phone pinged with a text message from the bank, reminding him that he was four-fifths into his arranged overdraft and detailing some of the payments that had gone out over the weekend. Chris sighed, the worry starting to cloud his mind once again. He'd have to find a backer soon if Halstead House was going to get off the ground. Olivia's life insurance and the profits from the sale of the last place they'd renovated had kept things afloat until now, but the money was starting to run out. Thankfully, Gabe's school fees were paid from funds that had been left in trust for Gabe for that purpose by Helena's husband, which was, at least, one less thing to worry about. Even so, Chris still had to find a substantial sum if he was going to complete the renovations. If only the British Heritage Fund had been interested in acquiring Halstead as well as Roseford Hall, but it wasn't of significant enough historical interest. Not that he'd have wanted strangers tramping around his house in perpetuity, anyway. He wondered how Simon and his family were able to put up with it.

He hadn't spoken to Simon in ages. It had been hard, since Olivia's sudden death, to reconnect with her old friends. The funeral had been full of people telling him to 'keep in touch', to 'let us know if you need anything', but how would they have felt if he'd actually done that? How would they have reacted if he'd rung them up, sobbing down the phone, asked them to help him, to take away the dreadful pain of losing someone as vital as Olivia? Most people had murmured the appropriate platitudes, and then drifted away.

He didn't blame them. Chris's loss was a reminder to them all of how fragile life was. And, although he hadn't seen Simon Treloar for nearly a year, despite their living barely half a mile from one another, Chris was sure that Simon would have made time for him and Gabe, such was his fondness for Olivia. Chris often wondered, in his more restless moments, if Simon and Olivia had ever been more than just friends, but Olivia had always denied it, claiming their friendship was purely platonic. He'd believed her, of course, but that sense of insecurity that Olivia had chosen him, the gauche young man from Brighton, to fall in love with, rather than the infinitely more confident and self-assured member of the landed gentry from the West Country still remained.

Realising he hadn't picked up the post since last week, Chris got up and wandered through to the entrance hall, where a bundle of letters lay on the doormat. He tended to ignore the post for as long as he could; there were usually far too many final reminders and requests for money from creditors for him to deal with, but they couldn't be ignored forever.

Riffling through the collection of envelopes and assorted junk mail, putting the brown ones to the back of the pile, Chris's eye was caught by a thick cream-coloured envelope with his name and address in embossed type on the front of it. Convinced it could only be a cleverly disguised advertising campaign for a bathroom company or some other aspirational outlet looking for new customers, he was on the point of chucking it straight in the recycling bin by the front door when the logo for the British Heritage

Fund caught his eye on the back. Curious, he slid a thumb under the flap, and pulled out a prettily crafted card.

The Treloar family, in association with the British Heritage Fund,
invite Christopher Charlton and guest
to the grand opening ball at Roseford Hall on Saturday 21st July.
Arrive from 7pm for drinks in the courtyard.
Black tie essential
RSVP

Chris's hand started to tremble and he thrust the invitation fiercely down into the green paper recycling bin. There was no way he was going to get all dressed up in a penguin suit to ponce around for an evening at Roseford Hall! It was an odd coincidence that he'd thought about Simon and then received this invitation, but that coincidence certainly wasn't enough to induce him to get dressed up and make small talk with people he didn't know. There was no way he was ready for *that*.

As he headed back to the kitchen to grab a cup of tea and a last biscuit, he tried to put the invitation out of his mind. It wasn't so much the idea of getting dressed up for the party itself that had jolted him, he reluctantly conceded as the kettle boiled, it was the way the invitation had casually appended 'and guest' to his name. Surely bloody Simon should have known better? After all, he'd been friends with Olivia for years. Surely Simon should have had the good sense to check the guest list that was being sent out in his name? Swallowing a mouthful of still too hot tea, Chris felt his eyes brimming as the liquid scalded his throat. He shook his head and abandoned the mug on the kitchen counter. Tea would only keep him up all night, anyway.

As he mounted the stairs to put a few items of Gabe's clothing back into his new room before turning in himself, Chris paused at the window where he'd seen Stella early that morning. He remembered how she'd looked: hair scrunched back in a ponytail, trainers and pair of jean shorts paired with a scruffy pale pink T-shirt, Fitz scampering ahead of her through the woods at 5 a.m., probably not expecting anyone to see her at that hour. He'd had a good night's sleep, but had woken early, and, not wanting to wake Gabe, had been caught by the movement in the woods that had turned out to be Stella and Fitz on their morning constitutional. Raising a hand in response to her smile, he'd found himself also smiling back. He was amazed at how easily that smile had been exchanged; they'd barely said a word to each other in the time she'd been at Halstead, apart from that angry first meeting and a friendlier chat at Helena's when, despite the fact that she could have dropped him in it, she'd remained discreet about the previous day's confrontation. He was grateful for that, but he really did feel he should try to make amends. When he saw her again, he'd apologise properly to her.

Chris lingered in Gabe's new room for a few moments after he'd put his clothes away in the chest of drawers. He missed his son, and yet again wished he was at home with him, rather than boarding. But Gabe seemed to like it, and, after the past couple of years, he wanted to ensure that Gabe was as happy and secure as he could be. After all, what eleven-year-old boy wouldn't want to be living at a school that had sports on tap and all his mates around him? Why on earth would he want to come and live permanently in a draughty old house with nothing but his grieving father and granny for company? It was a no-brainer, really. Feeling disconsolate again, Chris headed back out of Gabe's room and to his own bedroom on the north side of the house. Really, he thought, Gabe's happiness was all that mattered. His own happiness, after everything that had happened, was completely immaterial. He just didn't deserve to be happy.

17

After another busy and inspiring few days at Roseford Hall, Stella was just putting the bins out at the bottom of the winding driveway that led to Halstead House when she heard the unmistakable rumbling of a wheelie bin coming down the tarmac. Glancing behind her, her heart gave a little flip. She squished the last of her cardboard waste into the green box and tried to be out of the way and back on her own garden path before Chris reached her. Then she realised she still had her own black wheelie bin to put out, and sighed in resignation.

'Evening,' she muttered as Chris drew nearer. He might have been nicer to her at Helena's house last weekend, but she felt a sting of embarrassment as she recalled the idiotic wave she'd given him when she'd seen him at the window on Monday morning, and she still didn't entirely trust that he wasn't going to turn on her again over some other perceived irritation.

'Hi,' Chris replied. He pushed the black bin neatly next to green ones and then gave a brief grin. 'I could drive the bins to the road-side but it seems a bit lazy, so I'm committed to taking several trips from the house.'

'A real hardship,' Stella said, a little more sarcastically than she'd intended.

Chris looked surprised at the bite back, and then grinned. 'First world problems, eh?'

'Well, I must get on,' Stella replied. She had no desire to prolong this conversation any further, no matter how different Chris had seemed in front of Helena.

'Stella?' Chris walked briskly after her. 'Look, do you have a moment?'

'Why? Has my dog got out again? Sorry, my *fucking* dog?'

Chris looked apologetic. 'I've been meaning to say sorry about that. I shouldn't have spoken to you and Fitz like that, especially since it was your first day here. It was rude and stupid and you didn't deserve it. I'm sorry. I wasn't having the greatest day.'

He seemed completely sincere, and such a contrast to the angry bloke she'd nicknamed 'Mitsubishi Warrior Twat' that Stella smiled despite herself and decided to thaw. 'Apology accepted. Fitz doesn't usually bark like that, either. He's quite protective of me, and he didn't know what to do when you started shouting at us. And he was excited to explore the space, of course.'

'Did you not have much garden where you were before?'

Stella shook her head. 'There was a small garden, but not enough for a working collie like Fitz. He had a walk around the park twice a day. I worked from home, which helped a lot, but when the post came up at Roseford Hall it seemed the perfect way to give both me and Fitz some much needed fresh air and a change of scene. And a bit of peace and quiet.' She conveniently edited out the part about her mother applying for the job on her behalf – in hindsight, it made her feel like the saddest human being on the planet.

Chris grinned. 'And then, on your first day, your idiot landlord, who should have remembered you were moving in, shouts at both of you. I really am sorry.'

The sunlight caught the grey of Chris's eyes as he said this, turning them the blue colour of a warm summer sky, and Stella felt a flutter of something other than just irritation. Something different; entirely, pleasingly different. 'Apology accepted,' she replied, plunging her hands into the green bin again and trying to squash the last pieces of card that had stubbornly refused to sit well in the box. 'Everyone's allowed at least one bad day.' Especially now I know about your wife, she added silently.

'Look, Stella,' Chris began again as she straightened back up. He rubbed a hand on the back of his head as he looked at her. 'I know you've been sticking to the path around the woods when you walk Fitz, but there's so much land here, and there's four acres of woodland and another three of fields behind the house that came with it when I bought it. If you want to walk him around the place, then please do. The only thing I'd ask is that you keep him under control around the vegetable garden that's near the back of the house. Olivia—' He paused briefly before continuing. 'My wife, she planted it up the summer before she died, and Gabe likes to tend to it with Helena when he comes home from school at the weekends.' He swallowed. 'It's kind of like their memorial to her.'

Stella felt compassion rise inside her for a man whose loss was obviously still so raw. 'Of course. I'll be careful, I promise. I'm so sorry about your wife.'

'Thank you,' Chris said. 'She died two years ago last Christmas. It still takes me by surprise sometimes.'

'I'm sure,' Stella replied. 'And thank you. Fitz will go nuts when he realises how much space there is for him to play in.'

'Well, someone needs to use it. After all, there's enough room for all of us.' Chris, obviously keen to move on from the painful subject of his wife, added, 'And if you happen to spot any fences down, or anything that shouldn't be there, please let me know. I'm getting enough hassle from the Parish Council as it is for not maintaining this place to their standards; I don't want to give them any more ammunition.'

'Tricky job to manage all of this on your own, though,' Stella mused. 'Have you thought about getting some help?'

'It's on the list, like everything else.' Chris gave a hollow laugh. 'Honestly, you'd never believe how long that list is getting now.'

'Well, I walk Fitz at least twice a day, three times if he's particularly hyper, so I'll let you know if I spot anything amiss.'

'Thanks,' Chris said. 'Oh, and there might be the odd few sheep grazing up in the first field behind the wood, so it's probably worth keeping an eye out for them. I don't know how Fitz is with them.'

'Wary, mostly!' Stella laughed. 'He stung his nose on an electric fence once and hasn't been able to look a ewe in the eye since!'

Chris laughed properly then, and Stella had the feeling that it wasn't something he did very often. 'Poor old boy. That'd be enough to put anyone off!'

Stella realised, with a jolt, that she liked the sound of his laughter.

'He wasn't terribly happy about it, no.'

'Well, I'd better get these other bins down,' Chris said, after a short pause. 'See you soon.'

'Yeah,' Stella replied. 'See you.'

As she headed back to the gatehouse, she reflected how different he'd seemed to the shouting, aggressive idiot she'd encountered on her first day in Roseford. Perhaps, now they'd actually spoken calmly, she'd begun to understand his bad temper a little.

When she got through her back door, she sat down at the kitchen table and grabbed her notebook. 'A stream tumbling down a dark, mossy bank into a lake as deep as oblivion itself,' was what had immediately sprung to mind about the sound of Chris's laughter just now. It certainly read better than her angry scrawl of moving day, when she'd written, in block capitals in her journal: 'I'd love to shoot that fucking man out of the cannon he thinks he sounds like.' Both were ridiculously cheesy lines, she thought, grinning, but practice made perfect, didn't it?

18

The next couple of weeks were both exciting and informative. Stella quickly got into a routine: walking Fitz at about 7 a.m., cycling down to Roseford Hall to start work by nine, gathering notes and observations about the current state of the restoration works, and then updating the Writer in Residence blog most afternoons to reflect what she'd learned. The BHF expected her to produce a minimum of two blog posts a week to document the progress the hall was making, but, in the early weeks at least, Stella found herself writing more than that, so taken was she by her surroundings.

Simon Treloar was a regular visitor to her small office, and talking to him Stella began to realise just what a wrench it had been to make the decision to put Roseford Hall into the care of the British Heritage Fund. Simon's easy manner and welcoming smile instantly put Stella at ease, and though she was meant to go to John Handley with any questions or issues, she soon found herself instead emailing Simon, or asking him when he popped in to touch base.

One morning, about three weeks after she'd started work, Simon put his head around her office door, holding an envelope.

Stella, who was just checking the stats on her blog post of the day before, looked up as she noticed his intrusion.

'I hope I'm not interrupting anything?' Simon asked as he hovered in the doorway.

'No, not much,' Stella replied, jotting down the stats in a notebook before closing the browser window. 'What can I do for you?'

'Well, this is a bit embarrassing, really,' Simon said, edging into the tiny space past the filing cabinet, a new addition that seemed to take up half the room. He reached her desk and when his eyes flickered to the seat in front of it, Stella grinned. 'Have a seat.'

Simon folded himself into the chair and then passed Stella the envelope. 'I meant to give this to you the week you joined us, but it got lost underneath a huge pile of paperwork to do with the restoration of the artwork in the Long Gallery. I'm sorry it's taken me so long to find it again.'

Curious, Stella furrowed a finger under the flap of the envelope and pulled out an invitation on embossed card to the opening celebration ball.

'Oh, crikey!' she said as her eyes scanned the details. 'I'd forgotten that it was this weekend.' She hadn't expected an invite, so she'd been happy to watch the preparations for it from a distance.

'Yup.' Simon smiled ruefully. 'I'm sorry you didn't get the full time to RSVP, like everyone else.'

'Is attendance, er, mandatory?' Stella asked, wondering if she'd blot her copy book with both Simon and the Fund if she said no. She wasn't madly keen on dressy occasions, having attended a few too many formals at university that had usually ended in someone being chucked into the river off a punt.

Simon grinned at her. 'Not at all,' he said. 'Although it might be good for you to show your face – let people know about the residency and your plans for it. A good way to drum up some trade for the workshops.'

'So you're basically telling me it is, then?' Stella grinned back.

'Well, okay, maybe I am...' Simon raised an eyebrow. 'But only if you're happy to.'

'I'll have to dig out a frock,' Stella mused, 'but yes, count me in.'

'Great!' Simon stood up. 'And I'm sorry it's such short notice – totally my fault.'

'No worries,' Stella said. 'These things happen.'

As Simon stood up again, his fair hair was caught by a stray shaft of sunlight that suddenly streamed in from the small window behind her. She wondered why he hadn't been snapped up by some attractive girl in need of a lord of the manor, complete with his own stately home.

'I wasn't sure if you had a plus one,' Simon said. 'But it's perfectly fine to bring them if you do. Just let me know so I can sort out the seating plans for the tables.'

'No, it's just me,' Stella said hurriedly. 'No, er, plus one just yet.'

'Great,' Simon said. 'I mean, not great that you're not, er, you know, needing the plus one, but...' he trailed off, suddenly looking endearingly embarrassed.

Stella couldn't help but laugh. 'It's fine, Simon,' she said. 'I know what you meant. See you later.'

Simon shook his head and ambled out of the door, saying goodbye as he did so. She wondered if he was bringing a plus one, and was curious to see what he or she might be like. Then, realising her imagination was going to get the better of her if she spent too long musing on Simon's love life, she wondered who else might be at the Roseford Hall ball. Perhaps it would provide inspiration for a blog post or two?

19

Chris, in contrast, was not feeling so well disposed towards Simon Treloar. He knew, when he thought about it rationally, that the 'plus one' part of the invitation had probably just been an oversight on Simon's part, but it still hurt. Not having Gabe around this week hadn't helped him – somehow, knowing he was having a great time in Shropshire in a 'normal' house with his 'normal' friends just seemed to rub salt in the already open wounds. However, Gabe was due back on Saturday from Toby's house and Chris would be pleased to have him home again.

As it was, on the Thursday before the party, Helena came sauntering through the front door, bearing a quiche she'd baked 'because I know you've probably not eaten anything decent this week, and you probably won't until Gabe comes back' and carrying the invitation, which she'd obviously clocked and retrieved from the recycling bin by the front door.

'No,' Chris stated adamantly, when Helena presented him with a plate of quiche and the invitation tucked carefully underneath it as a kind of place mat.

'What? I thought asparagus quiche was your favourite?'

Feigning innocence, Helena picked up a fork and delicately poked at her slice, murmuring appreciatively at her own baking prowess.

'Don't play games with me, Helena,' Chris replied, picking up his slice in his hands and taking a big bite, just to piss her off. She was forever giving him old-fashioned looks about his and Gabe's table manners; claiming the two of them were descending into some kind uncivilised blokeish oblivion without a consistent female influence in their lives, her own notwithstanding.

'I don't know what you mean,' Helena said, taking a sip from the glass of water she'd poured. 'I just assumed this had fallen into the wrong bin when the postman delivered it.'

Chris raised an eyebrow, and looked Helena directly in the eye until she wavered, and put her glass back down on the table with a clunk.

'Well, all right then, perhaps that's not entirely true.'

'I'm not going to Simon Treloar's fucking lord of the manor booze-up,' Chris said mutinously. 'Especially since he doesn't even own the place any more.'

'It might do you good to get out,' Helena said, picking up her fork and taking another delicate bite of the quiche. 'After all, when was the last time you actually got away from this place for a few hours? I can't remember you even going down the pub since...'

'Since Olivia died, Helena?' Chris, realising that he was getting angry at the wrong person, but, too afraid that the anger might give way to something else if he dropped his guard, chose anger as the best course.

Helena looked away, and Chris immediately knew he'd gone too far, but he could feel a spark smouldering inside him, about to burst into wild, uncontrollable flames.

'That's not fair, Chris,' Helena said quietly. 'You can't blame me for worrying about you, day after day, week after week in this house, alone most of the time, fighting a very difficult battle.

Halstead is dragging you down, darling, and you're letting it. Why not get away from that, just for an evening? Catch up with Simon and your other friends for a bit.'

'Simon was Olivia's friend,' Chris muttered.

'Maybe initially,' Helena observed, 'but he was just as fond of you as well. It'd do you good to get out. I'll even take your dinner jacket down to Southgate's Stores if you like – they've got a dry-cleaning service. It'll be spick and span by tomorrow if you dig it out for me now.'

Chris jumped up from the table. 'No, Helena,' he said eventually. 'The invitation was in exactly the right place. I'm not going to his fucking ball. And nothing you can say will convince me otherwise.'

Helena, seemingly unperturbed by Chris's anger, stood as well, picking up the plates and popping them on the side above the dishwasher. 'I don't think you're being terribly fair, Christopher.'

'You just don't get it, do you?' Chris's voice raised a notch as he paced around the room, and he knew deep down that he was aiming at entirely the wrong target, but at this point he didn't care. And Helena using his full name irked him, too. 'I couldn't care less if I never see anyone else again. I'm quite happy in this house, crappy as it is, with Gabe, trying to make it into something slightly less crappy as best I can.'

'But are you?' Helena's voice softened, and she drew closer to Chris, who'd paced so far he figured he might as well keep going, out into the hallway and towards the small lounge on the first floor.

'Well, maybe happy's the wrong word,' Chris admitted, 'but what else am I supposed to do?' He stopped, and ran a hand over his eyes.

'Oh, darling,' Helena murmured. 'It was a stupid idea. I don't know why I thought it was anything else.'

Chris shook his head. 'It's all right, Helena. It's just that I can't do this on my own. This house was Olivia's vision, and she drove so much of the work on it forward. How am I supposed to complete it when all I can think about is the fact she's not here to see it? And that fucking invite from Simon with its stupid plus one was yet another trigger.' He crumpled down onto the threadbare chaise lounge that faced out through the large windows overlooking the grounds at the front of the house.

Helena walked carefully over to where Chris now sat. She perched herself on the other end of the chaise lounge, mindful to give him space. 'She was my daughter,' she said quietly. 'There is not a day that goes by that I don't miss her.' She paused as Chris put his head in his hands. Moving slightly closer to him, she placed a gentle hand on his shoulder. 'I know you miss her, and I know you feel lost without her, and I do too. But Gabe needs you, Chris. He needs you to be there for him, to love him enough for the both of you.'

'I can't,' Chris groaned. 'Every time I see him, I see her, staring out from behind his eyes, judging me for the fuck-ups I just keep making.' He raised his head again. The tears hadn't fallen, but the frustration and hurt were written all over his face. 'I can't go on like this.'

'No,' Helena agreed. 'You can't. But the question is, what *are* you going to do? It's been over two years. Olivia wouldn't want to see you like this, stagnating in this draughty shell of a house, losing your rag at the drop of a hat, pouring good money after bad. Something has to change.'

'I can't sell Halstead House,' Chris said flatly, beginning to pace again. 'For one thing, it's unsaleable in its current condition, except to a property developer, who'd raze it to the ground. And much as this place is driving me mental, I won't let that happen.'

'But you're not *living* here, are you? You're just existing in this shell of a place, with no real destination in mind. And keeping

Gabe at boarding school is just a way of delaying making any firm decisions about what happens next in both of your lives. Are you sure that's fair? To either of you?'

'Oh, I don't know, Helena.' Chris looked at his mother-in-law. 'And that's the problem, isn't it? I just don't know. It's like, ever since Olivia died, I've been in a kind of stasis, hoping that, if I keep everything the way it was when she was alive, she might magically come back to life and we can pick up where we left off. Even though I know that's completely insane.'

'She was a wonderful woman.' Helena was blinking back tears, and Chris felt that old, familiar churning self-loathing and guilt that he was putting her through this again. He knew he shouldn't have to keep reminding himself that she'd lost her daughter, too, but at times, when the walls of the house felt as though they were closing in on him, it was hard to remember.

'She was,' Chris murmured. He rose to his feet and took her hands in his. 'And I'm sorry. I know I'm not the only one who misses her.'

'We were lucky to have her,' Helena said softly. 'But she *is* gone, Chris. But Gabe, and this house, and me, if you need me… we're all still here. You owe it to yourself, and your son, if nothing else, to make some decisions. You can't stay in this paralysis for the rest of your life. Olivia wouldn't want that.'

Chris nodded his head. 'I know. I do *know* that, Helena. Really. But knowing it and actually doing something about it are two entirely different things.' He glanced around the room. 'I mean, where do I even start?'

'With this.' Helena, who'd somehow managed to pick up the invitation from the table, pushed it into his hand. 'I know you said you didn't want to go, but I really do think it'll do you good to get out. Simon's bound to have invited the movers and shakers, and at the very least he'll have some of his wealthy mates going, so it's the perfect chance to put yourself and this place out there. If you want to make something of Halstead House, even if it's not the artists' retreat you originally planned, then this is a good place to start.'

Chris shook his head. 'I can't. Even if Southgate's dry-cleaning service could make my dinner jacket presentable, the last time I wore it, was... well, a long time ago. It probably won't even fit.' The previous occasion when he'd worn black tie, it was to some function at Olivia's firm, and he knew he'd need to belt in the trousers – he'd lost a lot of weight since Olivia had died.

'Well, you've got time to have a shave and get a good night's sleep and I said I'll get your dinner jacket dry-cleaned just in case, so let's hear no more excuses,' Helena continued briskly. 'I can babysit Gabe – he can spend the night at the bungalow with me. He's due back on Saturday anyway, isn't he?'

'I'm not going to get out of this, am I?' Chris said, allowing his mother-in-law a rueful smile.

'No. You're not.'

Chris sighed. 'Okay, okay. But I can't promise to enjoy myself. It'll be strictly a networking thing. And since I don't even know what I want to do about this house, I don't even know who I should target.'

'Well, perhaps that's your other job over the next couple of days,' Helena replied. 'It's high time you decided what to do, if you're insisting on keeping hold of it.' Squeezing Chris's hand one more time, she gestured to the desk that was shoved unceremoniously in the corner of the lounge. 'I bet you haven't looked at the plans for months. Why don't you have a think? Decide what you think it really needs?'

Chris shook his head. 'I don't know, Helena. I don't know if I'm ready for that yet.'

'No time like the present,' Helena said briskly, but her face softened swiftly. 'Losing Olivia taught me that you can't wait for things to happen because everything might change beyond your control in an instant. Don't you think it's worth just making a little start on where you see Halstead House going? What you really want to do with it? I know the artists' retreat was Olivia's idea, but you are free to think of your own plans, too. Her ghost won't haunt the place if you decide to turn it into a spa, or a bed and breakfast. Or if you just want to make it a proper home for you and Gabe, that's fine too.'

'I'm not sure I could afford the upkeep if it ended up being just Gabe and me here.' Chris smiled wryly. 'We always knew we'd have to subsidise living here somehow. Perhaps it is time to really put some thought into where it goes in the future.'

'That's my boy,' Helena said, all briskness again. 'Now, dig out your dinner suit and I'll pop it down the dry cleaner's this afternoon. That way you've got no excuse to duck out.'

Chris rolled his eyes. 'Okay, okay,' he repeated, glancing back at his mother-in-law. 'Thank you, Helena.'

'Oh, get on with you,' Helena replied. 'Someone's got to keep you and Gabe on the straight and narrow.'

As Chris reluctantly made his way to the bedroom he was using to store the non-essential wardrobe items, he wondered how Helena always had the knack of getting him to do the things she wanted him to do. He knew, had Olivia still been alive to witness their conversation, she'd have been laughing herself senseless by now. Surprised to find that he himself was smiling at that thought, he hurried off to dig out his dinner suit.

20

Later that afternoon, Stella jumped as there was a knock on the stable door of her kitchen. Smiling as she saw Helena through the window, she crossed the kitchen to let her in.

'Busy?' Helena asked as she wandered in.

'Just catching up on a few outstanding projects.' Stella glanced self-consciously at the kitchen table, where the detritus of a day's work lay. She'd chosen to work from home and she'd usually be in the second bedroom where her desk was, but she'd wanted to sit somewhere different, to try to kickstart her creative juices. Unfortunately, sitting in the kitchen had really only kickstarted her appetite for toast and coffee, and work had come a distant second. It would have to be back to the office tomorrow. The table was littered with four half-empty coffee cups, a plate that had contained a swift toast and jam breakfast, more toast for lunch, and her battered moleskin notebook, spine sprained open and pages held down by the Venetian glass paperweight that Briony had brought back for her from her last holiday. 'Sorry about the mess.'

'My late husband was an artist,' Helena said. 'I'm used to the messiness of the creative process. At least you're not likely to end up splattering the furniture with oil paint.'

'True, although it must have been lovely to be married to someone so artistic.' Stella smiled. 'I do tend to get rather caught up in projects, though, to the detriment of everything else.'

'Oh, we muddled along.' Helena laughed. 'And the kids found it fascinating, the way he approached things. My daughter, Olivia, was keen to set up Halstead House as an artists' retreat.'

'Wow!' Stella said. 'It's the perfect place for something like that, or at least it would be if it wasn't so...' She trailed off, embarrassed.

'Shabby?' Helena kept smiling. 'It's all right. Things have been, er, put on hold, since she died, as you can probably tell.'

Stella's heart ached for Helena as she made such a frank admission. 'So, was Olivia an artist?' she asked gently.

Helena nodded. 'She loved watching David when he was painting. She used to sit in his studio all the time during her school holidays. In the end he set up a short easel for her, so she could occupy herself while he worked. As she got older, she moved from art to numbers, did a mathematics degree and that was that. But when she and Chris saw Halstead House, she wanted to do something to support other artists. We'd lost David about a year before they found it, but when she first clapped eyes on it, she knew it would be perfect.'

'I'm so sorry, Helena,' Stella said softly. 'It must be awful to have such a stark reminder of what could have been.'

Helena shook her head. 'It's getting better. It's just frustrating that Chris is in a state of paralysis about the house. He needs to make some real decisions about it, for his sake and Gabe's, and soon. They can't do another winter there. Gabe spent most of the Christmas holidays at mine last year, Halstead House being as cold as it was. And don't get me wrong, I adore him, but being a parent to him wasn't quite what I had in mind for my twilight years.' She took the proffered cup of tea from Stella's grasp. 'But enough dwelling. That's not why I'm here.'

Stella raised an eyebrow. 'Not just passing, then?'

'Not exactly.' Helena took a sip of her tea. 'Wondered if you could do me a favour?'

'Sure,' Stella said. Helena, whilst undeniably spry, was old enough that Stella wouldn't hesitate to help her if she could. 'What can I do for you?'

'Well, I suppose you know about this ball at Roseford Hall?'

'Yes, of course,' Stella replied. 'In fact, Simon dropped me in an invite to it recently. Said I should probably show my face and chat up a few patrons, promote my position at the house.'

'Sounds a bit of a bore,' Helena observed.

'Well, I guess it's going to mean talking shop a fair bit,' Stella replied. 'Anyway, what about it? Have you been invited, too? Shall we go together?' She quite liked the idea of hanging out with Helena for the evening; she reckoned she'd be a lot of fun with a few glasses of fizz inside her.

'Well, er, it's not exactly me I'd like you to go with,' Helena said. 'I was wondering if you could keep an eye on Chris for me? He's not wild about going, but I've managed to talk him into it for the sake of Halstead House's future. He might find a backer there willing to invest, help him to turn it into something more lucrative.'

Stella's heart gave a thump. She'd met Chris precisely three times since she'd moved in; the first time he'd yelled at her, the second time he'd implored her with his eyes not to shop him to Helena for his poor behaviour, and the third he'd apologised, but it still hadn't exactly been an easy conversation. Not to mention the whole weird waving thing they'd done. Hardly the basis for spending a decent evening with someone.

'I don't know, Helena,' Stella said dubiously. 'I mean, I barely know him. And why would he need a chaperone, anyway? Is he likely to lamp someone or something?' Stella wouldn't have put it past him.

'No, nothing like that,' Helena said hurriedly. 'It's just... he doesn't get out much these days, and he'd never admit it in a million years, but he's probably quite nervous about going on his own. When Olivia was alive, she was always dragging him out to places, but he'd never really go out under his own steam. Now she's not here...'

'Even so, Helena, I don't know if I'm the best person to, er, *drag him out*. Doesn't he know anyone else around here?'

'Oh, he knows Simon quite well, but Simon'll be up to his ears pressing the flesh all night. Chris just needs a familiar face to touch base with during the evening. And, since you don't know very many people...' She trailed off again hopefully.

'Hmmm.' Stella was still non-committal. She might be going to the ball, but accompanying Prince Not So Charming wasn't part of the deal.

Helena, obviously sensing that Stella might need a little more convincing, tried another tack. 'Chris might not want to admit it, but he needs to do some networking if he's going to have any hope of getting Halstead House's future secured. The trouble is, he's just not very good at it.'

Stella sighed. 'Helena, I've been in Roseford for barely a month! He's lived here for a lot longer. How am I supposed to know who he should speak to? Surely he must have a little black book to help him? Or a LinkedIn profile?'

'I'm not asking you to make any introductions,' Helena replied, 'but if you could just... I don't know, watch out for him?'

'If you're that concerned, why don't *you* go with him?'

Helena grinned. 'He's long past listening to his mother-in-law. Besides, I'm washing my hair that night and I'll have Gabe. You need a jaunt – Chris definitely does. I'm not asking you to be his date.'

Stella sighed. Something told her that Helena wasn't going to take no for an answer, so it wasn't even worth trying. 'Okay, I might do it. But only because you asked me to.'

Helena laughed. 'I'm flattered. And I'll make sure he's on his best behaviour.'

'I've no idea what that even looks like,' Stella said wryly.

'He's capable of great kindness, and immense joy,' Helena said thoughtfully. 'He's just forgotten that.'

Stella's heart went out to the woman in front of her, and before she knew it, she'd agreed to be Chris's not-date date for the evening.

'I promise you, he's really good company when he gets going.'

'That's as may be, but I need to put on my game face at this do to promote my own work, too, so I doubt we'll get much of a chance to find out.'

'Well, just having you there will put my mind at rest,' Helena said.

Stella sighed in good-natured resignation. 'Good job I dug out my only decent party dress, then. Let's hope it still fits!'

Helena smiled. 'Let me know if you need any help finding something to wear. I've got a few things stashed away that you could borrow.'

Stella nodded, slightly tickled that Helena would think that any of her clothes would fit her, but said thank you. Helena was tall and elegant, with beautifully cut and styled white hair. Stella was considerably shorter and curvier and had never considered elegance part of her repertoire.

'And I'll dog-sit for you too, if you like,' Helena continued. 'Can't have poor Fitz on his own all night.'

'Thanks,' Stella said. 'I'm beginning to feel like you're my Fairy Godmother in disguise!'

Helena laughed. 'I don't know about that! I have just asked you to chaperone my son-in-law, after all.'

'That's true!' Stella laughed as well.

'You know,' Helena said thoughtfully, 'Chris has popped down to the builder's merchant in Taunton. I could show you over Halstead House if you like. I've spent so much time telling you why Olivia was inspired by it – maybe, as a writer, you might find something in it to inspire you, too.' She gestured to the table again. 'That's if you're not too busy?'

'Won't Chris mind me nosing around his house?' Stella asked warily. 'I don't want to intrude.' All the same, she was curious to see the inside of the place; she remembered the way her imagination had fired when she'd seen the one light on after she'd moved in. She couldn't help wondering what the rest of it was like.

'What he doesn't know won't hurt him,' Helena replied briskly. 'Come on, come and take a look.'

'Oh, all right then.' Stella smiled. 'But I'm blaming you if he comes back early and springs us.'

'I'm happy to, er, what is it they say, *take one for the team*.' Helena smiled. 'And don't worry, Fitz can come, too. He can't do any damage.'

As Stella and Helena walked together up to Halstead House, Stella couldn't help reflecting that, so far as mothers-in-law went, she wouldn't have minded having one like Helena one day. Chris was lucky to have her, even if he didn't seem to realise that at times.

21

Stella was blown away by the proportions of Halstead House. Helena had taken her to the top of the house, and then worked her way down, showing Stella the five bedrooms on the second floor, all gorgeously proportioned and full of light from the huge windows, if dated, shabby and rather damp now, down a creaky yet beautifully carved oak staircase to the first floor, where she paused.

'This is what we fondly call the Rogues' Dining Room,' Helena announced as she led Stella across a large, wide room that stretched the length of the first floor, with a couple of bedrooms leading off to the back of the house.

'Wow!' Stella breathed as she wandered through the generous space that looked out over the sprawling front lawns and across the valley to the Quantock Hills beyond. 'That's quite a view. I can see why Olivia wanted to make the house a retreat for artists. There's certainly a lot of inspiration right outside the window.'

Helena smiled sadly. 'She had such plans. Every day, when I wake up, just for a moment I forget that she's gone, and then it all comes rushing back to me.' She turned away from where she'd joined Stella at the large bay window and busied herself with shaking out the dusty curtain that framed it.

'I'm so sorry, Helena,' Stella said softly. 'I can't imagine what it's like to lose a child.'

'It was a horrible thing,' Helena replied, 'but also such a random, unexpected occurrence. If she'd had a gradual illness, we could have prepared ourselves – me, Gabe, Chris, Olivia herself – for the end, but there was no time. She was gone, in a few moments, because of the aneurysm. Chris witnessed it all.' She shook her head. 'It takes a long time to process something like that.'

Helena, clearly wanting to focus on something else, turned her attention to the other curtain. 'I don't know why Chris just doesn't take these damned things down,' she said as she shook it and motes of dust flew out, catching in the warm sunlight that was gently radiating through the room as the sun turned on its predictable journey across the front of the house. 'They must have been up here at least twenty years.' She turned back to Stella. 'Sorry, dear, I say it every time I come into this room. Must be losing my faculties at long last!' She looked back at Stella.

Stella, mindful that there really was nothing she could offer in the way of comfort, merely murmured, 'I'm so sorry, Helena.'

Helena smiled. 'I know. And I know it's difficult to know what to say, so please don't worry.'

'Oh, Helena,' Stella said. She ached to reach out and give the older woman a hug, but she didn't feel she knew her well enough to do that, yet. 'You must miss her.'

'I do,' Helena replied. 'But it is what it is. I had Olivia for thirty-four years. I was lucky.'

Stella was shocked at Helena's fortitude in the most tragic of circumstances. Then her mind drifted to Chris, who had seen his wife die in front of his eyes and been unable to save her. What must that do to someone? And poor, poor Gabe, who lost his mother at the age of nine years old. She felt her own eyes fill with tears as she tried to process the full extent of that loss to a family.

'But enough about the past,' Helena said firmly. 'We've got plenty of house to look around while his majesty is in Taunton. Come on!'

Stella was grateful for the change of subject, and for Helena's calm control of the situation. She supposed that the older woman had needed to take control of a lot of things after her daughter had died, and, to a certain extent, was probably still doing so, if her close relationship with Gabe and her careful eye on Chris were anything to go by. Trailing after Helena as she continued walking through the generous, airy space of the Rogues' Dining Room, Stella's mind was racing as fast as her heart.

'This was where the main studio for the retreat was intended to be,' Helena said. 'It's got such stunning light throughout the day – the sun moves around the front of the house, so those shade lovers can hide in one corner, and those who want the sun can have it bathing their canvases with light for as long as the sun is up.'

'It's perfect,' Stella breathed. She could sense the possibilities in this room, in the proportions, and the balance of it. The high ceilings and large, elegant rectangular windows did indeed let in the light, and although she painted with words, rather than paints, she could immediately imagine herself spending time in this room, at her desk, creating stories that were inspired by the beautiful view from the windows.

'And it's going nowhere.' Helena sighed. 'Chris is so entrenched, he just can't take it forward. If he's not careful, the running costs alone will wipe him out and he'll have to sell it anyway.'

'What'll happen to your bungalow and the gatehouse then?' Stella asked. She was only renting the gatehouse, but she still couldn't bear the thought of leaving it.

'Oh, I own my bungalow outright,' Stella said. 'When I sold my house to come and live here, I made sure of that. It's not that I didn't trust Chris, but I needed the security of owning my own home. If Chris does end up selling, I've got my place, and the garden, and the access rights to the driveway, so I'll be fine.'

'And the gatehouse?'

'Depends how desperate he is for the money at the end of all this,' Helena replied. 'By my estimation, he's got about six months until the cash runs out and then he might have to sell, if he can't make this place work financially.'

Stella's heart thumped in her chest. The salary she received for the Writer in Residence post only worked because the gatehouse was thrown in with the job. What would happen if Chris decided he had to sell it before Stella's year-long post was up?

The sudden uncertainty must have been written all over her face as Helena put a hand on her arm. 'Don't worry,' she said briskly. 'Even if Chris does have to put the gatehouse on the market, he'd have to give you notice. And the powers that be would have to rehome you for the duration of your contract here. You'll be fine.'

Stella shook her head. 'I know it seems selfish, given everything you've had to contend with over the last couple of years, but I really feel as though I'm settling here. I'd hate to have to move out so soon.'

'I'm sure it won't come to that,' Helena replied. 'Chris, for all of his faults, wouldn't evict you without knowing you had somewhere to go.'

Stella laughed. 'That's a relief. Although perhaps he's the one who needs a new home – or, at least, the chance to make this one a bit warmer!'

'You're definitely seeing it in its best light at the moment,' Helena said. 'The times last winter I had to strategically insist that Gabe came to stay with me, for fear the poor lad would freeze to death in his bed.' She shook her head. 'Chris claims he doesn't feel the cold, but I'm not sure if I believe him.'

Privately, Stella thought that, judging from the amount of empty wine and whisky bottles in Halstead House's recycling bins every week, it was no wonder that Chris seemed immune to the lower temperatures in the winter. Even in the summer, he seemed to get through enough booze to floor an elephant. Although, perhaps, given what he'd been through, that wasn't entirely surprising. Alcohol was a great temporary painkiller, after all, even if, in the long term, it made things infinitely worse.

'I'd still love to write in here, though,' Stella mused. 'It's got such a wonderful view of the hills, and there's such peace. If I lived in this house, I'd probably never get anything done other than writing. The gatehouse is stunning, but the back bedroom I use as a study is so small, and it faces north so it's chilly too, even in the summer.'

'Why don't you ask Chris if you can use this room as a work-space?' Helena said. 'It's not as if he's in this part of the house a lot – most of the renovation work he's doing at the moment is focused on the other side of the house. He tends to avoid this room, anyway. Too many memories and frustrations about what could have been.'

'I wouldn't want to impose on him,' Stella said, thinking that Chris was probably sick to the back teeth of seeing her and Fitz flat-footing all over his land. 'I'm sure he's got enough to think about without worrying about what I'm up to in the house.'

'No harm in asking,' Helena said briskly. 'After all, no one else is using this room, except for Gabe occasionally when he wants an indoor space to ride his skateboard, and, between you and me, I'm not convinced the floorboards are up to that!'

'Okay, I'll definitely think about it,' Stella said, knowing absolutely that she wouldn't. Gorgeous as the room was, there was no way she could ask Chris to use it, knowing what he and Olivia had planned for it. The whole house was riven with that awful, permeating grief, and despite the beauty of the summer's day outside, there was no escaping it. Stella could sense it in the air, and felt as though she could almost touch the memories that the walls must have witnessed, including Olivia's final, dreadful moments. It would be so easy to get drawn into the tragedy here, to revel and wallow in it as a writer, to draw inspiration from it. But these were real people, with a real history; how could she possibly allow herself to be inspired by it?

'If you're worried about being here, then don't be,' Helena said gently, as if reading Stella's mind. 'Olivia often got drawn into places, and their history. A lot of her own artwork was very intimate, and told stories that people who saw her paintings found difficult to see. She had a darkness, and she tapped into it regularly to inspire her. Try to think of Halstead like that, at the moment. It's crying out for a new voice inside it, a new beginning. The trouble is, I'm not sure Chris is in the right place to give it that new start.' She shook her head. 'Maybe having another creative soul here is just what the house needs.'

Stella smiled. 'You're very persuasive, Helena. Give me time. I might swap the bedrooms around and use the front one as a study instead. Lovely as this room is, I do feel as though it might put me off from writing the happy, optimistic public relations pieces that I'm under contract to produce for my employers about Roseford Hall!'

'You should take inspiration where you find it, surely?' Helena asked. 'And there's plenty of history here; not just my own family's.'

Stella looked around again at the room. 'It *is* a beautiful room, and a wonderful view,' she said wistfully. 'I'll definitely think about it.' And this time, when she said it, she was almost convinced she would.

22

Stella didn't have much time to dwell more on the Rogues' Dining Room, though, as the day of the ball came swiftly around. On the Saturday evening, she looked critically at herself in the mirror. She had to concede that she looked all right, considering she hadn't worn the dress since her last formal at Oxford. It was a black satin strappy, knee-skimming number with a flared skirt, which she dressed up with a scarlet pashmina and kitten heels. She'd swept her hair up into a loose bun, mostly to get it off her neck as the night was very humid, and it felt as though there was a storm coming. For a moment, she dithered about taking a coat, but decided against it; she had a taxi booked for midnight, and Helena had offered to give her a lift to Roseford Hall, so she probably wouldn't need one. And if she wanted to come home earlier, she could always walk – it was only three-quarters of a mile, after all.

Just as she was checking her make-up, her phone pinged with a message from Helena:

Gabe and I are running a bit late after the cinema – sorry! Have rung

Chris and asked him to pick you up. Leave Fitz in the conservatory and I'll get him on the way by. Hope that's OK! x

Great, Stella thought. So babysitting Chris starts right now, does it? She felt a bit annoyed with Helena, and was half tempted to text her back and tell her to tell Chris not to worry. She could just wear her flat shoes to walk, and take her heels in a bag to change into once she got there. It wasn't far, after all. Yes, she'd do that.

Checking her face one last time in the bathroom mirror, she hurried back into the bedroom to find her black ballerina flats, slipped them on and then headed downstairs to lock up.

'See you later, Fitzy,' she said to the collie, as she led him out into the conservatory, locked the kitchen door and opened the one to the back garden, adding, as all dog owners tend to, on the assumption that the canine in question understands, 'Helena's going to pick you up in a bit.'

Just as she was dropping the latch on the garden gate, there was a toot from behind her, further up the drive. Stella turned to see a significantly cleaner Mitsubishi Warrior approaching from Halstead House, with, as it approached, an observably more spruced-up Chris Charlton in the driver's seat. Her heart gave a thump as he approached, Matrix-style shades now more flatteringly offset by a beautifully cut black dinner jacket, bowtie and freshly ironed white shirt. He looked like Laurence Rickard dressed as James Bond, and Stella swallowed at the totally unexpected reaction she had, just catching sight at him.

'Hi,' Chris said as he drew closer and wound down the window. 'I take it Helena's been in touch?'

'Yes, but it's fine – I don't need a lift,' Stella said, beginning to walk briskly down the rest of the driveway towards the main road. 'It's not far to walk.'

'Don't be daft.' Keeping up with her from the Warrior, Chris,

Stella noticed, looked her up and down before returning his eyes to the road ahead. 'We're both going the same way. You might as well get in.'

'No, honestly, I'd rather walk. I need to clear my head.' Stella picked up the pace as she neared the end of the driveway. 'Simon dropped an impromptu speech on me for this evening, which I've been working on all afternoon, and I need to get myself psyched up for it.'

'Typical Simon.' Chris turned his eyes back to her and grinned. 'Always delegating the things he can't be bothered to do himself. Used to do it all the time when he was a student, apparently.'

'I think he's got to make an even bigger speech,' Stella said, grinning back at Chris, despite herself. 'But he thought it might be good publicity for me and the writing project if I said a few words.'

'And who could resist the lord of the manor?' Chris's grin turned swiftly into a grimace, but only for a split second. He brightened again and gestured to the passenger seat. 'Seriously, Stella, get in the car, please? I promised Helena I'd make sure you got there in one piece, and I assure you I'm not some kind of kidnapper in a dinner suit.'

'That's exactly what a kidnapper would say,' Stella said. 'Oh, all right then. And Helena did ask me to keep an eye on you, after all.' She pulled open the passenger door and hopped up into the Warrior.

'Did she indeed?' Chris shook his head as he pulled out of the driveway and onto the main road. 'That doesn't surprise me. She's always trying to find ways to keep me on the straight and narrow.'

'Does it work?' Stella asked.

'Not really.'

A small silence fell between them, before Chris, obviously feeling the need for small talk, spoke again. 'So what do you have to say in this speech of yours?'

Stella grimaced. 'It's basically about my early observations of Roseford Hall. I've got some lovely little anecdotes about the place – one of them involving Bert and Ernie—'

'Bert and Ernie?'

'The Roseford Hall peacocks. Simon says they go pretty much everywhere in the village.'

'Yup,' Chris replied. 'The bloody things got into Helena's back garden a year or so back and demolished her herbaceous border. Simon really ought to put up a fence or something.'

'I think they're pretty much a law unto themselves,' Stella said, remembering what Simon had told her about their liking for marmalade on toast.

'I wonder if they'll put in an appearance tonight then?' Chris smiled.

'Hopefully they'll crow through my entire speech and drown me out,' Stella replied. 'I'm sure anything they have to say will be far more interesting.' She leaned forward and changed back into her kitten heels as they approached the turning to Roseford Hall.

'Don't put yourself down,' Chris said gently as they turned right into the lane that would bring them to Roseford Hall's sweeping driveway. As they did, a steward in a hi-vis vest directed them to a parking spot on the newly laid gravel car park off to the left of the drive.

'Looks like we'll have a bit of a walk to the party, after all,' Chris said wryly as he parked the Warrior. 'I hope my dress shoes are up to it.' He switched the engine off and pushed open the door, and before Stella could gather up her pashmina and her handbag, and wonder whether she should change back into her flats for the trawl up the driveway, he'd come around to her side and pulled open her door. Scrabbling around for her belongings, Stella was glad of the hand he offered her to help her to step down from the pickup truck;

climbing in had been fine, but in these shoes she was concerned about turning an ankle.

'Thanks,' she said as his hand closed around hers. It was warm and dry, and she felt a slight tingle as he helped her down from the running board.

'You're welcome.' Chris smiled down at her. 'See? I promised I wasn't going to kidnap you.'

'I'm very relieved.' Stella smiled back. 'No chance you could give this speech for me as well, is there?' Her hand was still clasped in his as she said it, and she felt a shiver of... *something...* running down her spine.

'I'm afraid not,' Chris said, seeming to remember his hand after a beat too long and gently letting go of Stella's. 'That's all on you, I'm afraid.'

'Well, let's get on with it, then,' Stella said, tucking her pashmina over her arm. 'Hopefully Simon will be so entertaining that no one'll bother listening to me.'

'I hate to tell you this, but Simon thinks he's far more entertaining than he actually is.' Chris gave a short laugh. 'Olivia always used to tell him off for hogging the limelight at people's weddings when they asked him to be best man, even though he can't tell a story to save his life. It might be down to you to wake the audience back up, I'm afraid!'

'Great,' Stella groaned. Working behind a screen, writing lists and puff pieces for AllFeed, had never felt so enticing. Then she remembered what her mother had said about living her own life, rather than just writing about other people's, and conceded that, if nothing else, she was certainly doing that right now.

23

As they walked up to the Hall, Stella scrabbled in her handbag to retrieve her speech so she could look at it, and possibly edit it, one last time, even though she'd checked the copy at least a hundred times and she knew it was the best she could write. She knew she'd captured her first impressions of Roseford in all of its glory, and yet she still felt nervous.

'You're going to be great,' Chris said gently, as if reading her thoughts. He'd adjusted his naturally longer stride to accommodate her shorter one, especially in her heels, and she turned to him, grateful for the vote of confidence.

'I'd settle for merely okay,' she replied. 'If I can get through this without stumbling over my own words, and these ridiculous heels, I'll be happy.'

'I doubt you've ever settled for okay in your life,' Chris said as they walked through the iron gates that had been pushed back to the stone walls for the night, and headed towards the courtyard area in front of Roseford Hall's impressive frontage where the evening was taking place. 'You don't strike me as the under-achieving type.'

'Maybe that was true, once,' Stella replied. 'But being a perfectionist isn't exactly the most relaxing of life choices. This residency was supposed to be a chance to have some time to take stock, while still being creative.'

'What did you do before?' Chris asked.

Stella realised, with a jolt, that this was actually the first time she and Chris had had a proper conversation. 'I was a journalist,' Stella replied. 'I got what I thought would be my big break on a large international news and entertainment website.'

'The kind of thing that reports regularly on those ripped nobodies from *Love Island* and the like?'

Stella felt affronted. 'Well, it wasn't always things like that. We did cover some more weighty stuff as well. I once went to interview a woman who'd climbed Kilimanjaro with her eight-month-old son strapped to her back, and made him the youngest summiteer ever.'

'And I bet he was thoroughly enriched by the experience,' Chris said dryly, 'and when he grows up he'll be able to brag to all his mates about having his nappy changed with a view of the Himalayas!'

Stella, despite herself, laughed. 'Well, perhaps it does all seem a bit pointless, but every person has a story. Not all of them are epic or worthy, but stories are what make people, and I've always been fascinated by them.'

'So what made you give up a life like that and decide to be Roseford's Writer in Residence, then?' They were heading towards a group of people that included Simon, who were all hovering around a white-clothed table waiting for their complimentary glasses of fizz.

'Would you believe me if I told you that my mum applied for the job on my behalf?'

'What?' Chris gave her an incredulous look. 'And you still took it?'

Stella laughed. 'I know. But, after I'd made a fool of myself on the phone to John Handley and told him he'd made a mistake, she took the opportunity to tell me a few home truths.'

Chris looked wary. 'Helena has a habit of doing that to me. I usually ignore her, though.'

'The worst thing was, although I wanted to ignore her, she was actually right.'

'Parents usually are,' Chris replied, 'although we often don't admit that until later!'

They were nearly at the drinks table, and as they approached, Simon broke away from the group to greet them.

'Watch out,' Chris murmured so that only Stella could hear. 'Lord of the manor incoming.'

'Ssh!' Stella chided. 'He is my boss, after all.'

'No, he isn't,' Chris muttered back. 'The British Heritage Fund is your boss. He's just a rather pretty figurehead, remember.'

'That's as may be, but he still asked me to speak,' Stella said hurriedly, before Simon made it over to them.

'Stella! You made it all right, then?' Simon, cutting quite a dashing figure in his dinner jacket, fair hair brushed and gleaming in the light from the skeins of fairy bulbs that had been strung over the courtyard, smiled down at her. She was rather surprised when he leaned forward and kissed her on the cheek. They'd become friends, but she was still an employee. But before she could think about it too closely, Simon had turned his attention to Chris.

'Chris! So good to see you. It's been too long, mate.'

'It has.' Chris extended a rather stiff hand to Simon, whose face, as he took it, showcased a complex set of emotions. Stella, newly aware of the history between the two men, and feeling uncomfortable that this was clearly the first time they'd seen each other in a while, watched with a mixture of apprehension and fascination.

'I'm so glad you could come. We really ought to have had a

drink together long before this.' Simon's voice, injected with a note of false heartiness, seemed entirely different to his usual casual tone.

'Yes. We should.' Chris, clearly not wanting to give anything away, withdrew his hand as quickly as was polite.

'How's my gorgeous godson?' Simon asked.

'Good, thank you. Well, as good as could be expected, under the circumstances.'

Simon's expression changed dramatically in a split second. 'Look, Chris...'

'Not now, Simon,' Chris said. 'Let's talk later. I'm sure you've got more important people than me to waste your time on.' He turned his attention back to Stella. 'What can I get you to drink?'

'A glass of fizz, please,' Stella replied, trying to ignore the very obvious cross-currents between the two men in front of her.

Chris strode the final few yards to the drinks table and waited to be served. Stella, still standing in Simon's company, gave what she hoped was a bright smile. 'Are you all set for your speech?'

Simon grimaced good-naturedly. 'As ready as I'll ever be. You?'

'Just about,' Stella replied. As she was about to open her mouth to reassure him about his speech, and take her mind off her own, Chris returned, bearing two glasses.

'Proper champagne, Simon,' he said, handing Stella her glass. 'I assume the Fund is picking up the tab for that?'

Simon's expression remained carefully friendly, but Stella noticed a slight tightening of his jaw as he replied. 'Well, this is their place now, after all.' He turned his gaze back to Stella. 'I'll be officially opening this thing in about a quarter of an hour. Are you okay to meet me by the front steps then?'

'Sure,' Stella replied, suddenly keen for Simon to leave, so that the undeniable atmosphere between the two men would dissipate. She felt as though she was missing huge puzzle pieces, and she couldn't make any sense of what she was seeing. And the last thing she needed before she had to give her speech was to get caught up in it, whatever *it* was.

'Don't ask,' Chris said, clocking the expression on Stella's face. 'It's a long, long story.'

'Fair enough,' Stella replied. 'Shall we get on with what we're both here for, then? Pressing the flesh and trying to further our own agendas?'

'Such a venal way of putting it!' Chris gave a laugh. 'You don't look the type.'

'Must be a hangover from my days as a scurrilous journalist.' Stella found herself laughing at his surprised expression.

'Remind me never to get on your bad side, then.' Chris gave her a smile, and it was clear that, with Simon's departure, some of his tension had left him. Maybe it was the dinner suit, maybe it was just that Chris made her curious, or maybe it was the warm night and the auspicious surroundings, but she couldn't deny the sudden attraction that seemed to be knocking at her heart and brain.

No, she thought. There's too much, way too much there to unpack, whichever way you try to approach it. She might be beginning to make a friend of Chris, but it couldn't be anything more. Taking a good gulp of her champagne, she tried to focus on being in the moment, enjoying the buzz of people around her, attempting to commit the sights and sounds to memory, for the next Roseford Hall blog post.

24

Just as Stella was finishing her glass of Dutch courage, people started to move towards the front of the house, where Simon was already standing, getting ready to officially open the event. Stella felt a flutter of nerves in her stomach as she saw the guests, all in black tie or evening dresses of various splendid colours, assembling, waiting to hear first Simon, and then herself.

'You'll be fine,' Chris said, leaning in towards her ear just before they moved towards the steps. His breath, tinged with the aroma of the champagne, sent a shiver down her neck. 'Just picture them all starkers, or only in their socks.'

Stella burst out laughing. 'That's not helping!'

'I'll get you another drink in, for when it's all over,' Chris said. He turned to face her. 'I'll be back in a tick. Go and join Simon.' His eyes twinkled mischievously. 'After he's spoken, the crowd'll be gagging to hear someone who's actually entertaining, believe me.'

'I'm not sure I'll fit the bill,' Stella muttered, but she felt encouraged by his vote of confidence, and the knowledge that, if she did this well, she'd have a whole lot more sign-ups for the workshops she'd be running over the next year. Handing her glass to Chris, who whispered a last 'good luck', she took a deep breath and walked towards the edge of the steps leading up to the front door. Simon, who was just getting into position, holding the radio mic, glanced at her and smiled. He paused to allow her to join him at the top of the steps, and then flipped the switch on the mic.

'Good evening, ladies and gentlemen,' Simon began. 'And thank you for joining us tonight for the official opening celebration here at Roseford Hall.'

Naughty Chris, Stella thought, as Simon looked around, totally relaxed, and completely in command of his audience. He was a great speaker, and he had the crowd in the palm of his hand with his diction, gentle, self-deprecating humour and welcoming air. She felt fresh nerves wash over her as she listened, and wondered how she was going to be able to follow him.

'Of course, had my great-grandfather known that Grandad was going to make the first in a series of dreadful financial decisions that led to this place falling down around our ears for the next couple of generations, he'd have cut the old bugger off immediately!' Simon laughed, and the crowd, many of them local and well versed in the history of the man in question, laughed along with him. They knew what a wrench it had been for Simon to make the choice to work with the British Heritage Fund, and they were pleased to see him so at ease, now, with the transition.

As Simon wound up his speech, and began to introduce her, and her new role, Stella's eyes scanned the crowd, looking out for familiar faces and something to focus on. She saw John Handley, looking like Mount Everest in his dinner jacket, a pint of real ale in one of his large hands, standing with a diminutive woman who must be his wife. Various other volunteers and paid staff were dotted around the place, and, just off centre of her eyeline, Chris had taken up a position with a glass of champagne for her and a pint of Coke for himself. Stella, waiting for Simon to finish, found her gaze drawn to him. His expression, fixed on Simon, was unreadable. Yet again, she wondered what the undercurrents between the two men really were; there was obviously something she was missing. But then, she reasoned, she hadn't lived in Roseford very long; this place clearly had an intriguing history. She was looking forward to unravelling it.

'Er... Stella?' Simon's voice brought her back to the moment and she gave a start. She could feel a blush creeping up her cheeks as she turned from observing the crowd back to the man holding the microphone.

'Sorry,' Stella said, keeping the mic down so only Simon could hear. 'I was miles away.'

'That interesting, was it?' Simon smiled wryly at her.

'No, I mean, you were great,' Stella stammered, cursing, yet again, her tendency to lose sight of the present. She really did need to get a grip.

Bringing the mic up, she turned back to face the crowd. For a moment, her eyes fixed on Chris again. This time, his expression was far more amenable, and as their eyes met across the heads of the audience, he gave her a smile, mouthing 'good luck' again. Stella felt a tremor in her knees that wasn't entirely to do with nerves.

'Hello,' she said brightly, wishing she'd paid more attention to what Simon had said when he'd handed over to her. The tone of her voice made a few people chuckle good-naturedly, and she smiled in reciprocation. She drew a calming breath, and began to speak.

'It's so lovely to be here tonight, in this glorious place, waiting to embark on this new adventure, here at Roseford Hall...'

As she settled into her speech, she remembered what her mother had once said to her about moving her sight line around an audience, so you didn't just focus on one person and make them feel self-conscious. But, much as she tried not to fix her gaze on him, she kept flitting back to Chris, who was standing and listening, eyes completely focused on her. She found herself getting distracted as she caught his eye, and he gave a smile and slight nod that was sweet, and so unlike his normal pensive expression that she stumbled and lost her place. Glancing down to consult her cue cards, she couldn't remember how far she'd got. She decided to cut her losses.

'Well, er, that's about all I have to say for now,' she stammered, 'but please do consider joining me for one of the workshops I'll be holding over the next year. You may find a few things out about Roseford Hall that might surprise you.'

As the applause rippled from the courtyard, Stella, despite her disorientation, smiled and once again caught Chris's eye. He smiled back more broadly and mouthed, 'Well done.' She felt absurdly pleased.

'Great stuff, Stella,' Simon said, gently removing the microphone from her hand, which was still clenched around it from nerves. 'I've left a sign-up sheet over on the publicity stand, so hopefully that'll bring in a few punters.'

'Thanks,' Stella replied. Her knees had started to shake as she'd finished speaking, as the adrenaline subsided, and she was keen to get back to Chris and that second glass of champagne. 'Do you need me for anything else?'

'No, I don't think so,' Simon said. 'Go and grab a drink and we can touch base later.'

As Stella turned to walk carefully back down the stone steps, trying hard not to trip on the combination of age-worn stone, high heels and wobbly legs, she realised she couldn't remember a word of what she'd just said. And then she froze on the spot. The creeping sense of dread and shame she felt in that moment threatened to overwhelm her. There, having just arrived, and thankfully, she hoped, having missed her speech, was absolutely the last person she ever wanted to see again.

25

The world seemed to slow down as Stella stood rooted to the spot, unable to work out even how to put one foot in front of another. What was *he* doing here? Why hadn't she thought to check the guest list? If she'd known *he* was going to be in attendance, she'd have fought harder to remain in the background, to stay anonymous. She was only a writer, after all, she didn't need to be thrust into the limelight like this. She wrote about other people, other things; she didn't want to be centre stage.

Her knees, already knocking from the adrenaline rush of giving the speech, threatened to buckle as she realised she was within a few metres of someone she never thought she'd see in the flesh. Her palms, suddenly sweaty, clenched in the folds of her dress as she tried, abortively, to wipe them. Telling herself that, in person, he wouldn't know who she was unless she told him, didn't seem to stop her immediate reaction.

Then, thank goodness, Chris was approaching with that very welcome glass of champagne for her. Stella grabbed it from him and, in two gulps, downed most of it.

'Whoa!' Chris said, looking shocked. 'Was it really that bad?' He took a sip of his pint of Coke.

Stella shook her head. 'It's not that.' She glanced behind him, about twenty feet away, to where the object of her unease was standing, now chatting to Simon, who was obviously an ace networker, and a couple of other local bigwigs.

'Stella,' Chris said gently. He reached up a hand to stop her from downing the rest of the champagne. 'Tell me what's wrong.'

Stella's eyes were darting around, trying to find an escape route that wouldn't take her anywhere near the one person she needed to avoid. 'Nothing,' she said. 'I'm fine.'

'No.' Chris's voice was low, and he was clearly worried about her, and for a moment, Stella just wanted to sag against him, to feel his arms around her, protecting her from the horror of who she'd seen across the party. 'You're not fine.' Gently, he took her arm and led her away from the crowd, finding them a table in a secluded part of the courtyard, under a spreading horse chestnut tree, affording them a bit of shade from the still strong evening sun.

'You look like you've seen a ghost,' Chris said, his face a picture of concern. 'Are you feeling all right?'

'I'm fine,' Stella said hurriedly. The last thing she wanted to do was explain to Chris, who she still didn't know very well.

'Come and sit down for a minute,' he said.

'I think I just want to leave,' Stella said, but, since her heart was thumping fit to burst and her legs felt like jelly, that didn't seem to be an option, at least right now.

'Just sit for a bit,' Chris repeated. 'I'll get you a glass of water.' Stella watched as he walked briskly to the bar and was given a pint glass of water in short order. Within a minute or so, he was back. He passed her the glass, and she took a more measured sip, trying to still her racing heart.

'There are a lot of important people here tonight,' Chris said, obviously trying to take her mind off whatever it was that had spooked her. 'You and I should be networking instead of skulking under a tree. Helena'll want to hear that we made good use of the evening.'

'Feel free,' Stella muttered. 'I can find my own way home.'

Chris looked surprised at her defensive tone. 'That's not what I meant.' He regarded her levelly. 'Look, I know that you and I don't know each other that well, but if there's something I can do to help, please just ask. Or tell me what's wrong.'

Stella's eyes were still darting over the crowd, hoping against hope that the man she'd spotted would be so occupied he wouldn't think about coming to talk to her. She didn't know what she was going to do if he did.

'There's someone here I *really* don't want to see,' Stella replied eventually, sensing that Chris wasn't going to let this go.

'Oh, yes?' Chris raised an eyebrow. 'Sounds... intriguing.'

'It's not something I want to revisit.' Stella sighed. 'And I had hoped, moving here, that I wouldn't ever have to think about it, or him, again. I should have realised he'd be coming to a gig like this.' Her heart thumped again as the crowd in the courtyard milled around, and the object of her anxiety came briefly into view.

Chris followed her gaze. 'So,' he said gently. 'Do you want to tell me what's up?'

'I can't,' Stella said. Her eyes felt hot with tears and her throat grew suddenly sore. She took another large gulp of water and, in her haste, spilled it down her front, the iciness of the water making her draw in a sudden breath, which made her head spin. Telling anyone outside of her former job what had happened would be uncomfortable on a number of levels, not least because she found the whole situation so embarrassing. Now, as the subject of her embarrassment came fully into view, she felt the burning hot lava of mortification running over her. Charlie Thorpe, local MP and Junior Health Minister in the flesh.

'Yes, you can,' Chris said gently. 'No one's listening to us. Tell me what's wrong. Did something happen with our Mr Thorpe over there? Is he not quite the upstanding politician we all think he is? Has he got a guilty secret or two? Sleaze up his sleeve? Backhanders in his back pocket?'

'No! It was nothing like that.' Stella glanced around hastily. She realised Chris was right, and that there really wasn't anyone else in earshot, and relaxed a fraction.

'So what was it, then?' Chris's flippant expression softened, and he reached out a hand to take one of hers, where it was clenched on the table. 'Why are you so off balance?'

Stella took a deep breath. Chris's gentle response, and the fact that he'd been so kind to her when he saw her in such distress, made her want to share her reasons for not wanting to interact with Charlie Thorpe. She'd only known him for a little while, but he was looking at her in concern and curiosity, and she felt that perhaps she should take a risk and tell him.

'You know I told you that before I took up the Writer in Residence position I was a journalist in London?'

'Yeah. But I thought you were more about writing about Z-list celebs falling out of nightclubs, or having meltdowns on social media type of reporter?' Chris said.

'Thanks,' Stella muttered, although, to be fair, that's what she'd told him.

'Well, I don't know if you remember, but a few years ago, a story came out on AllFeed, one of the online news sites, about Charlie and his, um, motivations for helping a young woman out with the Cystic Fibrosis drug campaign.'

'I vaguely remember,' Chris said. 'I wasn't actually living in this part of the world at the time. Olivia and I were renovating a property in Salisbury, and I was up to my neck in planning regs and expensive wallpaper.'

'Well, anyway,' Stella said, eager just to get this out in the open and move on. 'I was working for AllFeed and they put me on Charlie's trail. We were all given a handful of the new intake to parliament to research, with a view to uncovering anything newsworthy, positive or negative, that would serve as clickbait and get our revenues up. That's how sites like AllFeed work, you see – we have to skirt the right side of the law, of course, but there's a lexicon, a linguistic framework that allows us to play with language, and then manipulate readers into clicking through to an article.'

'I get it,' Chris said. 'Like those dodgy fake news Facebook posts, "You wouldn't believe what you can do to build your muscles in a week," that sort of thing.'

'Exactly,' Stella replied. 'And so long as the punters keep clicking, and we hang on to the bare bones of a story, we were allowed to operate.'

'So where does Charlie fit into this?'

Stella paused and took another gulp of water before she replied. 'There was a story that came out at the height of the Cystic Fibrosis drugs campaign. It was generated by a so-called *concerned* third party, who contacted AllFeed about a possible sleaze case involving him. As a member of parliament who had, hitherto, been squeaky clean, AllFeed was all over it. The third party claimed that Charlie had taken advantage of a constituent to gain influence in the campaign, and then done the dirty on her when she'd outlived her usefulness, and turned his back on the campaign when it no longer suited his purposes.'

'And that constituent was his now wife, Holly, I suppose.' Chris filled in the blanks. 'She was pretty high profile in the campaign, if I recall. Didn't she end up with some crazy nickname?'

'The Green Goddess,' Stella said. 'She was all over the national news at the time, and once the media got wind that she and Charlie had had a thing, we were all systems go to find some dirt. AllFeed loves to discredit those in power, and Charlie had been too good to be true up to that point. Everyone wanted something on him.'

'So when you got the source saying he'd abused his power, it seemed the perfect opportunity,' Chris said. 'All you had to do was join the dots.'

'Well, it took a bit more than that,' Stella said, feeling momentarily resentful that he could be quite so dismissive of her former job. 'But, essentially, with some photographs we found on an Instagram feed that showed Charlie in an apparently compromising position with Holly, and this source's corroboration, it was straightforward enough to conflate the two. And then the story went viral.'

'You wrote the story, didn't you?' Chris's gaze was clear and calm.

Stella nodded. 'I'm not proud of it, but it was just work. And we had enough from this source, who checked out at the time, for us to believe in its veracity. Five paragraphs later, Charlie's a manipulative sleazebag, and Holly's a victim. Perfect clickbait.'

'Wow,' Chris said. 'No wonder you don't want to go and talk to him. If I was him, I'd be spitting feathers if I came face to face with the person who'd stitched me up in the media like that.'

'Exactly,' Stella said. 'Not to mention the fact that AllFeed later found out, through Charlie himself, that the source was someone with an axe to grind – some local business owner who'd been screwed over on a property deal by Charlie's predecessor – and we did fuck all to set the record straight except issue an amendment in eight-point type in a sidebar sometime later, which makes it all the more reprehensible.'

'Look,' Chris said. 'I'm sure every MP in the country is well used to having dirt chucked at them in the press. They wouldn't go into the profession if they couldn't handle it. There's always going to be a reporter on the corner, looking for that one bad decision, or that one embarrassing moment, and then making headlines with it. But it doesn't last forever. Unless you're Jeffrey Archer, of course!'

Stella smiled, despite herself. 'I just don't think I can look him in the eye, and shake his hand, knowing that the story I wrote caused such embarrassment. Somehow, just saying *yeah, but it's my job* doesn't seem to cut it, you know.'

'I get that,' Chris replied. 'And, despite his reputation for diplomacy, now might not be the best time to make that revelation. After all, you might need his help over the next year when it comes to access to local events.'

'Exactly. So I think I'll keep my distance from Charlie and his wife tonight, if you're okay with that.'

Chris smiled. 'Of course.' He looked thoughtful for a moment. 'Although, you never know... if he lost the plot at you, that might be a good story for AllFeed!' His eyes twinkled.

'Not a chance,' Stella said firmly. 'I learned my lesson working for those guys, and came pretty close to selling my soul. I won't go back there.'

'Fair enough. Was that why you decided to come out to the sticks and do this Writer in Residence job?'

'Mostly.' Stella nodded. 'I don't agree with that Samuel Johnson adage about being tired of life when you're tired of London – actually, I find a slower pace is good for me. And not having a deadline every twenty-four hours, too. I can really take the time to craft things, to give them the attention they deserve, and not just have my copy cut to shreds by content editors who have to meet their own deadlines.'

'Serious words, there,' Chris said. He turned back around to glance briefly over at where Charlie and Holly were talking to who appeared to be another local dignitary, and then shaking her hand.

'Looks like our Mr Thorpe has a prior engagement anyway,' Chris said. 'They're on their way out, I think.'

Stella followed his gaze and, much to her relief, Chris was right. Charlie had put his arm around his wife and was heading back out towards the gates. She breathed a huge sigh of relief. 'Well, this is one night where I won't have to keep watching my back, then.'

'You were just a byline on a website,' Chris said. 'He's not going to know who you are in person, is he?'

'I suppose not,' Stella said. 'But I know who I am, and what I wrote, and that doesn't sit well with me these days.'

'Well, he's off now,' Chris said. 'So shall we get another drink and a bite from the buffet? And then we can both do what Helena wants us so badly to do and get talking to people who might advance our individual causes.' He grimaced. 'Christ, I hate networking.'

'Me too,' Stella replied. 'But needs must.'

As they stood up and headed to where a wide variety of food was being served at the buffet, Stella felt a little lighter. She wasn't sure if telling Chris about her connection to Charlie Thorpe had been a good idea, but it did feel better to get it off her chest to someone. She only hoped he wouldn't go shouting about it to anyone else, but then he didn't really seem the type.

A short time later, as she tucked into a plate of warm hog roast and a variety of side dishes, she found her appetite had returned. She was relieved. She had been rattled by the reminder of an episode in her previous life that she was ashamed of, but as the moon began to rise, and the magic of the evening took over, she felt as though she could finally relax. After all, it wasn't every day you got invited to an event in the grounds of such a wonderful venue, was it? And in the right light, in his black tie and with his hair swept back off his forehead, her attraction to Chris was becoming more obvious to her.

She shushed that thought instantly. He was off limits as her next-door neighbour and a widower who, from what Helena had said, clearly had a long way to go before he got over his dead wife. And that was fine. She needed an ally, not a lover, and if Chris became a friend, then that was a perfectly acceptable compromise.

All the same, she thought as he took her now empty plate from her and put it on a table nearby, he was effortlessly courteous, and really seemed concerned that she was all right, and enjoying herself. As he loped back toward her, dark brown hair lifting in the slight breeze and eyes smiling as he drew closer, she again found herself thinking about just how attractive he was, and she stood up a little straighter. What an entirely confusing evening it had been so far. Could it possibly get any stranger?

26

Just as Chris reached her, the next musical interlude started. The string quartet that had been playing at the start of the evening had been replaced by a jazz band, and plenty of party guests, well lubricated and their inhibitions lowered by a drink or three, had begun to take to the dance floor.

Chris paused in front of her and looked endearingly unsure of himself in the low light from the fairy lights that cast everything in their golden glow. 'Um... you can say no if you want, but since we're here... would you like to dance?'

'How could I refuse an offer like that?' Stella laughed. Putting her now empty glass down on the nearest trestle table, she made her way with Chris to the dance floor, where there were already small groups and other pairs swaying to the music. As Chris reached out his hand for her to take, Stella felt a jolt of electricity as their fingers touched. She drew in a short breath, wondering if he'd felt it too, then hushed her mind and tried to breathe normally.

Then, she really did feel like a Regency heroine from one of those television adaptations she'd been glued to on Netflix. They might not have been wearing the costumes, but Chris looked good enough in his dinner jacket to play the role of some Regency buck, guiding her with an assured hand onto the makeshift dance floor. In the shadow of the magnificent presence of Roseford Hall, he slid his other hand around her waist, resting just above her hip.

'Thought we might as well show our public faces,' Chris said. 'And since the chair of the Parish Council is also on the dance floor, you could make informal contact.'

'Good thinking,' Stella said, although she was struggling to think logically now that Chris had drawn her close in the dance. She knew her breath was shortening again, and tried to put it down to the Spanx underwear she was wearing under the dress, but it was no good. Her body was reacting to his closeness, even though her brain was willing it not to with every neuron. She found herself moving closer to him, ostensibly to look over his shoulder and observe the rest of the guests, but the warmth of his body was attracting her like a magnet.

The rhythm of the dance was slow and fluid, and Stella found that she didn't really need to concentrate on where to put her feet, which was just as well, really. She breathed in the deep, woody scent of his aftershave and felt her senses reel.

'Are you all right?' Chris murmured into her ear, sending a shiver down her neck. 'You've gone awfully quiet.'

'I'm fine,' Stella said, rather more breathily than she'd anticipated. 'I've not danced with anyone for a long time.'

'Me neither,' Chris said. He pulled back slightly, so that Stella could see his expression. 'I'm a bit rusty. Am I doing it right?'

'You're doing brilliantly,' Stella said. She was distracted by his lips, which were a turn of the head away from hers. What the hell was happening to her? Hurriedly, she tore her gaze away and looked over his shoulder again. She made eye contact with the chair of the Parish Council and smiled, and was pleased to get a smile in return. Clearly the speech had done its job and she was now recognisable to the people who could help to promote her work.

As the song finished, Chris pulled away from her slightly, and she was sure she wasn't imagining it that his gaze dipped momentarily to her lips before he remembered himself and looked her back in the eye. 'Another one?' he asked, a husky note in his voice.

'I'd love to.' Stella smiled, and as Chris smiled back, her heart thumped in her chest again. Hiding the flush that she could feel creeping up her cheeks, she rested her head on his shoulder, breathing in his scent and feeling the contours of his chest pressed lightly against her – there was no denying that she found him wildly, achingly attractive.

The sensation intensified when he dipped his head slightly so that his cheek was brushing against her ear. The gesture was very distracting, and she couldn't help it when she stumbled in his arms. As his hands tightened around her, helping her to right herself, she gave herself a mental shake. This would not do. It wouldn't do at all.

The song came to an end and they parted slightly again. Chris's eyes, when they met hers, were dark with what she could easily identify as desire.

'Do you want to call it a night?' he asked softly.

'What about all the networking Helena told you to do?' Stella asked.

'Sod it,' Chris said. 'I've talked to everyone I really want to.'

'Fair enough.' Stella smiled up at him. 'And I'm not exactly in the right frame of mind to talk to anyone else, either, after baring my soul about Charlie Thorpe.'

A loaded silence descended between them as they walked off the dance floor and towards the exit. It became even more charged as Chris drove the short journey back to Halstead House. Stella, whose senses were still reeling, felt like a teenager on her first date.

As they drew up to the turning to Halstead House, Chris turned off the engine and, before Stella could thank him for the lift, he'd hopped out of the truck and gone to open the passenger door for her. Stepping down from the cab, she stumbled in her heels and would have gone down on the driveway if Chris hadn't caught and righted her.

'Thanks,' she said, the breath temporarily knocked out of her by the shock of tripping and being caught by him. She'd ended up standing very, very close to him again, closer than they'd been dancing, and she caught another tantalising waft of his woody, aromatic cologne. 'And thanks for the lift. It was a good night, mostly.'

'It was surprisingly bearable,' Chris said wryly. 'It was nice, er, to have someone to share it with.'

A pause descended between them, and Stella realised that Chris still had hold of her arms, where he'd stopped her from hitting the deck.

'Well, I should probably go and get Fitz from Helena,' she said, shifting slightly in his hold. Chris, obviously realising that they were still touching, dropped his arms, and Stella felt a flickering regret. It had felt nice to be held by him, however innocuous the reason.

'Shall I give you a lift up the drive?' Chris asked. 'Sorry, I completely forgot you had to go and get the dog.'

'No thanks, it's fine,' Stella said. 'It's only a hundred yards up, after all.'

'Well, goodnight then, Stella,' Chris said. He paused and looked a little uncertain about what to do or say next. Eventually, he settled for reaching out and giving her forearm a brief squeeze, as if kissing her, even on the cheek, was a bit too much at this stage.

Stella felt the warmth of his hand on her arm and raised her eyes to meet his. There was a delicious, aching moment of anticipation before Chris removed his hand and gave her a smile. 'See you soon.'

'Goodnight,' Stella said.

As Chris walked back around to the driver's side of the truck, Stella, with a little more of a spring in her step, wandered up the driveway to retrieve Fitz. She felt the slight breeze as Chris passed her on his way home, and for a moment wondered how he would have reacted if she'd leaned up and kissed him.

27

The morning after the ball, Stella woke to the sound of the bell ringers from Roseford Hall's chapel giving it large with the pealing, and remembered that Simon had said the bells had been refurbished and restored as part of the general restoration of the village buildings. It was a heavenly sound to awake to, and she rolled over in bed, luxuriating in it for a few moments. Then, grabbing a notebook, she set about capturing some imagery she might use in a blog post next week. Musing gently on the 'sharp sweet sound of bells that had lain silent for too long, now making themselves heard in joyful voice', she laughed at the hyperbole. Her writing had taken an altogether more bucolic turn in the short time she'd lived in Roseford; it was quite a change from writing for AllFeed.

After a quick breakfast, she took Fitz out for a morning stroll. She wasn't planning on going too far, as her feet still hurt from wearing her high heels the night before, so she slipped on a pair of flip-flops and didn't bother taking a lead with her.

As she headed out of the back door of the gatehouse, she saw Gabe up ahead in the distance, mucking about with a skateboard on the drive. Jumping on and off again, he was clearly still learning, and Stella smiled. She remembered the scabs on her brother's knees, and worse, when he'd got his skateboard at about the same age. Eventually, he'd mastered it, but it had taken the whole summer.

'Hi,' she said as she and Fitz drew closer. 'How are you doing?'

'All right,' Gabe said. He grinned at her and then leaned down to stroke behind Fitz's ears. 'Bored...'

'Ah, the summer holidays.' Stella grinned back. 'I remember it well. You wait all year for them to come, and then when they do, you're desperate to get back to school.'

'All my friends live miles away,' grumbled Gabe. 'And most of them have gone on holiday anyway, so I'm stuck here. I got back last night from my friend Toby's house.'

'Did you have a good time?' asked Stella.

'Really good,' enthused Gabe. 'But being on my own now is really boring. I wish I had some mates who lived closer.'

'I remember that, too,' Stella replied. 'I was at boarding school from age eleven, and all of my friends were spread round the country. It sucked in the holidays and I really wanted to go to the nearby secondary school so I could have some local friends.'

'I keep trying to tell Dad I want to go to school here in Roseford,' Gabe nodded enthusiastically, 'but he reckons it's best for me to stay at Bruton for a bit longer, you know, until the house is better to live in.'

'And what do think about that?' Stella asked.

'I don't really mind,' Gabe replied. 'School's pretty cool anyway, and the house does get cold in the winter.'

'Well, why don't you show me some of the good bits of this place?' Stella asked. 'I bet there are a million little secret spots that only you know about.'

Gabe considered this for a moment. 'Okay,' he replied. 'Come on.' He ran ahead of Stella with Fitz hot on his heels. 'I'll show you the vegetable garden. Granny likes to keep it really nicely, and you can pick all the herbs you want to put in your dinner tonight.'

'I don't know, Gabe,' Stella said as the warning bells of memory started to ring. 'Your dad said to keep Fitz out of there in case he started digging.'

'Fitz wouldn't do that, would you, boy?' Gabe leaned down and ruffled the dog's fur. 'Anyway, can't you put him on a lead?'

'I left it at home,' Stella replied. 'I was only going to take him on the woodland path this morning, so I didn't think I'd need it.'

As they ambled towards the small kitchen garden that was tucked away at the side of the house, Stella felt the summer sun on her face, and an equally warm sense of contentment started to spread through her bones. She loved the summer, anyway, and never complained when the temperatures rose in London. But being in the countryside in high summer felt like a luxury, and she was determined to enjoy every moment of it while her residency lasted.

'Mum brought this bit of the garden back to life when we moved into the house,' Gabe continued as they reached the vegetable garden. It was a riot of scents and sights, with rosemary and thyme bushes up against the garden wall, tripods of bamboo poles with runner bean vines creeping up in one of the generous vegetable beds running vertically through the garden, their scarlet flowers vibrant in the summer sunlight, and terracotta tubs of courgettes and tomatoes that were just coming into fruit.

'Granny took it over after Mum died. She says it brings her closer to Mum.' Gabe glanced up at Stella and then away again.

'You must miss her,' Stella said softly.

'I do,' Gabe said matter-of-factly, 'but I don't really want to talk about it.'

'That's okay,' Stella said. 'I understand. We don't know each other very well, after all.'

'It's not that,' Gabe replied. 'I just get fed up of everyone I meet who finds out about Mum giving me *that look*. You know the one, the one with the sad eyes, and the sympathy. Mum's gone, and I'm really sad about it, but I don't want to be sad all the time.'

'I get it,' Stella said. She was, momentarily, taken aback by the boy's honesty, but she could see what he was getting at. No one wanted to be defined by a tragedy, and that's what Olivia's death undoubtedly was. His resilience made her alternately smile and her heart ache, though. She wondered if he and Chris ever really talked about Olivia, and she realised with a jolt that she hadn't seen one family photograph on the walls or side tables of Halstead House when Helena had given her the tour the other day. It might just have been because the house was in such a state, but it still seemed a little odd, now she came to think about it.

'Look, the carrots are coming up,' Gabe said, running ahead to the end of the long vegetable bed. 'I can see the tops already. Gran will be well happy.'

As Fitz padded along beside her, Stella smiled at how engaged Gabe clearly was with this garden. It had obviously given him and Helena a focus, and something to take their mind off their terrible loss, and now the patch of ground was literally bearing fruit.

'See, the raspberries are starting to ripen, too,' Gabe pointed out. He reached out and grabbed one smallish pink berry from the stems and popped it into his mouth. 'Not quite ready yet, though,' he grimaced.

'Give them time,' Stella said. Not that she was particularly well versed in gardening knowledge, but it seemed an appropriate mantra for a lot of things at Halstead House.

'My school's got a gardening club,' Gabe said as they continued to look around the kitchen garden. 'It meets at lunchtimes on a Tuesday and Thursday. Jo, the gardener, has taught us all kinds of things about looking after the plants in the grounds, and also we've been growing lettuces. She's got a cool dog like you. A white one.'

'I bet it's better behaved than this one!' Stella laughed. 'He can't believe his luck now he's got all of this countryside to explore. He wasn't really built for life in London.'

'He really likes it here, doesn't he?' Gabe mused.

'He does.' Stella smiled at the boy, who was once again petting Fitz. Fitz was loving every moment. Then, suddenly, Gabe's eyes were drawn to one of the large oak trees that bordered the garden and formed the entrance to the woodland at the back of the estate. 'Look, Fitz,' said Gabe. 'It's a—'

'Don't say it!' Stella said, a beat too late. Fitz, who had behaved impeccably up until now, took off through the vegetable bed, trampling the new carrots and spraying composted earth everywhere in pursuit.

'What? Squirrel?' Gabe repeated, eyes following Fitz in fascination.

'Yes,' Stella replied, through gritted teeth. 'It's his mission in life to catch one, and even the mention of the word sets him off into a spin.' She began to run after the dog, but jogging along the garden path, rather than flatfooting through the vegetable beds, she lost precious time. 'Fitz!' She hollered as she ran through the iron gate that separated the kitchen garden from the woodland behind. 'Fitz, come!'

She cursed under her breath, after checking that Gabe wasn't so close behind her that he could hear. Where had that bloody dog gone?

'Fitz!' she yelled again, forgetting the rule that you should be calm but assertive when dealing with a dog. Off lead, and in pursuit of a squirrel, God only knew where he'd end up. He'd never caught one yet, but there was always a first time. 'Where are you, you frigging idiot?'

Stella hurried into the wood, cursing the fact that she was only wearing flip-flops as she hadn't expected to be going too far when she'd left the house. Gabe, looking concerned, caught up with her after a minute or two.

'I'm sorry, Stella – I wouldn't have said anything if I'd known.'

'You weren't to know.' Stella turned back around to the boy and grinned briefly. 'It's my fault for not putting a lead on him. He's too clever for his own good sometimes.' She shouted the dog's name again, but no answering footsteps came pattering towards her.

'There's no stopping him once he gets a squirrel in his sights,' Stella said. 'Come on, let's see if we can see where he went.'

Just as they were heading into the woodland, and Stella was starting to worry that they'd find Fitz on the other side, trying to herd the sheep, a pained squeal broke through the humid summer air.

'Fitz!' Stella cried again. 'Fitz, you come here!'

This time, to her enormous relief, the collie came bounding back to her, skittering drunkenly down the wooded bank and back onto the path where she and Gabe were standing.

'Fitz, you rat!' Stella dropped to her knees to grab his collar and give it a shake, wondering if her summer dress was decent enough to whip off the leggings she was wearing underneath and use them as a makeshift lead. Figuring that Gabe would make a show of not noticing, even if he had, she thought it was better to be safe than sorry, and took them off. Then, she realised Fitz was bleeding profusely from his nose and looking very sorry for himself. She grabbed a tissue from her pocket and dabbed at the blood.

'So you finally got bitten, did you?' she admonished, gently wiping away the worst of it and spotting two tiny puncture wounds where the squirrel had obviously made contact with the sensitive flesh of the collie's snout. 'I bet it'll be the last one you ever chase, too.'

Fitz seemed outwardly unfazed by his entirely too close encounter with the bushy-tailed grey rodent, but Stella's heart lurched. She had no idea if squirrels carried communicable diseases, and she was far too attached to Fitz to take any chances. She thought it was best to get Fitz checked out. The only problem was, she didn't have a clue where the local vet was. Registering Fitz with a practice was another thing that had slipped down the list since she'd moved in. Dabbing at his nose again as the blood continued to seep from the wound, she tied one leg of her leggings though the dog's collar and started to lead him back down the woodland path.

'Will he be okay?' Gabe asked. The boy had gone rather pale at the sight of all of the blood coming from Fitz's snout, and Stella paused briefly on her hurried walk back and smiled what she hoped was a reassuring grin, despite her own worries for the dog.

'He'll be fine,' she said, trying to reassure Gabe as much as herself. 'It looks worse than it is, I'm sure. The squirrel just punctured the top of his nose, but it's bleeding like mad. I'm going to take him to the vet to check him over, but hopefully he'll be perfectly okay.'

As they made their way back the way they'd come, through the gate and the kitchen garden, they were confronted by the sight of Chris looking less than pleased.

'I thought we'd agreed that you'd keep Fitz out of this bit of the garden?'

Without missing a beat, Gabe stepped in. 'Sorry, Dad. It was my fault. Stella was going out to walk Fitz and I wanted to show her the new carrots and beans.'

'Even so, you really shouldn't have brought him in here.'

'I'm sorry, Chris. I should have turned Gabe down. It won't happen again.' The man facing her with the serious expression looked so different to the one she'd been dancing with at Roseford

Hall with last night, and she felt as though she was back at square one with him.

'Looks as though it already has,' Chris replied, gesturing over to where the carrot bed had been ransacked by Fitz's mad dash after the squirrel. 'Granny's not going to be happy that he smashed up her new carrots.'

'It wasn't Fitz's fault,' Gabe said quickly. 'He didn't do it. Honestly.'

'Then how did it happen?' Chris raised an inquisitive eyebrow.

'Fitz saw a squirrel and bolted off after it,' Stella said. 'I'm sorry about the carrots.'

'It was my fault, Dad,' Gabe added, obviously keen that Fitz didn't get all of the blame. 'I mentioned the S word, and Fitz took off. Then the squirrel bit him.'

'Okay,' Chris said dubiously, and Stella followed his gaze down to where two very obvious paw prints lay in the vegetable bed next to the carrots. Was she imagining it, or did his lips twitch in the faintest of smiles, which broadened a fraction when he caught sight of Stella's leggings being used as a makeshift lead?

'I'd better get Fitz to the vet,' Stella said. 'It's probably nothing, but I don't want to take any chances.'

As if he'd noticed the blood on the dog's muzzle for the first time, Chris's face suddenly registered concern. 'Is he okay?'

'He came off worst from the encounter with the squirrel,' Stella replied.

'Good for him for trying,' Chris said. 'I've got a Local Pages inside by the phone if you want to check it for the number. I can't remember what the village vet's name is, offhand.'

'It's okay,' Stella said quickly. 'I can Google it. Hopefully they can squeeze him in for a check-up.'

'How are you going to get there?' Chris asked. 'You don't have a car, do you?'

'I can call a taxi,' Stella said.

'A cab driver won't be too happy if that dog bleeds all over the upholstery,' Chris replied, taking a long look at Fitz's still dripping nose. 'Give the vet a call, and then let me know when you're going in. I'll drive you.'

Stella hesitated, knowing Chris was right but not wanting to impose on him. He seemed to sense her reticence, and added, 'You can't make this poor boy walk all the way to the vet with a wound like that.' He leaned over and stroked the collie's neck gently.

'All right. Thank you,' Stella replied. 'I'll give the vet a call and then let you know.'

Chris nodded. 'Do that.' He turned back to his son. 'You'd better re-plant those carrots before Granny sees them.'

'But I wanted to go with you and Stella to the vet,' Gabe protested. 'Can't I do it later, Dad?'

'I'm sure Stella doesn't want you hanging around, getting in the way,' Chris said. 'And I'm not sure, with Fitz in the cab, that there'd be much room for you anyway. Go and tell Gran what we're doing, and I'll see you later.'

'I can squeeze in, Dad... please?'

'No,' Chris said quickly. 'You can make a fuss of him when he gets back.'

'All right,' Gabe said sulkily. Then, turning back to Stella, 'But will you let me know how he is as soon as you can?'

'I will.' Stella smiled down at the boy. 'But honestly, Gabe, he'll be fine. It's just a precaution.'

Leaving father and son to continue their negotiations over repairing the carrot bed, Stella hoped the vet would be able to get Fitz in quickly. The poor dog was looking increasingly sorry for himself, now the thrill of the chase had worn off, and Stella hated seeing him so deflated.

28

In a few minutes, Stella had found the local vet's number and booked Fitz in as an emergency. He'd never actually caught a squirrel before, and, judging from his expression now the adrenaline had subsided, he wasn't likely to want to do it again, or so Stella hoped. She'd texted Chris, who'd given her his number before they'd parted in the vegetable garden, and was now waiting for him to collect her.

'That'll learn you,' Stella grinned at the dog, who had his sore nose tucked between his paws as he lay out on the stone floor of the hall.

A gentle knock at the front door brought her back into the moment, and she grabbed Fitz's lead from the hook, then opened it. Chris stood on the other side.

'Are you good to go?' he asked, glancing down at Fitz, who'd jumped up and padded beside Stella to the front door.

'Yes,' Stella replied. She glanced down at Fitz, and for the first time since he'd been bitten by the squirrel, she felt her eyes blurring with tears.

'Are you all right?' Chris asked.

Stella nodded and looked back up at him, blinking furiously. 'Sorry,' she replied. 'It's just... I hate seeing him injured like this.'

'Apart from the blood, he seems like he'll live,' Chris said. 'But let's get to the vet, just to be sure.' He paused for a moment, seemingly unsure what to do, before reaching out a tentative hand to Stella's bare forearm.

The contact made Stella's skin tingle, despite her worry over Fitz, and as she looked up into Chris's eyes, she smiled. 'I'm sorry,' she said softly. 'It must seem daft, getting so upset over a minor injury to a dog.'

'Not at all.' Chris's eyes seemed to warm a little as he looked down at her. 'It's one of the reasons I've not allowed Gabe to have any pets yet – given everything he's lost, losing an animal would be a step too far... for both of us.'

'But he can borrow Fitz anytime he likes.' Stella smiled. 'So long as he avoids touching his nose for a little bit.'

'Let's get this boy to the vet, then,' Chris said. 'I've, er, put a rug down in the cab, more for his comfort than anything else. I'm not worried about him bleeding on it.'

'Thanks,' Stella said. She couldn't help thinking, as she walked Fitz to the truck, how her opinions about Chris had changed over the short time she'd been his neighbour and tenant. He certainly hadn't lived up to her first impression of him. Smiling slightly as she approached the truck, Chris noticed her change of expression.

'Something funny?' he asked.

'Oh, you know,' Stella said, suddenly embarrassed to tell him what she'd nicknamed him after their first meeting. 'I didn't think, when we met that first day, that I'd voluntarily be getting into this truck. Not after what I called you!' She gave Fitz's lead a gentle tug and then stepped up into the cab after him, settling him on the blanket and slipping on her seat belt.

'I don't remember you calling me anything,' Chris said as he slammed the driver's side door, put on his seat belt and turned the ignition. 'But then I was in a really shitty mood that day.'

'Were you?' Stella grinned. 'I didn't notice.'

'So what was it you called me, then?' Chris asked as pulled down the drive.

'Er...' Stella paused. 'If I tell you, will you still give me a lift to the vet?'

Chris glanced at her and grinned back at her now slightly red face. 'I promise,' he said softly. 'I couldn't leave the old boy to struggle all the way there under his own steam, could I?'

'Well, er, for a fair while after that first meeting, I called you Mitsubishi Warrior Twat... in my head, at least!'

Chris's gravelly rumble of laughter made Stella laugh, too, albeit a touch self-consciously.

'I probably deserved that,' Chris replied. 'No. I *definitely* deserved it. Promise me it won't end up in a book someday?'

'I can't promise.' Stella shook her head. 'I was quite pleased with it, actually.'

'Fair enough.'

They drove for a few moments in companionable silence, Stella's attention directed more towards Fitz than Chris. Fitz had never been fond of going to the vet, and she was glad she'd thought to pick up a few of his favourite treats and put them in the pocket of her dress before she left. Realising that he was carefully sniffing her pocket for one now, she took one out and gently fed it to him. His poorly nose didn't seem to have affected his appetite. Again, she found herself in the slightly odd situation of being grateful to Chris for coming to her rescue. She couldn't allow herself to think back to last night, though – now was definitely not the time. Fitz was the priority.

Luckily, before her mind could go further off on any more

tangents, Chris was pulling into the car park at the Harper and Homefield veterinary surgery.

'Do you want me to come in with you?' Chris asked as he stopped the engine.

'No, we'll be fine,' Stella replied. 'Hopefully we won't be long.'

As she climbed out of the truck, gently tugging Fitz's lead to get him down, she smiled. 'Thanks for doing this, Chris. I appreciate it.'

'What are neighbours for?' he said. His voice had a slight gruffness that Stella kept finding both endearing and sexy. She tried to focus on Fitz, who was already slowing his pace slightly, clearly scenting the unsettling smells of the vet's practice.

'Come on, you big baby,' Stella murmured. 'If you don't like the vet's, you shouldn't chase squirrels!' Tugging briskly on his lead, she led him to the door.

29

A little time later, Mike Harper, the vet, a tall, friendly, capable man in his late forties, cleaned up the puncture marks and gave Fitz a shot of a mild painkiller just to take the edge off. Fitz, to his credit, looked perfectly fine apart from the blood-stained white fur. He'd even relaxed enough in the surgery to accept several treats from the vet and the veterinary nurse, and as Stella completed the paper-work to register Fitz with the practice, he waited quite calmly for her to finish.

'Bring him back in a day or two and I'll look him over once his nose has had a chance to heal,' Mike said. 'Squirrels don't carry any diseases you need to worry about, and his temperature's fine, but if he suddenly gets lethargic or goes seriously off his food, come in sooner and I'll take a look at him.'

'Thank you,' Stella said, feeling relieved that there would be no lasting consequences from the squirrel bite. 'And I'll try to keep him away from squirrels in future!'

'You'd think they'd learn, wouldn't you,' Mike sighed, 'but I've got a collie myself, and he still can't resist chasing them. He's been bitten twice!'

Stella laughed. 'You can't tell them.'

Stella got back into the truck, and filled Chris in on what the vet had said.

'Gabe'll be pleased Fitz didn't sustain any lasting injuries,' Chris said, as they drove the short distance to the gatehouse. 'He seems very fond of that dog already.'

'Fitz is very fond of him,' Stella replied. 'It's lovely to see.'

Chris turned briefly to glance at her, and she felt her stomach flip as he did so. He had such striking blue-grey eyes, especially when they were softened with kindness as they were now. They lapsed into silence again, but it didn't seem to matter. Stella absently stroked Fitz's neck, thinking vaguely about whether or not she should move his bed through to her room tonight, just to keep an eye on him. But he liked his spot by the Aga, even though it was too warm to light it. Perhaps she'd better just stick to routine; collies liked to know where they stood, or slept.

'Well, here we are,' Chris said a few minutes later as he stopped the truck. 'Do you need a hand settling him in?'

Stella shook her head. 'Thanks, but you've been helpful enough already. He'll be fine with a chew stick and a soft bed.'

'You know where we are. Give me a call if you need anything,' Chris replied. He paused, as if he wanted to add something else, but with a slight shake of his head, he obviously decided better of it.

'I will. Thank you, Chris.' Stella smiled at him. 'You've been really helpful.'

'Any time,' Chris replied. Clearing his throat, he glanced up the driveway to see Gabe running hell for leather down it. 'Looks like my son wants to check in on Fitz, too.'

'Is he okay?' Gabe gasped as he skidded to a halt a few feet from where Stella was now standing on the driveway.

Stella smiled. 'He's fine. Just needs some fuss and a rest.'

'Can I stroke him?'

'Sure, but just don't touch his nose.'

Gabe knelt down to Fitz's level and began to ruffle the fur around his neck, and Fitz, seemingly oblivious to his injury, shoved his nose into Gabe's face and gave him a huge lick.

'I think he's feeling better already!' Stella laughed as Gabe got to his feet and rubbed a hand over his cheek where Fitz had caught him.

'Come on then, Gabe,' Chris interjected. 'Stella wants to get the patient settled, and we need to think about lunch.'

'Oh, Gran said to come over to hers,' Gabe replied. 'She reckoned you probably wouldn't have thought about it, and she says we've had too many takeaways lately, so she's cooked a spag bol.'

Chris caught Stella's eye momentarily, and she noticed his mouth twitched up with a wry grin. 'Helena thinks of everything,' he said sardonically. Stella got the feeling that Helena's 'help' sometimes didn't entirely help, but at least Chris wouldn't have to cook.

'I'll see you soon,' Stella said. Her small smile grew wider as both returned the gesture, with identical grins.

Letting herself into the house, she fed Fitz, whose damaged nose didn't seem to deter him from wolfing down his food as normal. She grabbed something to eat herself, and then, feeling restless because of the humidity, she threw open the patio doors that led from her living room to the small front garden, and stretched out on the sofa, willing a breeze to reach her. The heaviness in the air was overwhelming, and as she took a sip of ice-cold water and tried to unwind from the drama of the morning, she wondered when the storm would break.

* * *

Stella didn't have long to wait. That evening, stealing in like a feral grey cat, the huge rain clouds began to assemble on the horizon, grumbling across the sky, closer and closer to the gatehouse. A warning rumble of thunder, still some distance off, heralded the break in the weather to come. The air crackled with electrical tension, and Stella remembered how, as a child, she'd relished thunderstorms, wrapped up in a blanket, sitting in the bay window of the London house, waiting for the storm to roar above the rooftops. Unlike her friends, who used to scream every time there was even the suggestion of thunder, Stella loved it; it made her feel as though her imagination was coming alive.

Fitz felt no such ease, however. He paced the living room, shaking his head and emitting a low growl in response to each noise. Stella had given him a calming tablet when the weather had started to close in, but it hadn't quite taken effect yet.

'It's all right, Fitzy,' Stella murmured, gesturing him to her and rubbing his back to reassure him. Perhaps she would let him sleep upstairs with her tonight. *Give him an inch and he'll take a mile*, the volunteer at Battersea Dogs' Home had said when Stella and her mother had adopted Fitz. *These collies are too clever for their own good.* Maybe she'd just leave the kitchen door open, in case he wanted to find her in the night...

A loud clap of thunder broke Stella's train of thought. She wandered through to the kitchen, stepping down onto the cool flagstones that lined the floor, and decided that a cup of tea was definitely in order, and perhaps a couple of his favourite treats for Fitz.

Although the air was still sultry and humid, the ground was so dry that the fat raindrops, when they did eventually begin to fall, bounced off the cracked earth of her back lawn that was revealed by the parched grass. The woodland behind Halstead House glowered down, shivering its branches in irritation (or was it ecstasy?) at the impromptu shower. As she stood at the kitchen door watching the rivulets of water sluicing rapidly down the long driveway towards her small gatehouse, Stella pulled her cashmere wrap more tightly around herself, caught up in the excitement of the moment. Fitz sat beside her, tongue lolling from his mouth as he debated whether or not to risk the rain and zip out for a pee. The break in the weather, despite his dislike of thunder, must be a relief to the thick-coated, shaggy-haired collie, Stella thought. He'd been lying in the shaded back garden for days as the hot weather had continued. Throwing open the double doors at the back of the kitchen, Stella stepped barefoot out onto the paved path that ran from there down to the bottom of the garden, where the gate was situated that led up to the woods. The slabs were still warm under her feet, with an echo of the oppressive heat of the past few days locked within them, and she wiggled her toes in the puddles that were rapidly forming.

The rain grew heavier, and Stella moved back under the cover of the kitchen doors. Glancing to her right, she noticed that the water running down the drive was turning into one continuous stream. She began to worry about the back of the house: the gatehouse was at the end of a long, sloping driveway and although the woodland could be relied upon to soak up most of the rain in normal times, it hadn't rained properly for weeks. Suddenly, the rain that had taken the edge off the heat and soothed her clammy body felt a whole lot more threatening.

Deciding that the writer in her was taking this entirely too many steps too far, she stepped away from the door and pulled it to. On cue, Fitz dashed out, large hairy paws splashing merrily in the puddles until he found his usual spot in the hedge to lift a leg. When he'd finished, Stella retreated to the living room, selected the latest episode of the drama she'd been watching on Netflix and settled down for the evening.

Two hours later, the rain hadn't let up and Stella was feeling considerably more concerned about the water getting into the gatehouse. It was an old Victorian construction, and while the windows had been updated a few years back, the roof looked as though it had seen better days. As she decided to call it a night, she settled Fitz in his bed in the kitchen, giving him an extra blanket to line his basket and then mooched upstairs to get her head down. She huddled up in bed that night hoping that the roof would hold as the rain battered down.

At 3 a.m., she was awakened by Fitz barking from the kitchen downstairs. Cursing under her breath, she padded down the straight staircase and wandered down the hallway to the kitchen. As she opened the door, assuming that Fitz would just be wanting a swift trip out to the back garden, she was met by the collie, paws deep in muddy water, barking his head off by his soaking wet bed.

'Shit!' Stella cursed. 'Come here, Fitz, quickly.'

Fitz needed no second invitation and scampered across the kitchen floor, which was now an inch deep in water. As he got to her side, he shook himself vigorously, covering Stella in muddy droplets.

'Thank you *so* much!' Stella admonished, but reached out a hand and ruffled his fur. 'Although at least you gave me some warning about all this.'

The kitchen was part of a more recent extension to the back of the house, and there was quite a deep step down to it from the rest of the gatehouse. Hopefully, unless the water continued to rise, that would mean that it would be the only part of the house that would flood. But the rain was still falling heavily, and Stella shivered, despite the fact that the temperature was still warm. She didn't have the first clue about trying to keep the water from the rest of the house; sandbags sprang to mind, but she wasn't sure where to get them or, indeed, what to do with them once she had them. At three o'clock in the morning, though, there didn't seem to be a great deal she could do.

At that moment, there was a knock at the front door. Wondering who the hell could be calling upon her at this hour, she jumped a mile. Surely, though, no self-respecting burglar would be knocking? As it came again, sounding more urgent this time, she hurried to the front of the house, pulling her pink waffled summer dressing gown around herself more tightly. She didn't tend to wear much to bed, so she'd just grabbed it on the way down out of habit.

Opening the door, she was glad she had covered up, at least a little, when she saw Chris on the other side. He was wearing a black T-shirt and cream shorts, and the rain had plastered his hair to his forehead in the time it had taken him to, presumably, walk from Halstead House.

'I saw the drain overflowing at the back of the gatehouse,' he said, without preamble. 'I thought the kitchen might have flooded again.'

'Again?' Stella said. 'As in, this has happened before?'

'Two years ago,' he replied. 'Fortunately, that time around, it was empty.'

'No such luck now,' Stella said. 'Fitz woke me up when his bed got wet.' She was about to ask him what the hell he was doing up at this early hour of the morning to notice the drains outside her house, but at this point she was distracted again by the steady creep of dirty brown water sliding under the kitchen patio door and rising ever closer towards the rest of the house.

'Christ,' she cursed. 'I'd better get dressed and sort that out.'

'I've got some sandbags in one of the outbuildings,' Chris said. 'I'll go and get them and at least we can put some against the kitchen step, as well as the back door and stop it getting any further, or worse.'

'Thanks,' Stella said. 'I appreciate the help.'

'Couldn't leave you to sink or swim in this,' Chris said. 'I'll be back in a tick.'

As Stella closed the door behind him and bolted up the stairs to put some clothes on, she again wondered why he'd been up so late, or early, but that was a question for another time. She grabbed the first things she could find, thanking goodness that her wellies were by the front door and not the back.

Chris returned quickly, and soon they were bagging up the step, as well as the kitchen door, and mopping up the water as quickly as they could. As they worked, Stella noticed that Chris was in pretty good shape, barely breaking a sweat as he hefted the sandbags into place.

'There, that should do it,' Chris said as they checked the last of Stella's towels that they'd used to soak up the water in the sink. 'I phoned Wessex Water while I was getting the sandbags and they're going to send someone out to look at the drains.'

'Thanks,' Stella said. 'And thanks for helping me sort this out.'

'You'll need at least one dehumidifier, too,' Chris continued. 'I know a firm who'll supply a decent one. I'll get them to drop one in and set it up later on.'

'And, again, thank you,' Stella replied. 'It was lucky that you, er, were awake and noticed the drain. It would have taken me twice as long to sort all of this out if you hadn't been.'

Chris grinned briefly. 'Insomnia's a pain in the arse. I'd been pacing around the first floor since the rain started, worrying about my own roof in this downpour, and when the drain went up, and the water from the woods started coming down, I knew what was going to happen.'

Stella smiled back. 'Well, I guess I have your insomnia to thank as well, then.'

There was a pause as the two of them, in wellies and shorts in a soaking wet kitchen, regarded each other.

'Well, since it's nearly sunrise, I might as well get up and start my day,' Stella said. 'It feels like it's going to be a long one.'

Chris paused before replying, rubbing the back of his head in a gesture that Stella was beginning to realise meant he was nervous.

It was strangely endearing, considering he'd just been her knight in shining, well, sopping wet, armour.

'Er... well, it's probably not safe to use this kitchen until it's fully dried out and an electrician's checked over the place. Do you want to come back up to the house for a cup of tea? Or coffee? Or something?'

Privately, Stella thought she could have done with a stiff whisky after the night she'd had, but she refrained from voicing that thought aloud. It wasn't that she doubted Chris would have a bottle stashed away, but that getting pissed in the small hours wasn't something she'd done since her student days, and she didn't want to go *there*.

'That would be great. Thank you,' Stella replied. 'I'll just go and get a jumper. It's starting to feel colder.'

'Okay,' Chris said. 'I'll pop back up to the house and put the kettle on. See you in a few minutes? Better bring the dog, too. Wouldn't want him biting through a cable and electrocuting himself.'

'Definitely,' Stella said. She watched as he turned away from her and wandered back down the hallway towards the front door with that long-legged lope of his. Perhaps it was just his perfect timing in showing up at her front door at precisely the right moment to help her with the flooding catastrophe, but she suddenly felt another very definite stirring of attraction towards him. That was three times he'd come to her rescue now, between the Charlie Thorpe thing, Fitz's injury and now the flooding. She tried to shush those thoughts back down; after all, he was still grieving, and she was a writer with an overactive imagination, but no, it definitely persisted, making her heart beat a little faster. She'd always been a sucker for a dashing hero in a romance novel – this was just another example of looking for something that wasn't there.

That said, when she went upstairs to get a jumper, she splashed some water on her face, pulled a brush through her hair, cleaned her teeth and sprayed on a bit of deodorant. After all, it had been a long night.

As Stella and Fitz reached the front door of Halstead House, she saw that the door had been left open for her. She wandered through and headed towards the kitchen.

'How do you take your tea?' Chris's voice emanated from the back of the room as she approached.

'Milk, no sugar, thanks,' Stella replied as she approached. She heard the pouring of water and the tinkling of the spoon against a china mug as she walked through the kitchen door and waited while Chris added some milk and then brought it over to her.

'Shall we go up to the living room on the first floor?' he said. 'It's a bit chilly down here.'

'Sounds good.'

'It's just down the hall, up the stairs and to the left,' Chris replied.

'Oh, I remember,' Stella said, then blushed at Chris's look of surprise. 'Helena kind of gave me a tour when you were at the builder's merchant the other day,' she explained. 'I hope you don't mind too much.'

Chris grinned briefly. 'My mother-in-law is a law unto herself sometimes.'

As the two of them reached the top of the stairs, the door to the living room was already open, and through it, Stella had a clear sightline through the large windows of the Rogues' Dining Room, highlighting a panorama of the hills. The sky had already turned a dusky rose pink as the sun began its gentle, sleepy ascent behind them, with the odd wispy cloud cast in smoky purple breaking up the wide expanse of sky behind the dark green hills.

'God, what a view,' Stella breathed, drawn, inexorably, to the warmth and light behind the windows. 'If I lived here, I'd get up early every summer morning to see this.' She took a deep breath and let it out slowly, eyes wide with the beauty of it.

'I often see it from the wrong side of the night,' Chris said, walking up to stand next to her, not too close, but near enough that she could sense his physical presence. 'Sleep isn't something I've been able to do regularly for quite a while. Helena thinks I avoid this part of the house, but watching the sun rise from here is... comforting.'

'It must be,' Stella said, eyes still on the sky and the hills. 'I mean, I can't imagine what you've been through, but seeing this every morning... is it some help?'

'A little.' Chris turned his head and Stella could see, from the corner of her eye, that he smiled. 'Olivia loved this spot, and standing here, sometimes, it feels as though she's still with me.'

Stella did turn her head then. 'I'm so sorry for your loss, Chris.'

Chris shook his head. 'They tell me it'll get easier. And some days it feels as though it is. Other days, not so much. At the moment, things are okay. Grief comes in waves, you know.'

Stella nodded. 'I can understand that.'

Chris took a step closer to her, and Stella felt that fizzing tingle again. He looked at her, and she saw a gentle smile in his eyes. 'It's nice, though, sharing this sunrise with someone else. With you. Gabe's never awake to see it, so I've seen enough of them alone. Seeing you falling in love with the view reminds me of happier times.'

Stella smiled back. 'I'm glad you wanted to share it with me. It really is beautiful.'

A pause settled between them then, as they both sipped their tea and watched the sky getting brighter.

'It's going to be a long day!' Stella said, glancing at her watch. 'And goodness knows what I'm going to do for food, if the kitchen's out of commission.'

'Come over for dinner tonight,' Chris said. 'It's my fault, really, that the kitchen flooded again. I should have made sure those drains were clear after the last time. Least I can do is give you something to eat by way of compensation.'

'If that's okay,' Stella replied. 'That would save me getting a takeaway and staring at four damp walls all night.'

'Gabe'll be here, of course, so he can make sure I don't put my foot in it.'

'Sounds good,' Stella replied, smiling. 'It's been ages since anyone cooked for me.'

'It's been ages since I cooked for anyone except Gabe, and on occasion Helena,' Chris replied, and then, at Stella's obvious look of concern, 'No, honestly, I didn't mean that in a maudlin way. I'd like to cook something for you, er, both. Gabe's used to far too many takeaway pizzas when he comes home at weekends as it is. It's about time I gave him a decent home-cooked meal, too.'

'Then I'll look forward to it,' Stella said. She yawned suddenly. 'God, what a night.'

'There's a guest bedroom down the hall if you want to crash out for a couple of hours,' Chris said.

Stella hesitated. 'I should probably get back to the gatehouse.' She wasn't sure how she felt about just crashing out in Chris's house, no matter how tired she was.

Chris looked wary. 'I'm not sure that's a good idea at the moment. The water could have got into the electrics. It could be risky. I wouldn't want you or Fitz injuring yourselves.'

Stella nodded, conceding reluctantly that he was right. 'Thanks, then. I think I'll take you up on that.'

'I'll show you the way,' Chris said.

As she followed Chris out of the living room and down the hall into one of the bedrooms on the north side of the house, Stella felt the weariness overtake her. She knew she'd have to sort the gatehouse out at some point today, but for the moment, all she wanted to do was sleep.

'I'll wake you in a couple of hours,' Chris said. 'And I'll ring the electrician who's doing the rewiring on this place, get him to check the gatehouse over and set up the dehumidifier.' He smiled down at her again. 'Don't worry. It'll be fine, I promise.'

Stella suddenly felt an overwhelming urge to cry. After the night she'd had, it really wasn't surprising, she thought. 'Thank you,' she managed to stammer out, before Chris had turned and closed the bedroom door quietly behind him. Flopping onto the double bed, she curled up, and within moments was fast asleep. She was too far out of it to even grumble when Fitz, weary from his own disturbed night, clambered up beside her on the bed and curled up into her back, with a martyred sigh.

30

'So do you want the good news or the bad news?' Chris said, once Stella had got her head together after a couple of hours' sleep, and her hands around another cup of tea. They were sitting in the first-floor living room again, and the sun was streaming in through the windows, casting the room in a much harsher light.

'I'm not sure,' Stella said. 'Bad news, I guess.'

Chris smiled ruefully. 'Well, the electrician nipped round early on his way to another job, and picked up a number of wiring faults that really should have been fixed before you moved in. As a result, he's said you can't go back in until the place is dry and he's done the work.'

Stella groaned. 'And the good news? And please tell me it is good.'

'As your landlord, I'm liable for the costs of the work, and it's something I really should have double-checked before I agreed to rent out the place. So I'm footing the bill, and I'll also pay for your alternative accommodation for the duration of the work.'

'But I'll have to find somewhere that'll take Fitz,' Stella said. 'So a B&B is probably out. And I barely know the area.' She put her head in her hands. 'This is the last thing I need.'

Chris said nothing for a moment, and Stella eventually looked back up at him.

'Maybe... oh, I don't know. You probably won't go for it, and the place is in a worse state than the gatehouse, but...'

Stella waited.

'There are plenty of rooms in this house, if you wanted to move in here temporarily. And of course, Fitz would be very welcome. He seems good with kids, and Gabe likes him. I mean, there's a mostly functioning bathroom down the hall from the room you slept this morning, and if that room isn't to your liking, you can take your pick from the other ones on the first or second floor. We'll have to work out some kind of kitchen rota, but I'm sure we'll sort something out.'

'And you wouldn't have to fork out for my rent elsewhere,' Stella pointed out. She knew, from what Helena had said, that Chris's finances weren't exactly bottomless, and had no wish to add to his money woes, even if he, as her landlord, *was* responsible for part of her current plight. She couldn't really hold him accountable for the rain, but the blocked drain and the wiring faults had definitely been his problem.

'Well, there is that,' Chris admitted. 'But, and I know this sounds ridiculous... the way you looked at the sunrise earlier made me realise that this place needs someone in it sometimes who might appreciate such things. And it means you can go back and forward to the gatehouse if you need to pick up stuff.'

'That's true,' Stella said thoughtfully. 'But are you sure I wouldn't be in your way? I mean, all I really need is a place to sleep and a desk somewhere to work. And I can definitely make sure I'm not in the kitchen when you need to be.'

Chris smiled. 'I'm working on the other side of the house at the moment, and I will be for most of the summer, so you won't be in my way at all. Come and go as you please.'

Stella sipped at her tea. 'It would be very convenient. And you're right,' she added, 'that view is definitely inspiring.' Standing up, she wandered over to one of the windows and looked out at the Quantock Hills, lit up by the late morning sun. It really was a spectacular view, and one she would love to look at while she was writing.

'Okay,' she said, after a short pause. 'I'll go over to the gatehouse and grab some things. Is there anywhere you'd like me to set up, work wise?'

'What about in here?' Chris replied. 'Plenty of room for a desk, and there are a couple of power sockets.'

Stella shook her head. 'It's a lovely room, but I'd rather be right out of your way. I like my own space when I'm working, and this feels too much like where you and Gabe relax.'

'Okay,' Chris said. 'Well, take your pick of any of the other rooms and set up where you'd like to.'

'Um... would it be okay to use the Rogues' Dining Room? I can put a desk right in the corner,' Stella asked. 'With that dual aspect, looking out over the hills as well as towards the village, it's perfect.'

Chris paused, and Stella saw a combination of emotions flit across his face, jaw tightening reflexively and then brow furrowing for the briefest of moments before, to her relief, a smile broke through. 'Of course. It's the least I can do. I'll just have to tell Gabe he'll have to practise his skateboarding outside from now on.'

'Helena told me he liked it in there,' Stella replied.

'He spent a lot of time in there after Olivia died,' Chris said. 'I think he just wanted to feel closer to her. She loved that room too, for exactly the reasons you've just mentioned.'

'I don't have to work there,' Stella said hurriedly, 'if it'll make things difficult for the two of you.'

Chris smiled briefly. 'It's fine – it's got the best view in the house, as you say.'

'Well, thank you,' Stella said. 'All I need is a table, a chair and a power socket and you won't even know I'm here.'

'You don't have to hide away, really!' Chris laughed softly. 'Please don't feel as though you're imposing. You're really not.'

Stella smiled. 'You might not say that when Fitz comes flat-footing into your living room of an evening. He gets bored if I work too late.'

'He's more than welcome.' Chris leaned down and ruffled the fur on the back of the dog's neck. 'I always wanted as dog as a kid, and Gabe's been mithering me to get one, even though he's not here most of the time. Perhaps Fitz might be able to convince me.'

'Or put you off forever!' Stella replied. 'Once you've tried washing him off after he's rolled in fox poo, you might very well find him less endearing!'

'I'll leave that job to you,' Chris said wryly. 'There's a hosepipe by the vegetable garden.'

'Noted.'

As Stella left to pick up a few things from the gatehouse, she wondered at how things had changed so swiftly. She felt twin prickles of excitement and unease about moving up to Halstead House, however temporary that move might be, and although part of her hoped it wouldn't be for too long, there was another part of her that had fallen in love with the view from the Rogues' Dining Room, and couldn't wait to set up her desk there.

31

After a surprisingly well-cooked meal the evening after the flood, Stella went to bed feeling more relaxed than she had in a long time. She'd enjoyed sitting in the kitchen with Chris and Gabe, and it was lovely to see and hear the banter between them. She slept well, and woke up feeling refreshed.

For the first few days after she moved into Halstead House, Stella tried to remain as unobtrusive as possible. She took Fitz with her on the days she needed to be at Roseford Hall and hid herself away in her borrowed bedroom of an evening, so as not to intrude on Chris and Gabe's family time. She also spent more time walking with Fitz. Chris had told her that she shouldn't feel as though she was imposing, but she couldn't help being very aware that this was his space, and Gabe's, of course.

On the fifth day, after the storm of the previous week, the weather finally felt as though it was beginning to cheer up once more. The sun shone, lighting up the leaves of the woodland in the mornings, and mellowing gently into warm, sultry evenings that Stella adored. The scent in the air of the stocks that Helena had planted around in pots at the edges of the patio drifted through the open window of the Rogues' Dining Room as she worked, and for a while, every evening, she could forget that she'd been displaced from her actual home, the gatehouse, and was camping out at Halstead House. Her imagination filled in the gaps; the previous inhabitants of the house, the sights and sounds of the family who grew up here, the love affairs and trysts that might have occurred if her own fictional version of Halstead's history had been true. If Roseford Hall had the obvious power, romance and appeals to the imagination, Halstead, on its smaller, more intimate scale, was the place where you'd have to work harder to discover its secrets.

But there were also the words unsaid, those hidden emotions of the present. One morning, up later than usual as she'd been working all night to put the finishing touches on the workshop that she was going to be running in a few days' time, Stella clambered out of the rickety shower at the end of the corridor where her bedroom was and cursed that she'd forgotten to bring her bathrobe with her. The towel she'd used to dry off barely covered the essentials, and her glasses had steamed up in the heat from the shower. Gingerly opening the bathroom door, she peered out into the corridor, whipping her glasses off to rub them on the front of the towel to make sure she wasn't revealing herself to Chris, or worse, Gabe. Convinced the coast was clear, she checked she hadn't left any underwear on the floor, shut the door behind her and began to scuttle down the hallway.

Just as she was almost home free, and back to her room, Gabe came barrelling around the corner on his skateboard, realising too late that he didn't have a clue, yet, how to stop. With a startled yell, he tried to dodge her, and the board slipped out from under him, depositing him on the floorboards at Stella's feet.

Clutching her towel, Stella gazed down at the boy at her feet. 'Are you all right?' she asked, not daring to stoop down to help him in case she gave him an eyeful.

'I'm fine.' Gabe grinned up at her. 'I'm just learning to turn corners.'

'Evidently,' Stella said dryly.

'Gabe!' Chris's voice boomed from further around the corner. 'What have I told you about riding that bloody skateboard in the house?'

'It's fine,' Stella called back, hoping frantically that Chris was far enough away from her not to suddenly appear and catch her with slipping towel and soaking wet hair. 'He's not hurt.'

'It's the floors I'm worried about,' Chris said, and there was no doubt, his voice was definitely closer this time. Stella tried pull her towel further around herself as she made a dash away from Gabe towards her bedroom door, but as she did so, Chris came striding around the corner, clearly hell-bent on remonstrating with his son about his skateboarding habits.

The collision was inevitable.

As Stella crashed into Chris's chest, she made a grab for her towel at the front, and felt it slip from the back. Hands flailing, she just about managed to retain the last shreds of her modesty as they both sprang back, apologising frantically to each other.

'Sorry!' Chris said hurriedly. 'I, er didn't realise you were... I mean, you're usually up by now...' he trailed off, obviously desperately trying to look anywhere other than Stella's towel-clad body.

'It's fine,' Stella stammered, wishing that, with wild, wet hair and still slightly steamed-up glasses, not to mention a completely inadequate bath towel, she'd just hurried to her room and slammed the door behind her. 'I, um, was up late finishing some work.'

They regarded each other for a moment, all thoughts of Gabe and his rogue skateboard forgotten in the sudden heat at the surprise physical contact. Stella saw Chris's eyes widen, and a warmth spreading over his face that looked as vibrant as the blush felt in her own cheeks. She hoped she could blame the hot water, although, in reality, it hadn't been all that hot. Chris really needed to get the boiler fixed, she thought irrationally. She pulled the towel tighter across her chest, and was sure she didn't imagine Chris's gaze flickering, for a split second, away from her face and down.

'I'll let you get on,' Chris said, clearing his throat as he did so. 'Sorry about...' he gestured rather helplessly.

'No harm done,' Stella said, and her voice, in contrast to his, sounded rather too bright. 'I'll, er... yes... well...' Trailing off, even more embarrassed now that she didn't have a clue what to say, she pushed past him, threw open her bedroom door and hurried into the room, closing the door firmly behind her.

32

Having successfully managed to stay out of Chris and Gabe's way for the rest of the day, dashing through the house to take Fitz for his afternoon run when they'd gone to get some more supplies for whatever job Chris was currently working on, Stella put the finishing touches on the workshop and decided, eventually, that she'd have to eat something. Chris had been more than generous with fridge and cupboard space in the kitchen, so she had plenty to choose from, but she'd been so mortified by basically being *nearly* naked in front of Gabe and, horrors, Chris, that her stomach had been far too churned up to eat anything.

However, Fitz was looking expectantly at her for his dinner, and her own stomach had started to growl, so she'd have to brave the kitchen at some point. Hopefully, Chris and Gabe would have already eaten and would be safely tucked out of the way in their little living room on the first floor.

Creeping out of her bedroom, past the living room and down the stairs towards the kitchen, Fitz close to her heels and keen to have his own dinner, she wondered what she had in the cupboards that would require the least time to prepare. At this stage, even a Pot Noodle seemed like an enticing prospect; quick to prepare and even quicker to eat. As she slunk down the back stairs towards the kitchen on the ground floor, the sound of the television blaring away in the distance reassured her. Hopefully neither Chris nor Gabe would get the munchies in the time it took her to feed herself and her dog. Even the damp that still remained in the gatehouse felt like a better option than coming face to face with them again today.

Just as she was buttering the bread for the fastest Marmite and cheese sandwich on record, having given Fitz his dinner, which he'd demolished in about ten seconds flat, she heard the door to the kitchen creaking open. *Shit.* She'd been trying to work out something to say to both of them all afternoon, and was still none the wiser; every time she pictured talking to them both, she felt a hot flush of mortification.

'Would it help if I just stripped off now and ran around with a flannel as a fig leaf?' Chris's voice came from across the kitchen, low and distinctly amused.

'It might,' Stella muttered. Glancing up to see him, she felt her face colouring yet again as she saw him leaning against the door frame, a look of gentle humour on his face. 'I don't think I'm quite ready to joke about nearly losing my modesty just yet, though.'

'Nothing to joke about,' Chris replied. 'Not from where I was standing, anyway.'

Stella was about to open her mouth to ask exactly what he meant by that when she felt a sharp pain as the knife she'd been cutting with slipped and gouged into her index finger.

'Bugger!' she exclaimed as blood dripped over the white bread. 'That was my last couple of slices, too.'

Chris was over to her side in an instant. He grabbed a clean tea towel from the drawer and took her hand in his, wrapping her finger tightly.

'Hold it above your heart,' he instructed. 'Do you feel faint? Even a little bit wobbly?'

'I'm all right,' Stella murmured, senses starting to reel because he was so close to her, and still had his hand over her tea towel-wrapped one. She could feel the warmth of him, and smell the late-evening scent of a sandalwood-infused deodorant mixing with the natural aroma of his summer-warmed body. 'Honestly, it's fine.' Even as the words left her mouth, she felt a wobble in her knees, and Chris slid an arm around her, steadying her and gently manoeuvring her to the nearest kitchen stool.

'Sit down,' he said softly, arm still around her.

'I've never been great with the sight of my own blood,' Stella said, feeling more and more light-headed. 'Everyone else's is fine, though,' she joked weakly. She hadn't eaten since last night, either, she realised, too late, which couldn't be helping matters.

Chris kept hold of her, the hand clutching the tea towel to Stella's firm in his grip. 'I'm going to let go of you in a sec, and get the first aid box from the cupboard by the sink,' he said. 'You're not going to pass out when I do, are you?'

Stella's head was swimming, and the throbbing in her finger, which seemed to be spreading down to her hand, was not helped by the lack of food in her system. 'I don't know,' she said shakily. 'I don't feel great, to be honest.'

'Okay,' Chris replied. 'In that case, I'll keep hold of you for a bit. Here, have some of that Coke you poured. It's the proper stuff, I take it?'

Stella nodded. She couldn't abide the taste of the diet alternative. Chris brought the glass to her lips and she sipped it, willing the sugar to hit her system and stop the shakes that were coursing through her body. After a couple more sips, she leaned back on the stool.

'I think you can let go of me now,' she said, feeling the sugar start to do its job.

Chris looked down at her. He shifted a little closer, and, almost as if it had a mind of its own, his other hand reached up and brushed a curly lock of hair out of her eyes, tucking it behind her ear, then came to rest on her cheek. Stella leaned into the touch, closing her eyes reflexively.

'Oh, no, you don't,' Chris said, the gravel in his voice a little more pronounced. 'I'm not having you fainting on me.'

Stella's eyes flew back open and she tilted her chin upwards to look him at him. As she did so, he brought his face down to hers and very, very gently kissed her forehead. It was a gesture of comfort, more than anything else, but it sent a shiver down her spine, and she had the sudden urge to want to feel his lips against her own.

'Just relax for a minute,' he murmured. 'I don't want you slipping off the stool when I go and get the plasters.' His voice, though serious, was laced with the barest thread of amusement, too. 'I'd have thought you'd have learned how to cut a sandwich by now.'

'Someone got me talking,' Stella replied, her voice, at least, not betraying the sudden tumult of emotions that were washing over her. Chris was still very, very close to her, and she could feel his breath on her forehead as he spoke.

'Sorry about that,' Chris replied. 'The offer of the flannel still stands, you know.'

There was a pause between them that felt loaded with so many things. Stella, felt, suddenly, emotionally, a lot clearer. She liked being held in Chris's arms; she couldn't deny it, despite the sore finger. Tilting her head upwards, her eyes locked with his, and before she could think better of it, she'd moved her lips to his, feeling their mouths meet in a gentle, tentative caress that sent her senses reeling again.

Chris stiffened momentarily, but then, to Stella's relief, he returned the pressure of her lips, the warmth and taste of his mouth sending her senses reeling. His arms tightened around her and she found herself pulled up off the stool, into his embrace, feeling the contours of his body as they pressed against one another.

Then, inexplicably, he pulled back from her, shaking his head and putting a little distance between them.

'I'm sorry,' he murmured, and Stella immediately saw the shutters come down. 'I shouldn't have.'

'You didn't,' Stella said softly. 'I did.' She tried to reach out to take his hand with her uninjured one, but he pulled back from her.

'I'll, er, get the first aid kit,' Chris said. He turned abruptly and crossed the large kitchen, which suddenly felt about a million miles wider, to rummage in the cupboard by the sink. In a few more moments, he was back by her side, but Stella noticed he was keeping his distance, putting the kitchen island in between them as he unwrapped an antibacterial wipe and then removed the tea towel from Stella's hand. Thankfully, the bleeding had stopped, so he gently wiped the cut, which made Stella wince as it stung, and then he put a suitable dressing on it.

'That should do it,' Chris said, zipping up the first aid kit again. 'Can I make you another sandwich, too? I've got some bread.' He was determinedly not meeting her gaze, and Stella felt as though he was trying to pretend the last couple of minutes hadn't happened.

'I can manage,' she said quickly. 'I've got a Pot Noodle stashed somewhere. I'll have that instead.'

Chris looked as though he was about to argue but, clearly desperate to get away from her, he gave her a brief smile. 'All right. I'll leave you to it.'

Before she could respond, he'd crossed the kitchen again and had vanished out of the door. Stella, sitting back down on the kitchen stool, couldn't help thinking that, in terms of awkwardness and embarrassment, the shoe was now most definitely on the other foot. She didn't regret kissing Chris in the heat of the moment, but it seemed as though he definitely regretted responding.

33

For the next twenty-four hours, Stella didn't see hide nor hair of Chris, or Gabe for that matter. It wasn't entirely surprising; she was gearing up for her first workshop at Roseford Hall and took Fitz up there with her, leaving earlier than her usual start time, and not returning until just before it started to go dark. She wasn't consciously trying to avoid Chris, it was just that work was a very convenient excuse at that precise moment. She tried not to think about the kiss she and Chris had shared, and his flummoxed reaction to it, but it was tricky not to. He *had* kissed her back, after all. Her impulsive decision to kiss him hadn't been *that* unwelcome. But she had to admit, if he had instantly regretted it, she could understand why. He was still coming to terms with losing his wife, after all, and perhaps she shouldn't have pushed him. But had she?

She'd spent the day in various rooms at Roseford Hall; the Long Gallery had been a particular draw for her, and she hoped it would be for her workshop attendees as well. She'd asked Simon if it would be all right to use one end of the Long Gallery for the first workshop, rather than the designated teaching rooms, which were a little small and out of the way, and he'd readily agreed, provided the British Heritage Fund reps were okay with it, too.

'Doesn't it grate on you, having to ask them permission for every decision?' she'd asked him as they'd walked the length of the Long Gallery together, and then headed outside to the beautifully manicured gardens that sprawled from the front of the house. 'I mean, this was – is – your family home.'

Simon smiled ruefully. 'I'd rather it was this way than having to sell the place. Can you imagine how much more awful it would be to have to live out my days watching someone else doing the work that the family could never afford to do?'

'You could have moved away,' Stella said. 'Had a new start somewhere else.'

'And be forever known as the Treloar who handed over the house and ran off?' Simon grimaced. 'I think I'd struggle to reconcile myself to that.' He kicked at a stray stone on the gravel path that led down between the lawns. Bert and Ernie, who were on the lawn a few feet away, looked at him with barely disguised disdain, and then strutted away. 'But enough about me. How's it going, living up at Halstead? Has the roof fallen in around your ears yet?'

Stella grinned. 'Not yet, but then I've been working in the Rogues' Dining Room, which is fairly sound.'

'Ah, Olivia had some great ideas for that part of the house,' Simon said. 'I remember her waxing lyrical, when she and Chris were at the planning stage for the artists' retreat, about the beauty of the light, and the proportions of the windows and a whole bunch of arty stuff I couldn't really understand but pretended to.' He paused, his expression becoming less jovial. 'It's a shame her vision never got to see the light of day.'

'Never say never,' Stella replied. 'Chris is still working on the house, after all.'

'Yeah, but his heart's not in it any more,' Simon replied. 'It wouldn't surprise me if he sold up in the next year or so to that developer who was sniffing around when they bought the place. There's too much baggage there for him to ever be truly happy.'

Stella, hating herself for asking, but feeling compelled to anyway, did. 'So there's not been anyone in Chris's life since Olivia, then?'

Simon shook his head. 'I'm not really the best person to ask. We used to be quite close, but... well, not so much any more.'

Stella's antennae for a good story couldn't help twitching. There was more to this than met the eye, she was sure. She'd sensed it the night of the Roseford Hall ball, and she was definitely getting that vibe again now.

'You can tell me to mind my own business, if you like,' Stella began, 'but am I missing something? What happened between you and Chris that means you don't talk much any more?'

Simon glanced at her. 'Are you asking as a writer, or as a friend?'

'A friend, of course,' Stella replied. 'Of both of you.'

Simon stopped walking and reached out to pluck one of the flowers from the lavender bed that was in full bloom in the summer sunshine. The pungent, heady scent drifted in the air, and Stella breathed it in, wondering what Simon was going to tell her.

'Chris was a bit unsure of me when we first met,' Simon began. 'I'd known Olivia since we were at university together, and I suppose he always wondered if she and I had ever, you know, been more than just friends.'

'And had you?' Stella asked. She wasn't sure if she expected a reply.

Simon shook his head. 'You don't pull your punches, do you?'

'I *am* a journalist by trade,' Stella replied. 'But as a friend, you don't have to tell me.'

'Well.' Simon began to shred the lavender petals in his hands before sprinkling them onto the grass. 'I fancied my chances, once upon a time, but she was never interested in me that way. So we ended up in this kind of brother-sister thing. She'd come and spend time here at Roseford during the university vacations, and I'd sometimes go and stay with her folks, but we were never more than friends. When she met Chris, I was happy for her. I could see how much she loved him, and they both had a passion for renovating places. From the first little house they took on to Halstead, they were the perfect match. At least, it seemed that way.'

'So what happened? Why do you and Chris have such an atmosphere these days?'

Simon sighed. 'Why does anyone drift apart from anyone?' He looked at her. 'Grief does awful things to people. Especially when they were never expecting to have to deal with it. Losing Olivia the way we did was such a dreadful experience for us all, but Chris was completely broken by it. I tried to get him to talk about it, to talk about her, but he just closed up, shut himself away up at Halstead with Gabe coming home at weekends, and wouldn't talk to anyone. Something didn't feel right about it all, but I didn't have the relationship with Chris to be able to get to the bottom of it. In the end I just gave up trying.'

'What do you mean, something didn't feel right?' Stella asked. 'Surely you're not suggesting—'

'No, no,' Simon cut in hurriedly. 'Nothing like that. We all knew what the coroner's report said. There was never any question of Chris having hurt her or caused her death. Besides, he adored her – Olivia and Gabe were his life. He'd never have done anything to either of them. But losing her... it nearly destroyed him. He pushed everyone who tried to help him away. In the end, in that situation, if you're not careful, you end up alone. And that's the way Chris was definitely going.'

'Was?' Stella asked.

Simon grinned crookedly at her, and if she'd fancied him, her heart would have melted. 'Let's just say that the Roseford Ball was the first time I've seen him out and about with anyone since Olivia died. And for some of the time, he actually looked as though he wasn't about to rip the heads off people who tried to talk to him. It was nice to see.'

'We went as friends,' Stella said, feeling her face start to flush as she remembered last night's kiss.

'Believe me,' Simon laughed, 'seeing Chris with any woman, friend or otherwise, was enough of a surprise. And you know what? He actually looked happy, next to you. That's something I didn't think I'd see again.'

'Well, I'm glad it looked that way, but it was nothing, really.'

'Whatever it was, it reminded me that he deserves to be happy again, and that I shouldn't have let my own grief, and my own frustrations with how he was handling his grief, drive us apart. He and Gabe needed me, and I stepped back. That's why you might have noticed a bit of, er, tension between us. Sometimes, when you lose someone important to you, it's difficult to speak the same language as other people mourning the same loss. It's hard to know what to say; how to communicate.'

'I understand,' Stella said softly. In later years, when her mother had talked about losing her father, she had told Stella about how people would run a mile in the opposite direction rather than try to discuss that loss with her. She could see how two men might have trouble connecting over a woman they both loved, albeit loved in different ways.

'Has he ever talked to anyone about Olivia?' Stella asked.

Simon shook his head. 'I honestly don't know. I think having his mother-in-law nearby helps, but he was just never the type to confide in people. His family isn't close, you see. He has a brother, but they don't really keep in contact, and his parents are divorced and live at opposite ends of the country, so really Gabe, Helena and

Olivia were his only family. Now Olivia's gone... well, he was lost for a long time. Perhaps, eventually, he'll find his way again.' Simon paused and looked speculatively at Stella.

'No,' Stella replied immediately, fully aware that she was starting to blush. 'I know what you're thinking, Simon, and just... no.'

'All right.' Simon grinned. 'Perhaps I'm just an old romantic, and it's all a bit too convenient, with you having to live up at Halstead at the moment, but I know Chris, and what he really, really needs is a proper home, with someone who gets it.'

Stella slapped Simon's arm playfully. 'You're way off.' She laughed. 'As if I'd ever be able to take Olivia's place. Not in a million years, and I wouldn't want to.'

'No one said you had to,' Simon replied, suddenly thoughtful. 'But people move on, don't they? And everyone needs a home. Not just a shell with a roof on it.'

As Stella shook her head again and wandered back to the Long Gallery, she mused on Simon's words. Home, she'd always thought, is where the heart is. Having been dragged around the world by Morwenna, quite regularly, and been at boarding school, too, Stella wondered if she'd ever really known what home actually was. And why Roseford was feeling more like home than the house in London ever had.

34

Later that day, Chris cursed as yet another splodge of plaster slipped from the trowel and plopped wetly onto the dust sheet under his feet. There was an art to plastering, and despite having been on a week's course, he could safely say that he hadn't mastered it. It didn't help, of course, that not a single wall in Halstead House appeared to be straight. Not for the first time, he wondered if it was worth just biting the bullet and getting a professional in to sort the walls in the main dining room, but there was a bit of him that absolutely refused to admit defeat. It was a skill he could develop; he was sure of it. And if he could, it would save him more than a few grand doing the rest of the house.

The problem was, his mind just wasn't on the job this morning. Every time he tried to focus on the wall in front of him, his mind drifted back to Stella, and just how good it had felt to kiss her. She'd taken the lead, and he'd followed for a few moments before his brain had overruled his heart and made him pull away from her.

Of course, he knew that the kiss had been the culmination of several rather convenient factors; living in the same house had meant they'd been seeing more of each other, despite the fact that he knew that Stella had been doing her best to keep out of his way as much as she could. Bumping into her in the hallway, where she'd struggled to cover her delicious curves under a really rather inadequate towel, had spiked a sharp surge of desire. It hadn't helped at all when Stella had crashed into him, her still damp body radiating heat and a scent that he found intoxicating. Then, holding her briefly in his arms, and later in the kitchen after she'd cut her finger, and the gentle kiss that had ensued, had made his senses come alive. He'd never felt so starved of touch, and he hadn't realised how much he'd missed the intimate contact from another human being until that moment. He'd deliberately cut himself off, made sure he didn't have the opportunity to engage with someone else on a romantic or sensual level, and now Stella was here, living in his house, sharing his life, through circumstances beyond her control, and he'd been thrown completely off balance by it.

But the real question was, what should he do about it now? He wasn't ready to answer that, even inside his own head.

But it's been over two years, another voice, from deep inside his heart, spoke. Isn't it about time you started living again?

Chris shook his head, aware that the whispering internal monologue only had a voice when he was starting to spiral. The grief counsellor had given him some strategies to stop this from happening, to stop the inevitable descent that had paralysed him for months after Olivia's sudden death, but, somehow, this voice sounded different to him. Whereas the 'usual' one was full of recriminations and guilt, this one sounded lighter, more optimistic.

He slammed the brakes on that line of thought straight away. He knew where that voice was coming from, and it wasn't his heart. It was from a place decidedly further south. Proximity to Stella, and circumstance, had caused these feelings; nothing more. It wouldn't be fair to drag her into his darkness – she deserved light, and fun, and someone who loved her. Not a terrified widower with more baggage than an EasyJet storage locker.

Savagely slopping more plaster onto his palette, he tried to clear his mind and concentrate on the walls in front of him. It was rather a Zen activity, he thought. Not boring at all. But then, perhaps boredom was what he needed; monotony as an escape from the conflict in his heart and in his brain. Determined to put the kiss with Stella out of his mind, he focused on the expanse of half-plastered wall in front of him.

There was another fat, wet plop as the replenished trowel deposited its contents on the dust sheet.

'Oh, for fuck's sake!' he exploded, chucking the trowel across the room.

'Everything going okay?' An amused voice came from the doorway that led out of the dining room and into the grounds at the back of the house.

'Fine, thank you, Helena,' Chris said shortly. 'Was there something you wanted?' Helena had a habit of popping up when he least needed or wanted her to. Now, a feeling of immense, familiar guilt washed over him, as if she could read his mind about Stella. What would she think if she knew he'd kissed someone else?

'I just wanted to see if you'd be all right for me to take Gabe away with me for a night or two,' she said. 'He's expressed a desire to go and see where Olivia grew up, and I've some friends in Hertfordshire I haven't seen in a while, so I thought I'd take him with me.'

'When?' Chris asked, fully aware that he still sounded snappy. Shaking his head, he tried again. 'I mean, that's great, Helena. I'm sure he'll have a lovely time. If you're definite you want him tagging along with you? Won't he be a bit out of place with, er, your friends?'

'What, with other old fogeys like me?' Helena raised a wry

eyebrow. 'Tiggy and Roland have got their grandchildren staying with them, too, and they're about Gabe's age. He won't have to hang out with the old crocks too much.'

Chris felt his face colouring. Helena was always careful not to remind him that she came from a rather more upper middle-class background than he did, but when she started making references to 'Tiggy and Roland', it hit him in the face again. He'd never been particularly comfortable with Helena's insistence that she pay for Gabe to be privately educated from the money that her husband, David, had left for that purpose, no matter how lovely his little independent school was, and now that Olivia was gone, he felt even more conflicted about some aspects of her life that seemed so impenetrable to him.

'Well, if he wants to go, then I'm happy for him to,' he replied eventually. Gabe had been asking more and more questions about Olivia as he'd been getting older, and Chris knew that the boy had an aching desire to know more about his mother with every year that passed, to keep his connection to her, for fear that he'd forget what she was like. Perhaps this little trip would help Gabe to feel more of that connection.

'Lovely,' Helena said. She paused, and Chris could feel himself being scrutinised.

'Was there something else?' he asked, aware of the plaster beginning to cake on his fingers and dry on the dust sheet.

'Oh, nothing,' Helena said quickly. 'You just look a little... different, that's all. Like you might actually have had a good night's sleep last night.'

Chris laughed. 'Do I look that rough normally?'

'Well, I wouldn't exactly say that.' Helena smiled at him. 'But you have been looking a bit tired lately. Is there something you want to tell me?'

'No,' Chris said, feigning a light tone. 'Not at all. But I'm glad you think I look less awful than usual.'

Helena grinned back at him. 'All right, then. If you can make sure Gabe's got everything he needs for a couple of days away, I'll pick him up later.'

'Will do,' Chris said. As he turned away from his mother-in-law and back to the wall, he cursed her perceptive nature. She always seemed to sense when something had changed. The question was, he thought as he scraped up the blob of plaster, how did *she* know, when he wasn't even sure himself?

35

That evening, having spent another busy day at Roseford Hall, which had included writing a blog post about the experience of the opening ball, a piece of flash fiction – in this instance a mere 250 words, from the imaginary point of view of one of the Edwardian Roseford ancestors, which Simon had, off the record, deemed to be 'somewhat glossing over the truth of the man's roving eye for the servants', Stella finally put the finishing touches on her workshop, which was kicking off at nine o'clock tomorrow. She felt the old, customary trepidation tingling beneath her skin as she looked over her notes for the final time, before sending them to John Handley and copying in Simon. When she'd finished a writing task, she was so used to moving straight on with the next; having to deliver her thoughts to an audience still made her nervous. But at least it wouldn't be as bad as giving the speech at the ball had been, she thought.

As she let herself in at the back door of Halstead House, which led directly into the kitchen, she thought she might as well get dinner ready now and disappear off to her room before Chris and Gabe needed the kitchen themselves. She'd bought some divine fresh tomatoes, onions and basil from Southgate's Stores on her way home, and with the wet garlic bulb the Roseford Hall gardener had presented her with before she'd left that night, and a smidgen of parmesan, she intended to elevate her dried spaghetti to a thing of beauty.

Grabbing one of the larger frying pans from the hanging rack over the worktop, she popped it on top of the large range-style gas hob and gave the pan a generous glug of olive oil. After a brief false start with the gas (Chris had warned her that, not being on the mains, the Butane gas bottles burned hotter and with more of a kick), she set to work finely chopping the onion and garlic, before adding them to the pan. The delicious smell of just those three ingredients made her stomach rumble.

She then carefully retrieved the plum tomatoes from the glass bowl of hot water she'd soaked them in to remove their skins, threw them into ice-cold water for a moment, then removed them and chopped them up, adding them to the pan swiftly. A touch of seasoning and she could leave them to cook down for the time it took to rehydrate the spaghetti. Chucking in a dash from the glass of red wine she'd poured too, on impulse, she then took a sip from it.

She'd successfully managed to avoid thinking too much about *that kiss* all the time she'd been up at Roseford Hall, but now, as she began to unwind from the day, and she was back in the kitchen where it had taken place, she couldn't help raising a finger to her lips, tracing their outline and remembering the sensation of Chris's mouth on hers. But it was clear, from the way Chris had all but run away afterwards, that he wasn't feeling the same as she did about it. Oh well, she thought. Not every kiss has to lead to happily ever after.

The philosophy was a sound one, but her heart would take a bit more persuading, especially since she'd grown really fond of, not just Chris, but Gabe and Helena as well. But perhaps it was just that they'd all been living so close together since she'd been forced to move into Halstead House. Maybe her feelings would diminish when she returned to the gatehouse to live.

Realising, during this reverie, that her tomato sauce was starting to catch, she hurried back to the hob and gave it good stir. The aroma was wonderful, now, and the addition of a generous handful of basil at the end of cooking would really set it off. The pasta was bubbling away nicely, too. As she gave the sauce another stir and then brought the wooden spoon to her lips to taste, she was aware that she was being watched from the kitchen door.

'Hi,' she said, as she turned around, spoon still by her mouth. 'How are you doing? Have you had a good day?' She hoped small talk would see them through whatever last night had meant to both of them.

Chris was just staring at her, gripping the door frame where he stood. He seemed completely incapable of answering.

Hurriedly, Stella put the spoon back down in the pan and turned back to him. 'Chris?' she asked gently. 'Are you all right?' He looked as though he'd seen a ghost.

Chris, seeming to come slightly back to himself, nodded his head. 'I'm fine,' he said, but there was a shake in his voice.

'I'm just finishing here,' Stella said, unnerved by his demeanour. 'Sorry to get in your way. I didn't think you and Gabe would be eating until later.' She glanced down at her sauce and pasta and turned both pans off. They would be a touch undercooked, but she was hugely conscious of being in his space, and just wanted to get out of his way.

'No, honestly, it's fine.' Chris had gone absolutely white as a sheet. 'I'll, er, come back later. Don't worry.'

'Are you sure you're all right?' she asked again, seeing the stricken look in his eyes. She took a few steps towards him, starting to feel really concerned.

'Yes, yes, I'm fine, honestly. Just a trick of the light,' he mumbled, still backing away towards the kitchen door.

'What do you mean?' Stella could see that Chris had started to shake. She took a careful step closer. 'Chris, wait.'

At the door frame, Chris paused. He looked as though he was going to pass out. 'It's nothing, honestly. I'll come back when you've finished.' He stumbled out of the door, and Stella, aware this was his house and his space, was left in a quandary. Should she go after him? Did he want to be left alone? What the hell had just happened?

Standing in the doorway, suddenly feeling as though she was a fifteen-year-old, emotionally illiterate teenager once more, she found that she, too, was shaking. And if she felt that bad, then how must Chris be feeling?

Padding through on bare feet from the kitchen, she looked around, but he'd vanished from the ground floor. Then, hearing a sob that made her heart wrench, she worked out exactly where he'd gone. Speeding up her footsteps, she hurried up the stairs and to the back bedroom where Chris slept. She pushed the door open slowly, and there, slumped on the ancient single bed, head in his hands, was Chris.

'Can I come in?' Stella asked softly, hesitating in the doorway.

Chris said nothing, but Stella was sure she saw the slightest incline of his head.

'What did I do wrong?'

Chris drew a shuddering breath. 'You didn't. I did. I should never have kissed you last night.'

Stella moved a little closer to where he sat, hunched over, head still in his hands. She wondered if she dared risk touching him.

'It was all too much,' he said quietly. 'I shouldn't have put you, and myself, in that position.'

'It was just a kiss,' Stella said gently. 'We can forget it and move on. It's no big deal.'

'No big deal?' Chris laughed bitterly. 'For you, maybe. I'm sure you kiss people all the time. But for me... you were the first. The first since... since she... and in the kitchen, just now... with the same aromas from the cooking... the same as the night she...' He trailed off as he choked on the last words, burying his face deeper into the palms of his hands.

Acting on instinct, Stella moved forward and wrapped her arms around him. He stiffened under her touch, and then, seemingly sensing that it was all right, he put his arms around her, pulling her close until his head was resting on her stomach. She could feel him trembling, and as she reached a hand up to caress his long, unruly mop of dark brown hair, he leaned into her touch.

'I'm sorry,' he whispered, over and over again, and Stella wasn't sure to whom he was apologising. He seemed so lost, at that moment, in his grief, and she'd never seen pain like it.

'It's all right,' she murmured softly, dropping her head and breathing in the scent of him. 'Just let it go, Chris.'

After a few moments, he began to speak. 'We'd argued that night,' he said brokenly. 'She wanted to push ahead with renovating the outbuilding at the back of the house, said it would make the perfect holiday let, and allow us to bring in a bit more cash to help with the renovations on the main house. We'd sold another property the previous October, over in Willowbury, and we had enough cash to keep on with the Halstead House renovation, but I thought it would be too much of a stretch. Olivia wanted to do everything, all at once, and mostly my job was reining her in.' He laughed brokenly. 'I told her to put the brakes on, but she was adamant. I worried all the time about the finances, about what would happen if we couldn't make the house everything we'd planned... but she couldn't see the sense in finishing the house first. We'd discussed it before, but I was exhausted from knocking down walls all day, and I couldn't face it again. I snapped back and told her that I wasn't prepared to tolerate any more pie-in-the-sky ideas until we'd got the retreat off the ground. She politely disagreed, and then confessed that she'd got our architect to draw up some plans. I was stunned when I heard that. We were paying out money left, right and centre for the place as it was – we simply couldn't afford to shell out more on some crappy barn in the back garden. Which was precisely what I told her.' He paused again, and looked up at her, eyes so full of pain that Stella knew exactly what was coming next.

'Olivia shook her head and told me I was being an idiot, that we had to be bold, or not do things at all. I, rather less than politely, disagreed. I told her I didn't want any dinner and I stormed out of the kitchen to ring the architect and tell him to put the outbuilding plans on hold. He wasn't answering his phone. I mean, why would he? It was Saturday night and we'd all had a hard week. When I went back to the kitchen, I was just in time to see her crashing to the floor. She'd had an aneurysm, and, to make it worse, she smashed her head on the kitchen counter as she fell.' He paused again, gulping back the emotions that were obviously desperately close to the surface. 'I dashed over to her and held her in my arms as she died. I never even got the chance to make things right with her.' He put his head down again, and Stella, now realising the depth of his guilt and his pain, held him even more tightly.

'It wasn't your fault,' she said gently. 'It could have happened at any time. You didn't make it happen.'

Chris said nothing, and Stella was suddenly, blindingly aware that he'd been carrying this dark responsibility around with him ever since Olivia had died. When Helena had told her what had happened to her daughter, she hadn't mentioned anything about

Chris and Olivia having rowed just before she'd died. Chris must have kept this to himself ever since it had happened. He evidently believed, despite whatever anyone could say, that he was responsible for his wife's death. Surely he must know that he wasn't, deep inside his heart?

'I couldn't tell anyone what had happened that night,' Chris replied. 'I never should have let things get that heated between us. I always knew it was better to walk away and let Olivia come to her senses in her own time, but I'd had it up to here with everything about this place by that point. I'd quite happily have sold the whole bloody lot to that developer who keeps sniffing around and bought a new build in the estate down the road, and the last thing I needed was more stress. She was a visionary, but she wasn't terribly practical.' He looked up at Stella again. 'And kissing you, letting myself think for one second that I could be happy again, knowing what had happened in that very room... I lost it.'

'You can't keep blaming yourself,' Stella said softly. 'I don't know much about aneurysms, but surely it could have happened at any time?'

'That's what the medics said,' Chris said wearily. 'But even knowing that, the cold hard facts of it, it doesn't make it any better in my head. And every time I see Olivia's eyes looking out from Gabe's face, I can't stop thinking that one day he's going to ask what happened to his mother that night, and I'm going to have to tell him that I was the one who caused it.' He choked again and put his head in his hands.

Stella fell to her knees in front of him, her hands clasping his in a desperate attempt to get him to look at her. 'It's not your fault, Chris. It isn't. You must accept that and try to forgive yourself.'

'I can't,' he whispered. 'No matter how many times I tell myself that, I just can't.'

Stella could feel his hands trembling and she knew he was

finding these admissions absolutely harrowing. Chris had obviously been holding this deep within himself for over two years, and his dark, misplaced guilt was holding him back from so much. She had no idea how to make it any better, though. She'd become his friend over the past couple of months, but she had no real concept of what he was like as a man, and no real idea how or where to start. Kneeling there in front of him, holding together his very, very broken pieces, she knew it would take a long time to help him put himself back together. Did she really have the strength to do it?

Eventually, when Chris had stopped shuddering, Stella drew back from him, allowing them both the space that they needed to re-establish the boundaries of whatever it was between them.

'I've made you ruin your dinner,' he said shakily, looking up at her with a brief, apologetic smile.

'It's all right,' Stella replied. 'It wasn't exactly gourmet cookery, anyway.'

'Smelled good enough to me, despite what I said,' Chris said. It was as if he was trying to pull back now, to construct a wall between his heart-breaking disclosure and the reality that the two of them found themselves in. Stella wondered if that wall would now remain in place for the duration of their relationship; if she'd had an insight into the man that, like staring out of a car window in the inner city, you got when you passed a house in the middle of a dark winter's night, was as fleeting as it was revealing.

'Would you like to share some with me?' Stella asked, as if the past half hour hadn't happened. 'There's plenty for you, and for Gabe, too, if he wants it.'

'Gabe's not here,' Chris replied, wiping an impatient hand over his eyes and then standing up from where he'd been sitting on the edge of the bed. 'Helena's taken him to stay with some friends of hers back where Olivia grew up. She thought it might help him to learn a bit more about her childhood.'

'He'll like that,' Stella replied. 'He's very close to Helena, isn't he?'

Chris nodded. 'She's the best link to his mother he's got.' He gave a brief, hollow laugh. 'I mean, I'm no bloody good to him, am I?'

'Don't say that,' Stella said quickly. 'He loves you. You've still got each other.'

'For what I'm worth,' he said, his voice still holding an extra trace of roughness from the tears. 'Sometimes I wish it'd been me who'd died, for his sake. Olivia would have had this place sorted and made into a proper home in no time.'

Stella doubted this, given what Chris had told her about Olivia's flights of fancy, and having witnessed first-hand the sheer size of the task. She merely replied, 'Don't say that. You're here, and he loves you.'

'Look, Stella.' Chris took one of her hands in his. His palm felt rough from all of the manual labour he'd done on the house, but his touch was warm and gentle. 'I'm so sorry to drag you into this mess. You have every right to want to walk out of here, find somewhere else to stay for the duration of the work on the gatehouse and never speak to me again. It's not fair of me to land my baggage on you.'

While he was talking, he was gazing at her with such an open, soft look in his still slightly red-rimmed eyes that Stella had to fight the urge to bring her mouth to his and kiss him again. But with a huge act of will, she steeled herself.

'I like it here,' she said softly. 'And so does Fitz.' As if on cue, the collie, obviously wondering where Stella had got to, poked his head around the bedroom door. 'And it won't be for much longer, anyway.'

Chris smiled. 'Well, if you change your mind, I'm happy to foot the bill, as your landlord, for you to go somewhere less broken and disorganised.'

For a moment Stella wondered if he was talking about himself or the house. She smiled back at him. 'I kind of like broken and disorganised. I always liked jigsaw puzzles as a child.' But, she thought immediately, Chris wasn't a puzzle to be solved, and neither was Halstead. They were more like one of those Japanese vases, which, when mended with precious metal, became all the more beautiful for the cracks. The question was, would she be the one to help mend them?

Dropping her hand once more, Chris wandered to the bedroom door. 'Take your time in the kitchen,' he said. 'I've got some work to finish in the dining room. I won't disturb you again.' As he passed Fitz, who was still standing in the doorway, tongue lolling in the heat of the evening, he dropped a hand to the dog's head and stroked it briefly as he passed. 'Keep your mistress company,' he said gently. Fitz, seeming to understand the reference to Stella, padded in to stand next to her.

Stella, glancing around at the contents of the room, which, except for a couple of stray items on the bed, had all been boxed up and stacked neatly against the walls, realised that while Chris might have contained Olivia's possessions into some sort of order, his own emotions were completely different. Shaking her head, she followed him out of the door, closing it softly behind her as she left.

Much later that night, Stella couldn't sleep. It wasn't just the thought of the workshop that was preoccupying her – she kept playing back the encounter with Chris over and over in her mind, trying to make some sense of it in her heart and brain. She surprised herself by wishing that her mother was around to talk to; she'd never really had the kind of relationship with Morwenna that a lot of her friends had had with their mothers. Morwenna, while affectionate, had always treated Stella as more of an equal than a daughter; certainly since she'd been in her teens. Stella couldn't escape the fact that Morwenna had probably confided more in her than she'd ever really needed to know; unfortunately, the reverse wasn't true. She'd rarely talked to her mother about relationships, for fear that Morwenna would start dispensing advice she was in no way ready to hear from the woman who gave birth to her. But tonight Stella felt out of her depth. Ringing Morwenna's mobile, knowing it was too late for her to answer and assuming that she would be safely tucked up in bed with Damon, she left a message, hoping that her mother would get back to her quickly.

Sighing in frustration a few minutes later, she got up and decided to risk the kitchen to make a cup of tea. Since she was wide awake, she might as well use the time to get some work done. The workshop was ready, but she'd been toying with the germ of another idea, a project that she thought might work as a novel. She felt guilty if she worked on it during 'office' hours, but the middle of the night seemed an apt time to put some thought in. She couldn't find her dressing gown, so she grabbed her dusky pink cashmere wrap from where it was slung at the end of the bed and threw it around her shoulders. The night was sultry, but the house retained a damp chill, even on the warmest nights. Padding through the Rogues' Dining Room and then down the flight of stairs towards the kitchen, she was distracted by the moonlight rising over the hills, bathing everything in a silvery green light that gave an impression of cold, even though she knew the night air was humid. She was tempted to sit outside on the terrace and drink her tea, as the house suddenly felt dank and weirdly claustrophobic.

Walking across the kitchen to the kettle, she swiftly made a cuppa and grabbed a biscuit from the barrel on the kitchen island.

Her heart thumped at the loud pop of the lid in the silent air. Realising that the French windows were locked, and the keys must have been put somewhere safe, so she wouldn't be able to get out onto the patio, she wearily headed back up to the first floor.

The moonlight cut across the floor of the Rogues' Dining Room like a knife as she mooched past the huge bay windows, stepping in the criss-crossed rectangles of light that shimmered through. She paused for a moment when she reached her desk in the corner of the room, and put her tea down. Sleep wasn't going to come any time soon, no matter how tired she felt, and the view across the valley to the hills beyond soothed her. In daylight it was picturesque, chocolate-boxy, even, but at night, when the road was quiet and the velvet blue-black of the evening sky had descended, allowing the silver moon to travel sedately across the top of the rearing hills, it was truly breathtaking. Surprised at the sudden rush of emotion, she felt tears prickling at her eyes as she imagined Olivia standing in this very spot with her artist's eye taking it all in, and thinking of the future that she and her family would have in this wonderful house with its spectacular view.

And now here she was, Stella Simpson, feeling like an intruder; an interloper, through circumstance, where the lines had been blurred in her relationship with Chris from the knowledge that he'd shared with her. You're not cut out to be the next Mrs de Winter, she thought wryly, despite her sudden rush of emotion. She pulled her wrap around her shoulders as it slipped against her nightdress and was just about to sit down at her desk and flash up her laptop for a brief session on her guilty pleasure writing project when a shadow fell across her and she jumped so hard she was relieved she'd put her tea on the desk.

'Sorry,' Chris said softly as he approached. 'I didn't mean to startle you. You couldn't sleep, either?'

'I hope I didn't wake you,' Stella stammered, nervous and

embarrassed to be caught *again* not exactly fully clothed. The nightdress was white cotton, and while it fell to just above her knees, she still pulled the wrap around herself more tightly, feeling a little exposed in the moonlight.

Chris shook his head. 'Insomnia kind of goes with the territory these days. What's your excuse?'

Stella laughed, not entirely covering her nerves. 'Too many ideas flying around my brain. Thought now was as good a time as any to try to pin one or two of them down.'

'I'll leave you to it, then,' Chris replied. 'I didn't want to disturb you. I just heard footsteps and thought…' He trailed off, shaking his head. 'I don't know what I thought.'

His ghosts don't just haunt his mind, Stella thought, looking at his pale face and the grey eyes that, in the draining light of the moon, looked cavernous.

As he turned to leave, he started slightly, his gaze tracking across the expanse of lawn at the front of the house. Stella, noticing immediately his change of body language, took a step closer to him, trying to see what had caught his eye.

'Look,' Chris whispered, pointing towards the end of the lawn, where it sloped gently down to meet the main road, separated by a stone wall.

'Where?' Stella shifted her glasses further up her nose and looked in the direction of Chris's pointed finger. There, its pelt bleached to a light fawn in the moonlight, stood a young roebuck, horns still needing a few months' growth before reaching their full maturity, but magnificent in its self-assurance, nonetheless. It was looking directly up at the house, and for a long, timeless moment, it felt as though its gaze was locked directly on them.

'Gabe'll be gutted,' Chris murmured. 'We were told, when we moved in, that there were deer around here, but none of us have ever seen one in the grounds.'

'Perhaps there's a herd in the woods,' Stella said. 'I'd better keep an eye on Fitz the next time I take him through there. I don't fancy his chances against those antlers.'

Chris shifted slightly next to her, his gaze moving to the left of the buck. 'He's not alone. Look.'

There, off in the shadow of the oak tree that was on the left of the front lawn, was a doe.

'Looks like there's a new family moving in,' Stella quipped, then instantly regretted it. 'I'm sorry, Chris.'

'Don't be,' Chris murmured, turning back to her. Stella shivered as he took her right hand in his, and drew her closer to him, so close that she could feel the heat of his body through the T-shirt and shorts he was wearing. 'You don't have anything to be sorry for, Stella.' And then, waiting a split second for her assent, he dipped his head and brought his mouth to hers.

Stella gasped as the warmth of his lips ignited something deep within her. His mouth was hot, and tasted of coffee with entirely too much sugar. The sweetness was in complete contrast to the fervour of his actions, which were those of a man who'd not been touched in a long, long time. The smouldering fire she'd been trying so hard to ignore since their encounter in the kitchen suddenly burst into life, and she kissed him back hard, relishing the feeling as the kiss deepened. Loosening her hand from his, she reached up to tangle her fingers through his hair, her other hand finding its way instinctively under his T-shirt to feel the warmth of his skin.

Once they were sure of one another, Chris's lips hungrily sought out her neck as her hand continued to rake through his too long, unruly brown hair. His hands were on her waist, and then down onto the backs of her thighs, grabbing her closely to him, and she could feel his body trembling as he drew her closer.

After that, there was no room for hesitation. Chris's body pressed up against her so that Stella only had time to catch a swift breath between kisses. She was grateful for the writing desk, as his hands roamed down her back. She pulled him ever closer, relishing the feeling of his body against hers.

'What are we doing?' he murmured as he came up for air.

'I'm not sure,' Stella replied. 'But whatever it is, I think we should keep doing it.'

'Agreed,' Chris murmured and kissed her again.

Soon, it was obvious that neither of them wanted to stop at kissing. Stella paused to pull Chris's T-shirt up over his head, and as he slid down the lace trimmed straps of her nightgown, she saw Chris's eyes widen.

'God, you look... incredible,' he stammered as he drank in the sight of her. 'I could lose it right now just looking at you.'

'Try to hold out a little longer.' Stella couldn't help the flattered pleasure in her voice. The nerves, the uncertainty about what they were doing, had all vanished in the moment he'd kissed her. Perhaps she was more like Morwenna than she thought. This felt completely, deliciously out of character, and she loved it.

'Oh, fuck it,' Chris murmured, and gathered her up in his arms, until her legs wrapped around him. They pressed tightly against each other, and if Stella had been in any doubt as to Chris's state of arousal, there was no doubt now as she felt his hardness press against her through his jersey shorts.

Chris staggered a few steps with Stella in his arms until she laughed and wriggled down. 'There's no way you can keep that up,' she said as she pressed herself against him where they stood. 'Come on. We'll need to keep the bedroom door open for Fitz, though. He hates being left out.'

'Canis interruptus.' Chris gave a low laugh. 'I'll be prepared.'

Stella grinned back, between kisses. 'Your Latin is impeccable.'

Chris's voice, as he whispered gentle, erotic nonsense into her ear, was gruff with desire. He manoeuvred Stella so that her back was against the wall, and before she could think better of it, was kissing her again.

'You will catch me if I fall,' she quipped, suddenly nervous that this could all go horribly wrong and they'd both end up in Magdalene Park A&E.

'I promise.'

It soon became clear, though, that both of them needed a softer, gentler surface. After some blissful kissing against the wall, Chris took Stella's hand and led her down the corridor, up the stairs to the second floor and towards the first bedroom they came to. Stella felt a moment's confusion, as she knew this wasn't Chris's room, but she quashed that thought. As he pulled the door open, a large, dark wooden king-sized bed was revealed. They melted down onto the top of the thick, springy duvet and rapidly lost the rest of their clothes and Stella felt sharp tingles of desire washing over her skin. Amidst kisses, both gentle and harder, and wandering touches, they were both soon breathing heavily, and Stella was more than ready to take the final step.

Stella scurried to her room and back again in record time to grab a condom from her handbag, hoping against hope that Chris wouldn't freak out again before she got back.

'Are you sure?' Chris asked softly, looking endearingly uncertain as she slipped under the covers again.

'Yes – definitely, yes.' Stella smiled up at him. 'Are you?'

In reply, Chris thrust into her, rocking his hips in a deep, regular rhythm that, combined with the ministrations of his fingers, had Stella gasping against him. She tightened one lifted thigh around him, and as the rhythm got frantic, and deeper, she felt herself peaking, just before he did. A few moments more, and with a groan, he came, burying his head in her shoulder as he did, and tightening his arms around her.

'Fuck...' he murmured. 'That was...'

Stella smiled into his neck, kissing the juncture between collar bone and throat. 'It was.' She felt him tense as he gently lowered her thigh, but kept his arms around her.

'I'm glad we're lying down,' she said softly.

He pulled back to look at her, and gave a broad, still achingly seductive smile. 'Where do we go from here, again?'

Stella grinned back. 'Well, I don't know about you, but I'm having a shower. Join me?'

Chris's smile got wider. 'Absolutely.'

Hand in hand, neither quite believing what had just happened, and the manner in which it had, they headed off to the bathroom on the first floor.

36

The next morning, Stella woke up in the large mahogany bed and stretched luxuriously. The bed must have been a relic that came with the house, she supposed, although the mattress felt surprisingly new and comfortable.

As she rolled over, she realised that she was alone. She wondered where Chris was, and hoped he wasn't having second thoughts about what they'd done. Just as she was girding her loins to get dressed and either slink out of the bedroom and back to her own, or go in search of Chris (she hadn't decided which yet), the bedroom door opened and in wandered Fitz, with Chris not far behind.

'This fella was scratching at the bedroom door, wanting to go out,' Chris said as he came back into the room. 'You seemed to be out for the count so I thought I'd better let him do what he needed to do.'

'Thank you.' Stella smiled. Her smile got broader as he passed her a freshly made cup of tea in a white porcelain mug. 'And thank you even more for this.' She took a sip. 'I'm usually completely anti-social in the morning until I've had at least one cup of tea.'

She looked up from her mug and saw Chris was looking rather adorably awkward, standing at the end of the bed, as if he was waiting for her permission to sit down.

'It's all right,' she said softly. 'This is your bed, after all. You can come a bit closer.'

'Actually, this is the guest bedroom.' Chris laughed nervously. 'My bed's nowhere near as decent as this. It was going to be the premium room for the artists' retreat, which is why it looks so much nicer than where I actually sleep.'

'I'm honoured, I think,' Stella replied. She rested her free hand on the expensive feeling duvet cover, and then looked up as something occurred to her. 'This bed linen... if this is the guest bedroom that hasn't been used for guests... why has it been made up?'

Chris laughed. 'Gabe was bored when he came home a couple of months ago and so he talked Helena into showing him how to do hospital corners. He wanted to practise on every bed in the house, including this one. He found the bed linen we'd bought and just went for it.' He looked down at her, still smiling. 'I don't think we ought to tell him exactly how it's been christened, though!'

'Probably best.' Stella smiled back. She still felt a slight prickle of unease that Chris had spent the night with her in this room, though. He was such a closed book to her, even now they'd made love, and she'd have appreciated the insight into him, even if it would just have been getting a glimpse of his actual bedroom.

'Look, Stella...' Chris began. He shifted awkwardly on the end of the bed where he'd perched. 'About last night...'

Stella burst out laughing. 'Did you really just say that?' She put her mug of tea down on the bedside table and pulled the sheet around herself before she moved down the bed to be closer to him.

Chris looked apologetically at her. 'I'm not very good at this. Olivia always said if I ever managed to remove the rod from my arse

I'd be a half-decent communicator, at best. I'm guessing she was right.'

'Why don't you give it a go?' Stella said gently. 'I can't really respond until you end that sentence you just started, anyway.'

Moving around slightly on the bed so he could face her, he raised a hand and tucked a strand of Stella's unruly dark hair behind her ear. She felt a shiver run down her spine at his touch as she remembered where else he'd touched her last night.

'Last night was something else,' he said softly. 'And, believe me, I want nothing more than to do it again, and again, until everything else in my life means absolutely nothing.'

'But...' Stella prompted.

Chris shook his head. 'But. It can't happen again.' He looked her straight in the eye, his own clear gaze reassuring her that he was trying his very best to be honest, without hurting her. 'I'm not ready, Stella. I thought I was... but I'm not. And it would be unfair to you, and unfair to Gabe, to convince myself that I could be anything other than a friend to you right now.'

Stella nodded. She'd asked him for honesty, so she could hardly blame him for giving it to her. And, to be fair, everything had happened so quickly, she felt as though she, too, needed time to process it all. She remembered how out of character she'd felt, and realised that, perhaps, that wasn't the greatest basis for a new relationship.

'I understand,' she said softly. 'I can't forget that last night happened – it was too lovely for that. But I don't expect anything of you, Chris. I know how hard all this is for you, and I'm happy to just be your friend.'

'Maybe one day...' Chris said.

Stella smiled. 'Don't say that. Let's just remember a wonderful night and move forward, shall we?' She reached up and laid a hand on his cheek, and was gratified when he leaned into her touch for a moment before remembering the conversation they were having.

'I'm sorry,' Chris said. 'I feel like a massive twat for getting cold feet the morning after, but I need to level with you. I don't want to hurt you, Stella. You mean too much to me for that.'

'Honestly, it's okay,' Stella said. 'We had a great time. Let's just leave it at that. After all, we've both got more than enough to be getting on with without adding a complication to the mix.'

Chris looked relieved. 'You're being very good to me.'

'Hey,' Stella admonished. 'I chose to sleep with you last night, remember? You didn't force me. And now, we can both, as adults, choose to walk away from that side of things. It's all right.'

'Well, the least I can do is get you some breakfast,' Chris said, standing up again. 'What would you say to some scrambled eggs?'

'It's all right, I don't feel like breakfast right now.'

'Fair enough,' Chris replied. 'I'm off out later to pick up some supplies. Is there anything I can get you?'

'I'm all good, thanks,' Stella replied. 'I'll see you later, yeah?'

Chris obviously took that as his cue to give her some privacy and nodded, before leaving the guest room. As he left, Stella's stomach gave an almighty rumble. Well, she ruminated, one white lie in order to get out of an awkward situation wasn't the end of the world, was it? She was glad she had a box of Sugar Puffs stashed in her desk drawer in the Rogues' Dining Room. Those, even without the milk, should see her through until an early lunch. Having breakfast together after the discussion they'd just had would be a whole lot more than just awkward. She threw on her nightdress and scuttled off to her own bedroom on the other side of the house, determined to put her encounter with Chris to the back of her mind. Pleasurable as it had been, he clearly wanted to move on, and although she felt a sharp pang of regret and sadness as she reflected on his words to her, there really wasn't much else she could do. After all, if Chris wasn't willing to take things further, what was the point in arguing?

37

Stella was glad she could escape to Roseford Hall for the rest of the day, even if her tiredness from the near-sleepless night wasn't exactly the best state in which to be heading up her first workshop. She hoped the lack of rest wouldn't tell on her concentration too much. She threw on some clothes, chugged some Sugar Puffs and then grabbed her laptop and Fitz's lead and made her way out of Halstead House. She had to file away her upset at Chris's rejection. She knew enough about his history, now, to realise that if a kiss could freak him out, then having full-blooded sex was going to send him into a tailspin. A relationship with Chris was clearly off the table, and she wasn't going to spend her time in Roseford pining for something she couldn't have. Sure, living with him at Halstead House was going to be a little weird, but that wouldn't be forever. And if the worst came to the worst, she was sure she could ask Simon if she could bunk in one of Roseford Hall's spare rooms.

Stunned that she was actually feeling less negative about the whole thing, and wondering if she was just in some ridiculous state of denial, she set to work making the final preparations for the workshop. She spent the first hour copying and collating the packs for the participants, which included the British Heritage Fund's brand-new Roseford Hall brochure, and a hard copy of her Power-Point presentation. She'd also requisitioned some beautiful floral notebooks from the BHF shop and some of their branded pens, and had got permission from Simon to make careful copies of some of the letters from the Treloar family archive that gave a fascinating insight into what life had been like in the house at the turn of the last century. The decade and a bit before the First World War, in particular, had seen the house play host to a number of interesting and infamous guests and social gatherings, and Stella hoped that the workshop participants would find as much inspiration in them as she had. One 'character', in particular, Edmund Treloar, Simon's great-great-uncle, had caught her eye. His resemblance to Simon was startling, from the portrait she'd seen when it had been uncovered in one of the anterooms off the main drawing room, and from the letters she'd read that mentioned him, he would make an excellent character for a novel. That had been the inspiration for her current side project, and she wondered how the Treloar family would react, should she suggest actually writing the story she had in mind.

'Everything all right for later?' Simon sidled up to where Stella was photocopying her resources and putting them into their plastic wallets.

'I think so,' Stella replied, trying to make sure she'd put the last of the carefully copied historical documents into the packs. 'I'm as ready as I'll ever be, at least.' She counted the packs, and then had to stifle a yawn.

'Late night?' Simon asked, raising an eyebrow.

Stella couldn't help the blush that spread across her cheeks at his implication. 'Sort of,' she admitted sheepishly. 'But then I can never sleep in the run up to something important.'

'What, the thought of a few old fogeys from the village showing you their creative etchings has kept you awake?' Simon laughed. 'Pull the other one.'

'I've not actually done a lot of teaching, up until now, unless you count a fairly disastrous creative writing session at my old school a few years ago,' Stella replied. 'So I hope they're going to be gentle with me.'

'You'll be great,' Simon replied. 'And your topic is absolutely perfect.'

'I'm glad you think so,' Stella said, feeling a flush of pleasure, which happily counteracted her blush, at his words. 'This place holds so many mysteries, "The Hidden Secrets of Roseford Hall" seemed to fit it perfectly.'

'Can I get you a cuppa?' Simon broke into her thoughts. 'You look as though you could do with the caffeine.'

'Thanks.' Stella swallowed. She felt nervous as well as tired all of a sudden, and she couldn't work out if it was carrying the knowledge about Olivia, getting ready to 'go live' to a group of strangers, or a combination of the two. A cup of tea would be most welcome.

'And there's some coffee cake in a tin in here somewhere,' Simon said. 'John's wife, Val, is the most incredible baker.'

'That sounds perfect,' Stella replied, sinking down into one of the chairs next to the window of the kitchen. 'She's done all of the baking for the workshop, too, so I guess I'm in for a treat.'

'You are.'

They munched their cake in silence for a minute or two, both of them lost in the lightness of the sponge and the intensity of the flavours.

'Stella...' Simon began, eventually.

'Yes?'

'You can tell me to eff off if you like,' he continued, between sips of tea, 'but I'm getting the impression there's something else bothering you besides the workshop. Are you really all right?'

Stella smiled. Over the time she'd been working at Roseford Hall, she'd begun to appreciate Simon's friendship more and more. He was kind and thoughtful and, despite the oddness of his situation, being the lord without a manor, he'd been nothing but helpful to her, even when her requests had been a little offbeat. But she couldn't talk to him about what she'd learned about Chris and Olivia. It wasn't her secret to tell.

'I'm fine,' she said gently. 'As I said... not enough sleep.'

'You know I'm here if you ever need to talk,' Simon said. 'You can trust me, Stella.'

'I can see why Olivia thought you were such a good friend to her,' Stella replied. 'I appreciate it, Simon. But I'm fine, really.'

'That was the last thing she said to me, the last time we talked before she...' Simon trailed off, shaking his head.

Stella's heart jumped. She wished she could level with Simon, but she didn't want to get caught up in the quagmire of past tragedies. It wasn't her place, no matter what had happened with Chris. Instead, she leaned over and squeezed Simon's forearm. 'Has anyone told you that you're a star?' she said gently.

'Not recently, but I'll take it,' Simon replied, giving a slightly shaky laugh. 'Now, can I help you get set up in the Long Gallery?'

'That would be great. Thank you.' They put their coffee cups and cake plates into the dishwasher and picked up the packs for the workshop. Stella still felt nervous but, fortified by the cake and coffee, she felt at least as though she'd be able to stay awake now.

38

Christ, you're a stupid, stupid twat. That was the constant, nagging refrain in Chris's brain as he tried to concentrate on today's less-than-inspiring job, which was sanding down and preparing the plasterwork in the dining room for its first coat of paint. Not that there seemed much point in doing that when the roof still leaked, but the top floor was most affected by that, so Chris had figured he might as well crack on. It might all be for nothing, anyway, if the money ran out before he could get the house completed. He felt although he was inside a huge hourglass, with the sand pouring slowly but resolutely onto his head, waiting to be buried by the responsibility of it all.

Because this house *was* a responsibility; it was the physical manifestation of Olivia's vision, and would be her legacy, as well as being his and Gabe's home. But now, having spent the night with Stella, that legacy felt even more remote. Olivia's memory glittered and sparkled, high above him, unreachable as the stars. Stella had brought him back to earth, reminded him that he had flesh and blood needs. That he was, still, a man – not just some broken shell. But the conflict he now felt, between honouring the past and tentatively hoping for a future, was ripping him apart. Knowing that *it had to happen sometime*, which was something Helena had said to him recently, was little comfort, especially when he knew he'd given Stella such a brush-off. She'd taken it better than he'd deserved, but that didn't help.

Sighing, he put down the sander and decided that coffee, while not the answer, was definitely a good start. A better one than cracking open another bottle of whisky, anyway. It was definitely too early for that. Just at that moment, his phone pinged with a text from Helena. Swiping the screen, he felt his throat start to ache. There, immediately, was a snapshot of Gabe, grinning outside the house in which Helena and her husband had raised Olivia. A rambling late-Victorian pile, it bore a striking resemblance to Halstead, and although Chris knew this was why Olivia had fallen so immediately in love with Halstead when it had come onto the market, he was assailed with a powerful sense of loss, and also of missing his son. Shaking his head, blinking back sudden tears, he knew, with a lightning-bolt sense of clarity, that this could not go on. It was time, finally, to get a grip on things, to make some positive decisions for himself, his son and the rest of their lives.

The first decision would be to see what progress had been made at the gatehouse, and whether Stella would be able to have her own space back anytime soon. The rented dehumidifier had been going day and night for a while now, so hopefully soon the gatehouse would be habitable again. As he was musing on this, he remembered that he had another dehumidifier in the attic of Halstead. Perhaps, if he could dig it out, it might help the gatehouse to dry a little quicker. Putting down his sander, he strode up the stairs to the top floor of the house, pulled open the rickety old door that had an uncarpeted set of wooden stairs behind it and headed up. The attic wasn't a space he frequented often; he'd told Gabe, in the strongest possible terms, to stay away from it, as it had been deemed unsafe in the survey they'd had before they bought the place, because of the state of the floorboards, which would definitely need replacing. Once it had been the servants' quarters, and the small, grimy windows that looked out over the back of the property did let in some light, but it had now been relegated to being a dumping ground.

Stepping carefully across the floor, he flashed up the little torch from his keychain and skimmed it across the vast area, which covered the footprint of the entire house. It had such potential as a usable space, but that would definitely have to come later. Most of the stuff he'd stored up here was situated close to the door, to mitigate the risk of the floor giving way, but a couple of items were propped near the windows on the left-hand side, in the area that was directly above the bedrooms on the floor below. Spotting the dehumidifier as part of that group, he hurried across the floorboards.

Too late, he realised that there was a reason he'd stopped Gabe from exploring up here. As the boards gave way, his last thought before he hit the floor in the room below was that, actually, he didn't really want Stella to move out, so why had he been looking for the extra dehumidifier in the first place?

39

Stella gazed out of the bevelled bay window of Roseford Hall's Long Gallery and breathed a sigh of relief. The participants, ten of them, had all shown up on time and were now engaged in the first task she'd set them: to fabricate a 'found history' of a resident of Roseford Hall from the documents and artefacts she'd amassed from the archives. Situated around the room were various relics from the house's history, mostly from the turn of the last century. She'd persuaded the art restoration team from the British Heritage Fund to relocate Edmund Treloar's portrait to the Long Gallery, and was pleased when a couple of the workshop's participants made the link between the man and the letters.

One participant in particular, a student from the local sixth form college, had taken the concept of 'found history' and written a whole series of letters in response to Edmund Treloar's from a fictional lover. Interestingly, she'd chosen to keep the gender of the writer unrevealed, which gave the letters, in that context, an added texture of mystery.

'These are wonderful,' Stella said as she read the work at the end. All of the doubts she'd had about the teaching side of her residency began to ebb away. If this place could inspire such creativity, then she wanted to be a part of it for as long as she could.

At the end of the afternoon, she returned to Halstead House feeling far more euphoric than when she'd left it. The buzz of having done her job well was almost enough to make her forget the awkwardness of having been given the brush-off by Chris, and as she passed the gatehouse, one of the guys working on the rewiring told her that, with a bit of luck, she'd be back home within a few days. Although on one level she felt sad at the prospect of leaving Halstead, she felt relieved that any awkward encounters with Chris would be escapable once she was back in her own home. She'd be able to close the door and focus on what was important: making her time in Roseford as happy and creative as it could be.

As she approached the front door of Helena's bungalow, on her way back up to Halstead, she saw a figure huddled on the doorstep. Surprised that she should be sitting out here when there was a perfectly serviceable patio set in the back garden, Stella's heart sped up a little.

The sight of Helena's ashen face, as Stella drew closer, brought her up even more short. Her heart started to thump uncomfortably in her chest. Had Helena found out about Chris and Stella's night together? Was she here to call her out? No, she chided herself, Helena wouldn't have an axe to grind – she'd been trying to get her and Chris together since Stella moved here. So what on earth was the matter? One thing was for certain; she wasn't going to find out by dawdling on the path.

'What's wrong?' she asked as she approached. Helena was staring into space, a cup of tea untouched on the step beside her.

'Oh, Stella!' Helena said, standing up so suddenly that she wobbled. Stella reached out a hand and steadied her, the panic starting to rise in her throat.

'What is it?' Stella asked, all kinds of dreadful things flashing across her mind. 'Is it Gabe? Is he all right?'

Helena shook her head. 'Stupid, stupid boy. I don't know what he was thinking.'

A feeling of such dread took hold of Stella as Helena's words sunk in, she felt her whole body go cold. 'Helena? Is Gabe all right?' She realised her voice sounded harsher than it should have, in her urgency to find out, and she took a deep breath. 'Please... tell me what's happened.'

Helena looked blankly at her for a long moment, and then, clearly still in shock, she spoke.

'He must have been looking for something in the attic rooms. They're unsafe, and he knows not to go up there. But for some reason, he did.' She paused, wiping at her eyes impatiently. 'When I went up to look for him, I found him unconscious in the master bedroom on the floor below, underneath a huge hole in the ceiling. God knows how long he'd been there.'

'Oh, my God!' Stella gasped, her own head starting to spin as her pulse thumped horribly.

'I called an ambulance immediately,' Helena continued, 'but I couldn't rouse him. The emergency responder told me not to move him in case he'd broken his back. He was breathing, but unconscious.' Helena sank back down on the step again, and, sitting with her, leaving Fitz to sniff around the front garden, Stella handed her the cup of tea she'd left. It was still just about warm enough to drink.

'He's been taken to Magdalene Park Hospital. They've just left.' Helena took a sip of the tea and then looked down at the gravel in front of her.

'Has Chris gone with him?' Stella asked gently.

Helena's head jerked up. 'It was Chris who had the fall,' she replied.

Stella's heart felt as though it was going to jump out of her chest as the world slowly closed in around her. In her horror, she'd leapt to the conclusion that it was Gabe who'd fallen through the ceiling. And now, it seemed, the poor boy might lose his father as well as his mother.

'Oh, my God,' she whispered. 'Poor, poor Gabe. What was Chris doing up there?'

'I don't know.' Helena's voice broke. 'I had to let him go in that ambulance, all alone, as Gabe was far too distressed to go with him. I persuaded him to go and get his Xbox from the house so he's got something to take his mind off things, and I'm going to grab a few things and get over to the hospital now.'

Stella imagined Chris, all alone in the hospital, with no one by his side, and her eyes filled with tears. She was so caught up in the image that she barely registered what Helena was saying next.

'So could you keep an eye on Gabe for me this evening?' Helena said. 'I don't think he should come to the hospital tonight. The paramedics couldn't rule out internal injuries, although they did diagnose a broken ankle and a couple of broken ribs.'

'Of course,' Stella replied. 'Anything you need. Does Chris have any family to contact? Any—' she swallowed, 'next of kin?'

Helena smiled briefly. 'I've rung his mother and she's getting a lift down from Staffordshire with his brother. They're going to ring as soon as they're close.'

'Oh, Helena.' Stella reached out and gave the older woman a huge hug. 'This must be so hard for you. I'll keep an eye on Gabe for as long as you need me to. But, please, keep me posted. I can't imagine what you're—'

'I know,' Helena cut her off, but not unkindly. 'And of course I will. I'll just grab a few things and I'll be off. Help yourself to whatever you'd like from the kitchen, and I'll be in touch.'

As Helena hurried off to sort some stuff out to take to Chris in the hospital, Stella's knees continued to tremble. Sending up a message to a god she wasn't sure she believed in, she prayed that Gabe wouldn't lose his father as well as his mother, and that Chris would pull through.

40

That evening felt like the longest of Stella's life. Gabe had engrossed himself in the Xbox for quite a while, and Stella felt worried about how calm he was, as he blasted zombies and then switched to the latest version of the FIFA football game. Was he in shock? Was he closing off his emotions to protect himself? She had made them both a cup of hot chocolate at around eight o'clock, complete with a mountain of whipped cream and sprinkles, more to give them something to focus on than because either of them really wanted it. They'd then watched some Marvel film on Helena's Netflix account, which both of them had seen before, but at least the predictability offered a certain amount of reassurance. At 9.30 p.m., Helena had phoned, finally.

'He's out of danger,' she said immediately. 'He's cracked some ribs and has a nasty bump on the head from where he must have hit a joist on the way down, and a fractured ankle, but thankfully no internal bleeding.'

'Oh, thank goodness!' Stella sagged back against the sofa cushions. 'Let me put you on speaker. Gabe's right next to me.'

'Can I come and see him?' Gabe asked immediately.

'Not tonight, darling,' Helena's voice emanated from the phone. 'They're even going to send me home in a minute. I'll bring you over in the morning.'

'But what if he doesn't wake up in the morning?' Gabe was suddenly hysterical, as if all of the emotions he'd been keeping in check in the hours since Chris's accident had burst through at once. 'What if he dies suddenly, like Mum did?'

Stella flung her arms around the distraught boy, trying to calm him, but he shrugged her off.

'No!' he shouted. 'Get off me. You don't know anything!'

Stella dropped her arms immediately. 'I'll call you back, Helena,' she said quickly, knowing that Helena would be just as distraught to hear Gabe's outburst and be too far away to help. Chucking her phone down on the coffee table by the sofa, she chanced a tentative hand on Gabe's upper arm. He'd collapsed against his side of the sofa and was hiding his face in the cushions.

'Your dad's going to be fine,' she said softly.

'How do you know?' Gabe's voice was muffled, but Stella could tell from the way his back was heaving that he was still crying. 'You're not a doctor.'

'He's fit, and he's strong. It was a horrible accident, but your gran said he's out of danger. Try to trust the doctors.'

'But what if they're wrong?' Gabe said. 'What if he's got a thing like Mum and they haven't found it yet?'

Stella's heart ached for the distressed boy. He'd been through so much in the past couple of years, and she knew that there was nothing she could say that could help to mitigate that. Instead, she gave his arm a little squeeze.

'It's all right to be frightened, Gabe,' she said softly. 'When... when my dad died, I was a couple of years older than you. He was gentle, and kind, and he got me in a way that no one else did. My mum was very, very sad for a long time, and one day, when I got home, she wasn't there.' Stella paused for a moment, the over-whelming force of the emotions she'd felt, coming home to an empty house temporarily knocking her off balance.

'Where'd she gone?' Gabe sniffed, turning a wary eye back towards her.

'She'd left me a note, saying she couldn't be in the house any longer, and that she was going away for a bit.' Stella shook her head, trying to chase away the demons that still lingered over that event. 'I was terrified, just like you are now. I thought she'd left me forever. I even thought that she'd...' She trailed off, not wanting to voice the fears to Gabe, who was still so young. He shouldn't have to think about things like that, after everything he'd been through.

'I spent the night calling her friends, and other people she might be with, and I didn't get any sleep. I've never been so scared. My dad was gone, and now my mum had disappeared.' Brushing her eyes impatiently, she paused to collect her thoughts and try to phrase what she was going to say next.

'Eventually, I fell asleep on the sofa, and when I woke up, early the next morning, she was coming through the front door, as if nothing had happened. She cooked me breakfast and we made conversation, and I so badly wanted to ask her where she'd been, but I just couldn't. I was so relieved to see her back that I just played along.'

'Where had she been?' Gabe asked, intrigued now, and calming down as he listened to Stella's story.

Stella shook her head. 'I still don't know. She never told me. But she came back, Gabe, and I was so happy to see her, that was all that mattered.' She chanced a hand on his arm again, and this time he didn't shrug her off.

'But that's different!' he retorted. 'She wasn't hurt.'

'But she was,' Stella said softly. 'Maybe she wasn't hurt physically, but mentally she was in so much pain. I... I thought I'd lost her, too. And I was just as scared as you are now.'

'But Dad fell through the ceiling! He could actually die!'

Stella was losing him again, she knew it. She felt the worry beginning to creep up on her as she wondered what the hell she could say. What *could* she say that could possibly make this dreadful situation any better for the scared eleven-year-old in front of her?

'Oh, Gabe,' she murmured, hoping that, if she put an arm around him, it might help, at least a little.

Just as she was about to pull him in for a hug, her phone rang again. Grabbing it from the coffee table why the side of the sofa, she was simultaneously relieved and nervous when Helena's name appeared onscreen. What if... but she stopped that thought in its tracks. Helena wouldn't tell them something that dreadful by phone.

Swiping the screen with a suddenly sweaty fingertip, she nearly dropped the phone as she brought it to her ear.

'Can you put me on speaker again?' Helena asked as the call connected. 'I want Gabe to be able to hear.'

'Of course, if you're sure,' Stella said. She hoped Helena knew what she was doing. Gabe was about two breaths away from a full-blown meltdown, and she didn't have a clue how to deal with him if Helena's call was going to tip him over the edge.

'I'm sure.'

'Okay, bear with me.'

Stella fumbled with the button on-screen, and then really did drop the phone, with a clatter, onto Helena's limed oak floorboards. Scrambling to pick it up, she eventually managed to get it onto loudspeaker.

'Are you trying to take my eardrums out as well as everything else?'

The voice, weaker than usual, but with that unmistakable trace of gravel that sent a relieved shiver down Stella's spine, was tired, but sounded sweeter than it ever had, to both Stella and Gabe.

'Dad!' Gabe exclaimed. He grabbed the phone off Stella, wanting, clearly, to hold proof in his own hands that his father was awake. 'How are you?'

'I fell through a ceiling,' Chris said, a dash of wryness in his tone. 'How do you think I am?'

'When can you come home?' Gabe asked, his face transformed by the sound of his dad's voice. The fear, for the moment at least, had been chased away.

'Not tonight,' Chris replied. 'But hopefully they'll let me out in a few days. Got to wait for the swelling to go down on my ankle first, so they can pin it and put a cast on.'

'Can I come and see you, then?' Gabe was bouncing up and down on the sofa cushions, jittery with relief.

'Maybe in the morning.' Chris sighed. 'It's been a long day and I need to send your grandmother home to get some sleep.'

'Oh, don't worry about me,' Helena's voice came from further away. 'I take crises like this in my stride.'

Stella resolved to make Helena a large gin and tonic when she got home, and not spare the gin. The poor woman had been through enough today, and it must all have been a dreadful scare for her.

'Well, we'd better let you get some sleep,' Stella said, finally finding her voice. 'We'll see you in the morning.'

'Goodnight, Dad,' Gabe said. 'See you in the morning.'

'Goodnight, munchkin,' Chris said. And this time, he really did sound tired as he added. 'Sweet dreams.'

Stella was about to end the call when Chris added, 'You too, Stella. And thank you.'

'Goodnight,' she murmured, oblivious for the moment to Gabe's presence beside her. She was lost in Chris's voice again. 'Sleep well.'

As she ended the call, she blinked away sudden tears, then turned back to face Gabe. 'He's going to be all right, Gabe. He's awake.'

Gabe reached out and nearly knocked the wind out of her as he hugged her. She felt him nodding in response to her statement, and realised that he couldn't say anything for fear of crying again. Holding him closer for a moment longer, she felt the relief wash over her that she wasn't sitting here trying to help him through far worse news.

'Right,' she said, a moment later when they broke apart. 'I think you need to get some rest if you're going to go to the hospital in the morning, don't you?'

Gabe started to grumble, but then nodded. 'You're right, I suppose.' As he got off the sofa, he turned back towards her. 'Thanks for staying with me. You didn't have to.'

'I wasn't going to leave you alone,' Stella said. 'What kind of a friend would I be if I did that?'

'I'm glad you're my friend.' Gabe smiled suddenly at her, and she felt her heart melt. 'And I'm glad you're Dad's friend, too. He needs friends.'

As Gabe turned away and headed off to the bedroom in Helena's house that had basically become his, Stella was left thinking about that comment. Yes, she thought, Chris *does* need friends. So why, when she knew that, did she still find herself hoping for something more? Realising she was very, very tired, and very, very emotional after everything that had happened that day, she tried to shush those thoughts. It was no use even allowing herself to think in that direction – Chris had made his feelings perfectly clear after their one-night stand. Even so, she still found herself imagining what it would be like to be with him as more than just a friendly neighbour. There was something there, something real between them, she was sure. But now, she said to herself firmly, was definitely not the time to pursue it. Perhaps it never would be.

41

About an hour later, the front door of the bungalow opened and Helena came into the living room. Stella, who'd been dozing with Fitz on the sofa, jumped up with a start as Helena's footsteps creaked on the floorboards.

'Hey,' she said, reaching for her glasses and sitting up quickly, feeling guilty that she'd dropped off, and let Fitz up on the furniture. 'How are you?'

Helena looked at her blankly for a long moment, and then, to Stella's horror, burst into tears.

It was like watching Notre Dame's spire collapsing. Jumping off the sofa, Stella threw her arms around Helena who, for just a moment, clung to her helplessly. Stella realised then how frail Helena actually was; she'd always exuded such calm, such confidence and such incredible resilience. This horrible accident had obviously taken it out of her.

'It's all right,' she said softly as they broke apart again. 'It's been an awful day. But it's over now.'

Helena glanced in the direction of the hallway, and Stella

realised that she was checking to see if Gabe had heard her come in.

'He crashed out a while ago,' she said, in answer to Helena's unspoken question. 'He was knackered.'

'Thank you for looking after him,' Helena said shakily. 'I didn't want him to witness his father being put back together again. Not after...' she trailed off.

'It was no trouble, honestly,' Stella replied. 'I wouldn't have left him by himself after what happened.'

'You're a good friend,' Helena replied, wiping her eyes with the back her sleeve. 'To all of us.'

'Come and sit down,' she said, guiding Helena to the sofa. 'I'll put the kettle on.'

'Actually,' Helena smiled briefly, 'I'd quite like something stronger. There's a bottle of sloe gin in the cupboard by the window, if you'll be so good as to fetch it, and a couple of glasses, if you'd like to join me? And bring the bottle over, too. We may need a top-up.'

Stella smiled back. 'I think that's a much better idea.' Doing as Helena directed, she'd soon poured two generous measures and brought them over to the sofa. She deposited the bottle on the coffee table and settled back down.

Helena took a gulp of the sloe gin and leaned back into the cushions, letting out a long sigh. 'Thank God that's over.'

'Is he really out of danger?' Stella asked, once she'd taken a more guarded sip of her own drink. The sweet, slightly medicinal taste was comforting, and she could feel it warming her.

Helena nodded. 'It was touch and go there for a while; the doctors wanted to rule out any internal bleeding, especially on his brain, since he'd taken such a knock to the head on the way down. That was a relief, you know, given what happened to Olivia.'

Stella nodded. She could only imagine how much today's events must have brought back for Helena. Gabe had been

distraught enough; Helena knew and understood the full implica-
tions of what could happen. 'I'm so sorry you've had to go through
this, Helena.'

'He should never have been up in the attic rooms,' Helena said,
taking a slightly more decorous sip of her gin. 'He knew damn well
it was dangerous up there. He's told Gabe to keep out often enough.
I don't know what possessed him.' She shook her head. 'And to do it
when no one else was around... imagine what could have happened
if Gabe and I hadn't found him?' She trailed off, swallowing back
more tears.

'But you did,' Stella said gently. She gestured to the gin bottle.
'Top-up?'

Helena nodded. 'I wouldn't, under normal circumstances, but I
feel as though I need it tonight.' She looked at Stella as she poured
them both a little more. 'It just brought back so many things about
the night Olivia died.' She shook her head impatiently, as if trying
to shake off the onslaught of memories that Chris's accident had
triggered. 'Seeing him lying there, unconscious, feeling so helpless
in the face of it.' She sipped her replenished gin. 'I'm not strong
enough to go through that again.'

'You're one of the strongest people I know,' Stella said gently.
'The way you've been supporting Gabe and Chris through all of this
is astonishing.'

'What else could I do?' Helena replied. 'They needed me. And I
needed them. Somehow, we helped each other through those
appalling, awful, early days, when we were all questioning how
something so hideously random could happen to the one person
we loved most in the world. And then, to think that poor Gabe
might have lost his father, too...' She closed her eyes as she trailed
off and took another sip.

Stella's heart ached for Helena, Gabe and for Chris, and how
close they'd nearly come to yet another tragedy. 'This must be so

hard for you,' she said gently. 'After the way you lost Olivia, you must have been terrified.'

Helena nodded into her glass. 'When you lose a child, almost your whole heart goes with them.' She paused, obviously trying to measure her words, to give some quantifiable meaning to an unquantifiable pain. 'Olivia's death was something I never, ever thought I'd get past. And, to a great extent, you never do. She was part of me, a link to the husband I loved so much, and her own, incredible, vital self, and to have her snatched from me was agony.' She gave a mirthless laugh. 'I wanted to howl. I wanted to rage at the unfairness of it all. How, if there is a God, could they ever allow this to happen? For a son to lose his mother, for a husband to lose his wife, and for me to lose my precious, beautiful baby girl.'

Stella remained silent. She had the feeling that Helena hadn't talked so openly about losing Olivia for a long while, and she had no wish to interrupt. Instead, she reached out and squeezed the hand that wasn't holding her glass.

'I did howl, too,' Helena said, talking almost to herself. 'When Gabe and Chris were out and about. I screamed my pain into the walls of that house, and I hated the world for taking her from me. My girl. The impulsive, vibrant, creative spark of light that had been snuffed out because of a seemingly random event. My despair was so dark, so dangerous, I had to hide it from Chris and Gabe. I knew it would consume them as it was me. I couldn't let that happen, when I knew how much they were both suffering, trying to come to terms with it. I wonder, sometimes, if they did the same, but we never talked about it.'

Knowing what she did about the guilt Chris was carrying about the night of Olivia's death, Stella thought that Chris probably had, but she kept that to herself. It wasn't her place to betray the confidences he'd entrusted her with. Eventually, she hoped, he'd do that himself.

'But I'm being maudlin, dwelling on all that,' Helena said, obviously noticing Stella's expression. 'It's got to be about moving forward, now. We've got to help Chris to get back on his feet.'

'When's he coming out of hospital?'

'Not for another few days, at least,' Helena replied. 'And what's he coming back to?' She sighed. 'The house is still a huge mess. I really do think Chris is going to have to make some decisions about the future of Halstead when he's better.'

'You mean whether to keep going or to sell?'

Helena nodded. 'Got it in one. Perhaps this fall will bring him to his senses, after all. Or at least shake him out of his paralysis about Halstead and make him realise he needs help if he's going to get it up and running as he wants to. If he still wants to. And if that doesn't, then seeing his mother tomorrow morning might.' She smiled ruefully. 'They don't exactly see eye to eye on many things.'

'What if he had some help?' Stella asked, the flicker of an idea beginning to form. 'What if he didn't have to try to do this all by himself?'

'He won't accept it.' Helena sighed. 'He wants to be involved in all the decisions, and he's determined to do as much of the work himself as he can. If we don't watch him like a hawk, he'll be up out of bed and painting or plastering before we can stop him.'

'Well, he'd better learn to accept help,' Stella said. The flicker of an idea was bursting into flames. 'It's about time he stopped burying his head in the sand and got Halstead sorted out. And if that means delegating some of the work, then so be it.'

'What have you got in mind?' Helena asked, looking at Stella curiously.

'Leave it with me,' Stella said, not wanting to share her idea with Helena until she was completely sure it was viable. 'I think I know just the person who can help.'

'Well, whatever you're thinking, I'll be pleased to hear about it in the morning,' Helena replied. To Stella's eyes, she suddenly looked exhausted, and every one of her years.

'I'll leave you to it, then, if you don't need anything else,' Stella said.

'Are you going to be okay in the big house on your own tonight?' Helena asked. 'I'm afraid there's only the one spare bedroom here, Gabe's room, but you're welcome to the sofa.'

Stella smiled. 'I'll be fine. I've got some stuff to finish up from the workshop today, and a couple of other things to plan, so I won't be in bed for a while, anyway.' She stood up and, suddenly, the effects of the sloe gin kicked in and she wobbled. 'Or perhaps I'll get up early and tackle them instead.'

'Goodnight, then.' Helena also stood. 'And thank you, again. You've gone above and beyond the call of duty for a neighbour today.'

'I like to think I'm more of a friend,' Stella said.

'Yes,' Helena replied. 'You definitely are. But even as a friend, it's been a hard day. You make sure you get some sleep, too.'

'I will.' On impulse, she leaned forward and kissed Helena's cheek. 'See you tomorrow.'

As Stella left and walked herself and Fitz wearily back to her room at Halstead, her mind was spinning with possibilities. It was time to see just how much store Simon Treloar set by his former friendship with Olivia, and whether he'd be prepared to help to get Halstead up and running as the retreat that Olivia had always wanted it to be. Whether or not Chris would agree to Simon's help, of course, was another matter entirely. But, lying in a hospital bed with a broken ankle, what did he really have to lose?

42

Fuck, fuck, fuck! Chris was so drugged-up on painkillers that he wasn't even sure if he was thinking it or saying it out loud when he woke up. What a bloody stupid thing to have done. And now here he was, flat on his back, left foot immobilised pending a hard cast, and head fuzzy, but mercifully not pounding because of the drugs.

For two years since Olivia's death, he'd dreaded being out of action. Although progress on Halstead had been unbearably slow at times, he'd been fit and well and able to tackle any job that needed doing. Now, with two cracked ribs and a broken ankle, he was going to be unable to work on it, and that worried him more than he was prepared to admit. Being in a state of emotional paralysis was one thing; being in a state of physical incapacity was entirely different. Maybe it was the painkillers, but he was torn between utter panic and a sense of *que sera, sera*. After all, what else could go wrong?

He found he was laughing. That must be the drugs. What the hell did he have to laugh about? The absurdity of his situation did not pass him by. But, right now, there was little he could do about it. For the next few days, at least, a hospital bed was his only option.

Gabe was coming in tomorrow, so he'd better get his head in order before he did. And he was sure Helena had mentioned something about his mother and brother, too. Great. But, more pressingly, how could he look his son in the eye, knowing he'd been so stupid? The thought that he could have left his eleven-year-old boy an orphan suddenly made the laughter stop and tears bloom in his eyes. Gabe – gentle, sweet, patient Gabe, who'd borne so much in his short life, but still kept smiling for him. He owed it to Gabe to give him a home, a proper home, not just a rotting shell of a house. But how could he do that now?

Helena had left about an hour ago, and he was glad to be out from under her scrutiny, however well-intentioned it was. She'd been incredibly patient with him over the years, both before and after Olivia's death, and had really become more of a mother figure to him than his own mum, at times. She'd accepted this sullen, chippy man into her family and made him welcome, even when his seemingly crackpot ideas about being a successful property developer were far from reach. After the first couple of projects, though, she'd realised that he'd been serious about creating a future for his family, and she'd supported him wholeheartedly. When Olivia had died, she'd carried him, even though he'd never truly opened up to her about the night it happened. She hadn't criticised his decisions, just been there with a calm head and a gentle admonishment when necessary. And now he'd let her down, too.

Telling himself his fall had been an accident didn't help. It was still a massive inconvenience and meant that he'd be out of action for weeks, if not months. But what did it matter, anyway? It wasn't as if he was *really* working to a schedule. He'd been faffing about for too long and not really achieving anything: happy to tinker at the edges of the project without truly making an impact. If he was going to have any hope of holding onto Halstead, he'd need to start making some decisions, getting some help.

One of the nurses was doing the late-night obs round, and he smiled briefly at her as she approached his bed and took his temperature and blood pressure.

'Seems fine,' she said, in response to his questioning eyebrow. 'And,' she continued, looking at his chart, 'looks like another hour or two before your next lot of painkillers. How are you feeling?'

'Like I fell through a ceiling,' Chris said wryly. He kept grinning when she smiled back at him.

'Well, you know where the call button is if you need anything,' the nurse replied. 'I'll let you get some shut-eye now.'

As she moved on to the next patient, Chris closed his eyes and willed the thumping in his head to subside. The painkillers had muted it, but the awareness that the ache was still there, almost hovering above him, drew him to keep it in focus. Eventually, when the drugs wore off, he'd feel it again, and the anticipation was enough to speed his heart up. He lay in that state between waking and sleeping, a kind of strange lucidity where he couldn't be sure what was real. Drifting in and out of sleep, he didn't know if he was dreaming when he pictured Olivia's face, her smile, her favourite black and red checked shirt that she wore when she painted. She was forever frozen in time at age thirty-four, blonde hair to her shoulders and the beginnings of laughter lines around her eyes. He blinked, and she was gone. He felt a sense of peace as he closed his eyes again; all too often, he'd woken, drenched in sweat with tears on his face, recalling the horror of her final moments. For once it was comforting to 'see' her as she had been in life; happy, bubbling over with enthusiasm for the artists' retreat that Halstead was going to be, and looking forward to the future.

Chris drifted into sleep, his body finally getting some of the rest it had been denied for a long, long time. He hadn't realised just how tired he'd been until he'd been forced to stop. The dreams he had, when he finally did fall asleep, weren't of Olivia, though. They were of someone quite different. Someone with curly brown hair, soft curves and piercing green eyes that seemed to see straight into his soul. Someone he'd run scared from not forty-eight hours previously, because he couldn't cope with the feelings that being with her so intimately had unleashed. He'd thrown his emotions into a box in the back of his mind, locked the box and sworn to deal with them some other time. But now, forced into inertia by his injuries, he had no choice but to unlock that box again. As he slept, he dreamed of the peace of her arms around him, and, even with the state of his injuries, he slept better than he had in a long time.

43

Stella did actually manage to crash out when she got back to her room at Halstead. The events and emotions of the day had taken their toll, and it was all she could do to feed Fitz and then stagger to bed, ready for oblivion. Whether it was the sloe gin, or just exhaustion, she was too tired to worry too much, and just grateful for the rest.

The next morning, she woke with the light streaming through her bedroom window, having completely neglected to shut the curtains. Thankfully, the sloe gin hadn't left any ill effects, and she sat up in bed, remembering the half-formed ideas that she'd been contemplating before she crashed out. In the cold light of day, she began to question them, but she fought the instinct to back off. She wanted to help Chris when he came home, and be useful.

Thankfully, for the next few days she was a free agent. She'd written a blog for the Roseford Hall website that wouldn't need updating until the end of next week, and her next workshop wasn't for a few weeks. While there were always plenty of opportunities for writing, she felt as though she'd contributed enough lately to take some time off. Not that rest and relaxation was anywhere near what she had in mind, though.

After grabbing a coffee and a slice of toast, she sat in the Rogues' Dining Room and tried to make a plan. But where to start? Chris had almost been overwhelmed by the enormity of the task of converting Halstead into Olivia's vision of an artists' retreat – what hope did she have of making it a bit more comfortable for him when he came out of hospital? And did she have any right to interfere? Deciding that she'd need help, she gave Helena a quick ring.

'Hi, yes, I'm fine. Did you sleep all right? So... I've got an idea, but I need to see if you think it's a good one. Can you come over after you've been to see Chris? And bring Gabe, too?'

While she waited for Gabe and Helena, she wandered around the house, trying to get a sense of what most needed doing. The kitchen, thankfully, was fully kitted out, and the small living room on the first floor was more or less complete. Structurally, the house was now nearly sound, but in terms of décor, not very much had been touched. Chris's bedroom and the newly decorated living room were on the first floor, but that would be no good for him while he was on crutches. Chris, for the time being, would need a suite of rooms on the ground floor; he didn't want to be struggling up and down stairs all the time.

Fortunately, this was an option. There was another small reception room and a bathroom close to the kitchen, so it was just a case of sorting out somewhere for him to sleep. The larger room at the end of the long corridor would do, and it looked out over the front lawn, so he'd have a decent view. As she pushed open the door to see what the state of the room was, she heard Helena and Gabe coming in the front door on the other side of the building. She hurried to meet them.

'Hey,' she said, giving first Helena, and then Gabe a hug. 'How are you doing?'

After they'd made coffee, Helena had filled Stella in on how Chris was doing and Gabe was slurping a glass of fizzy cranberry pop, Stella took a deep breath and tentatively began to outline her idea.

'We all know that this place isn't in a fit state for Chris to convalesce, so I was wondering if we could do some things for him, to help him with the renovation in the longer term, but also to give him a more comfortable space while he recovers.' She explained her idea about sorting out a room on the ground floor for him to sleep in, so he didn't have to go too far while he was still on crutches.

Helena nodded. 'You're right, of course. I was going to suggest he came and stayed with me, for the same reasons, but three of us in the bungalow would be a bit of a squeeze, and, knowing Chris, he'd refuse.'

'I hope you don't think I'm interfering,' Stella said, suddenly aware that she was at best a houseguest and at worst merely the gatehouse's tenant, even if Helena had called her a friend last night, 'but I've taken a bit of leave before the next event at Roseford, and I wanted to use it to help, if you're both okay with that?'

'It's a lovely offer,' Helena replied, 'and one that Chris is lucky to have. There's only so much Gabe and I can do by ourselves, so having someone to help sort things out for him is a real blessing.'

'Well, even the three of us can only go so far.' Stella smiled. 'So I thought I'd enlist a few more pairs of hands, if you're all right with that?'

'Of course!' Helena replied. 'Who do you have in mind?'

'Give me ten minutes,' she said. 'I need to make a couple of calls.'

'All right,' Helena replied. She turned to Gabe, who'd been silently listening all this time. 'Why don't you help me to see if we can get the end bedroom sorted out for Dad, and what needs doing, while Stella makes her calls.'

'Okay,' Gabe replied. He finished up his cranberry pop and looked at Stella. 'Why are you doing this?' he asked. 'I mean, you don't *have* to. You're not, like, family or anything.'

Stella felt the heat start to rise in her cheeks at Gabe's question. 'You and your dad are my friends,' she said softly. 'That's what friends do, isn't it? Help each other.'

Gabe looked unconvinced, but trotted down the corridor when Helena called him. Stella got the impression that Gabe was beginning to work out that something more had happened between herself and Chris, but she wasn't going to be the one to confirm it. After all, Chris had made it clear that he didn't want things to progress further between them. And anyway, that *was* what friends were for, wasn't it?

Tapping her phone, she located the number she needed, and waited for the call to connect.

'Simon? Hi, it's Stella. Look, Chris had an accident yesterday and is in hospital. No, he's fine, well, sort of, but I was wondering if I could ask you a favour or three...'

44

'Right,' Stella said, the following morning, once everyone had assembled. 'We've got about four days to make the back corridor of the ground floor reasonable for Chris to convalesce in. Do you think we can do it?'

Simon raised a wary eyebrow. 'Wouldn't it be easier just to pay for him to live in a hotel for the next six weeks?'

Stella laughed. 'Probably, but we still have to try.'

As she outlined her ideas for the ground floor, Gabe and Helena chipped in from time to time, and the jobs were quickly divided up. Simon had brought two handymen from Roseford Hall with him to tackle anything carpentry related, and they were already sizing up the hallway and sitting room and setting up. Simon, however, didn't seem as sure as Stella, Gabe and Helena that they were doing the right thing by taking charge of this part of the renovation.

'Look, Stella,' Simon said, once the rest of the group were out of earshot, 'I appreciate what you're trying to do here, and I know Helena's in full agreement with you, but I can't help wondering if maybe we're overstepping the mark by doing this without telling

Chris? He's a tricky bugger at the best of times, and I'm not sure he's going to take kindly to us messing about in his house, no matter how good our intentions are. Don't you think you, or Helena, should tell him what we're up to before he comes home and freaks out?'

Stella, who was spreading out the dust sheets on the floor of the bedroom that they were going to paint for Chris, paused. 'I know that this seems really out of line, but please, trust me. Sometimes a pair of fresh eyes on a situation is all that's needed. You and Helena know Chris so well – perhaps the fact that I don't is my strength. He needs our help, Simon, our real, practical help. Let's try to give it to him, instead of mouthing platitudes that make us feel better but don't do any real good.'

'Okay, okay, I'll trust you,' Simon said, 'but if he freaks out, I'm denying all responsibility!'

'It's a deal,' Stella replied. 'Now, help me get the lid off these paints, will you?' Helena had ordered the paint from Amazon Prime the previous morning, and it had, thankfully, turned up just before Simon and his team had arrived.

'Maybe you should consider a new career as a developer?' Simon teased. 'You're certainly adapting to the role of site manager.'

Stella shook her head and laughed. 'Crisis management is one thing, but I think I'll stick to being a writer!'

As they began to slap paint on the walls of the bedroom, a nice, neutral pale cream that would be easily painted over if Chris decided to redecorate later, Stella tried to shrug off the doubts that Simon's words had begun to create in her mind. What if she *was* wrong, and Chris really did go postal about the renovations they were doing behind his back? She knew, even from the short time that she'd known him, that having control of this project was everything; and even now, when he was lying in a hospital bed, having effectively had that control taken from him, would he take kindly at all to having his space invaded? But, having discussed it with Helena and Gabe, she hoped that Chris would see that they'd acted to try to help him, and that he wouldn't resent that. Swallowing down the sudden worry that threatened to make her put down her paintbrush and call the whole thing off, she hoped she was right.

45

Three days later, and the ground floor of Halstead House was beginning to look attractive and liveable for the first time in nearly twenty years. The damp carpets, some disintegrating into dust when they'd been moved, had been stripped away, the floorboards sanded and varnished, the walls painted and a couple of rugs had been thrown down to make the rooms feel cosier. The place was looking brighter, lighter and would be a whole lot more pleasant for Gabe and Chris to live in while Chris recovered and the rest of the house was renovated.

Stella's sense of unease was growing, though, and her airy assurances to Simon that Chris would appreciate all their hard work weren't really working on herself. She couldn't help feeling that, although they'd made amazing progress, they'd overstepped the mark in taking on this project without telling Chris about it. Helena and Gabe had visited Chris a few times, but they'd sworn themselves to secrecy. What if Chris came home and really wasn't happy about their interference?

Later that afternoon, the day before Chris was due to come home, Stella was unpacking a box that Helena had brought over from one of the outbuildings that contained the curtains to hang in the bedroom. Thankfully, they were clean and dry, and once they'd been shaken out and hung by the open windows, any residual mustiness would soon be eradicated. In a gorgeous dark William Morris print, they were a little austere for a bedroom, but they'd do until Chris decided what he wanted permanently. Somehow, she didn't imagine him as the chintz and flowers type, anyway.

As she was pulling out the second curtain, something clattered to the floor from within its deep folds. Putting the curtain down again, Stella reached down, worried that some old ornament had been shoved in with the curtains for safekeeping and she'd broken something precious. She burrowed amongst the heavy material until she laid hands on the object, which turned out to be a plain silver photo frame. Turning it over, she caught her breath. Inside the frame was a picture of Chris and Olivia, clearly a studio job, and Gabe aged about eight, his still chubby cheeks and sweet smile trained on Olivia's face as she smiled down at him, not looking directly at the camera, but turned sideways on, with Chris looking adoringly at the pair of them, over her shoulder. Stella's heart ached as she saw the happiness in Chris's eyes; the way he looked so complete, with his wife and young son next to him. The photographer had captured the softness in his gaze, and the protective yet gentle body language told her so much about what this family had been. She felt kicked in the gut with sadness, both for what she'd missed out on because her own father had died when she'd been only a few years older than Gabe was in this photograph, and for Chris, whose loss was perfectly counterpointed by this loving family snap. A deeper, more subtle emotion, that she could vaguely identify as longing, settled in her stomach, too. There was a part of her that desperately wanted to make Chris as happy as he appeared in the forgotten photograph.

'Everything all right?' Helena's voice snapped Stella quickly out of her own thoughts as she poked her head around the door frame of the bedroom.

'Fine,' Stella replied, hurriedly hiding the photo frame beneath the folds of the curtains once more. She felt guilty, as if she'd been caught looking at something she had no business to see. She also didn't know how Helena would react to the picture; perhaps it had been hidden in the box for a reason.

'Simon's doing a run to Southgate's for some lunch – their paninis are fabulous. Did you want him to get you one?'

'Yes, thanks, that would be lovely. Any flavour'll do,' Stella replied. She took a moment to look around the room which, hopefully, by the end of the day would be a great temporary bedroom for Chris to recuperate in. Even with the dark curtains, the pale walls and newly sanded and varnished floor made the room light and airy. It should mean that Chris got a few decent nights' sleep while his ankle was in plaster.

'If we can move the bed in this afternoon, and get it made, when Chris comes home he can let us know what else he needs in here. You know, clothes and stuff.'

'I can't believe how much the team has done in such a short space of time,' Helena said, looking around the room. 'When I think of how hard Chris has worked, single-handed, on this house, and we've pulled together and created something decent in just a few days.' Stella knew that Helena was trying to be diplomatic about her son-in-law's refusal to accept all but the most essential help on this project, but she was grateful for her approval nonetheless.

'Imagine...' she smiled back at Helena, 'if we put our minds to it, we could have the whole house done in a few months!'

Helena laughed. 'I think Chris might like to have a say in it before we make any more ambitious plans!'

'What time do you have to pick him up?' Stella picked up the first of the curtains and headed towards the window. She ascended the ladder and began hooking them to the curtain pole. There was no time to spare.

'Around four o'clock,' Helena said. 'I'll ask a couple of those boys Simon's brought over to bring the bed down – the double from the guest suite on the second floor's the most comfortable, I think, and a damn sight better than the one in his usual room.'

Stella hoped that Helena couldn't see her face flushing at the mention of the guest bed. Chris *had* said it was the best one in the house, so clearly it would be the best to sleep in while he recovered.

Lost in her reverie, she'd totally zoned out from Helena. Snapping back to reality when she realised Helena was speaking to her, she shook her head. 'Sorry,' she said. 'I was miles away.'

Helena was looking at her shrewdly. 'I was just saying,' she replied, 'that I'm so glad Chris has made a friend in you, Stella. I haven't seen him so happy in a long time. Just having someone new in his life has been such a tonic. He's been so alone for the past couple of years.' She raised a hand to cut off Stella's instant response. 'Yes, I know you're just friends, but that's just what he's needed, and I'm glad he's found one in you.'

Sighing with relief when Helena bustled off to organise the logistics of another of the rooms they were renovating, Stella retrieved the photograph from the folds of the other curtain and put it carefully on the windowsill. She wasn't quite sure what to do with it, but since there wasn't any furniture in the room yet, she couldn't exactly put it away. Making a note to herself to be brave and show it to Helena when she returned, she cracked on with hanging the last curtain.

46

Chris was more than ready to come home by the time his release came around. With a heavy cast on his left ankle, and enough painkillers in his possession to anaesthetise a Shire horse, he was keen to get back to Halstead and Gabe. He'd missed his son so much during the time he'd been laid up, and when Gabe had come to visit him, they'd talked more than they had in years. Something about being flat out in a hospital bed made them both lose their reserve, and Chris was keen to keep these new lines of communication open when he got home.

Being away from Halstead had given him a bit of perspective on the house and its challenges, too. He now felt as though he had a clearer sense of how to approach things, and where he needed to enlist some outside help. After an expensive two years, the house was, attic rooms notwithstanding, structurally sound, and before his fall he had actually finished most of the plastering. There were windows that needed replacing, and the heating system definitely needed fixing up, if not ripping out altogether, but he did at least feel as though there might be light at the end of the very dark tunnel he'd been travelling for the past couple of years.

There was something to be said for a change of scene, however traumatic the circumstances. He'd thought a lot about Stella, too, and was kicking himself for being so offhand with her after their night together. There was no need to call things to such an abrupt halt; he liked her company, and their night had been wonderful. Maybe, in time, they'd have become something more than one night of passion if he hadn't shut things down so quickly. Perhaps he'd try to speak to her when he was back on his feet – if she still wanted to speak to him, of course.

He was fully dressed and waiting in the armchair beside his hospital bed when the door to the ward opened and Simon Treloar walked in. Immediately, Chris felt himself bristle, the calm perspectives of the previous minutes flying out of the very clean window beside the bed. Before he could open his mouth to ask what the hell Simon was doing there, Simon, with typical ease, got there first.

'All ready to go? Good. Helena's been caught up with something at home, so I said I'd run you back, if you're okay with that?'

Chris nodded, realising he didn't have much of a choice. A taxi from Magdalene Park to Roseford would be a needless expense with Simon standing right there in front of him, although the prospect of a stilted conversation for the whole of the half-hour drive was making him want to fork out for it. 'Thanks for coming,' he said gruffly. 'I appreciate it.'

Simon smiled briefly, clearly aware that this was a less than ideal situation for Chris, and went to grab the holdall that contained all of Chris's things he'd accumulated during his hospital stay. After he'd officially been discharged, Simon went to get his car from the car park, and in no time, Chris found himself settled back against the deep leather seats of Simon's Range Rover, heading for home.

'Well, this was a bit of bad luck, eh?' Simon said as they pulled out of the car park and onto the main road. 'What on earth were you doing up in the attic in the first place?'

'Looking for something for a friend,' Chris muttered.

'Well, at least they've let you out now.' There was a rather less than companionable silence as the Range Rover devoured the miles, but Chris wasn't inclined to fill it. Ever since Olivia had died, he'd found it increasingly difficult to connect with Simon; he had always been more her friend than his. She'd tried so hard to bring them together, but after her death, Chris had more or less stopped trying. It was just easier, in the very early days, than feeling that dreadful urge to break down every time her name came up in conversation. Even two years on, he still wasn't sure he wouldn't lose it.

'Look,' Simon said suddenly, just before the turning off to Roseford and home. 'I know I probably shouldn't be saying anything, but I think it's only fair to give you some warning, before you walk into something completely unexpected.'

'What is it?' Chris replied. It was nearly time for him to take some more painkillers, and his ribs were beginning to break through the comfortable numbness that the last lot had induced.

'Well, Stella and Helena, and Gabe, of course, wanted to keep it a surprise, but I'm not entirely sure, in your current state, that a surprise is what you need, so I'm coming clean with you now, so you can act the appropriate level of shock and wonder when you actually do get home.'

'Stop beating about the bush, Simon, and just tell me what the fuck's been going on while I've been laid up,' Chris growled. Surprises were the last thing he needed. What he really wanted to do was climb into his own bed, pull the covers over his head and sleep until it was time to take the cast off his ankle.

Simon slowed the car and pulled up into the driveway to Halstead House.

'Stella, Helena and Gabe thought you needed somewhere a bit more comfortable to rest when you came home, so they borrowed a couple of my guys and have spent the past few days slapping some paint on the walls of the back corridor, near the kitchen, and making the rooms more, er, liveable for you and Gabe.'

Chris let out a long sigh. 'And you've been lending a hand too, I suppose?'

'Where I could.'

Chris shook his head. 'Why can't you all just get it into your heads that I want to be left alone? There was no need for any of this. I'm fine.'

'Says the man with pins in his ankle and more cracked ribs than a TGI Friday's joint. Don't be so fucking stubborn.'

They were drawing up to the back entrance to Halstead, and Simon turned to him. 'Are you going to behave yourself?'

Chris said nothing. He was feeling hugely overwhelmed, despite Simon's attempt to prepare him. His very real fear – that Stella, Helena and Gabe's handiwork over the past week would show him up to be the hopeless, useless bastard he feared he was – was taking over, and he could feel his blood running hot and cold in his veins. What was he going to find when he walked through the door, and how on earth was he going to react?

47

'He's here!' Gabe peeked around the corner of the building, and beckoned excitedly to Stella and Helena, who were frantically putting the finishing touches on a High Tea of sandwiches, butterfly cakes and other sugar-laden treats, ready for Chris's return.

'Now, go steady,' Helena said as Gabe started to jump up and down on the spot. 'He's in no fit state to be jumped on and squeezed, remember?'

'I know.' Gabe rolled his eyes, all impatience.

Stella put down the kettle, with which she was filling the teapot ready for the table, and wandered over to the back door, suddenly feeling uncertain as to whether or not she should stick around. She was a friend, but not family. This felt like a very intimate moment, despite her involvement in the work on the rooms over the past days, and she hadn't seen Chris since before this had all happened. Standing behind Helena, she watched as Simon hurried around to the passenger side of the Range Rover, before opening it and then handing Chris his crutches from the back seat. It seemed an age before Chris emerged, and when he finally did make his way around the other side of the car towards the back door, she felt her heart start to race. Clearly still very unsteady on his feet, he looked as though he'd lost another half stone in hospital, and the dark shadows under his eyes told of the physical pain he was still enduring. Frozen to the spot, she nonetheless fought the urge to race up to him and help him into the house, and then throw her arms around him. She'd never felt so protective of anyone in her life.

'Dad!' Gabe exclaimed, unable to help himself any longer. He darted out of the back door and met Chris on the path, stopping short of him by about a foot and just staring.

'It's all right,' Chris said, his voice even more gruff than usual at the sight of his boy. 'You can hug me. I won't break, I promise.'

Stella's eyes filled with tears as Gabe gingerly moved forwards and Chris leaned all of his weight on his good side so he could slide an arm around his son. She caught sight of the grimace on Chris's face as Gabe squeezed him, even though the boy was clearly trying to be as gentle as he could.

'Let's get you into the house,' Simon said, and Stella could tell from the tremor in his voice that he was having trouble speaking, too.

'I can manage,' Chris growled as Simon went to help him with the crutch he'd slipped his arm out of to hug Gabe. Simon caught Stella's eye and raised his eyes to heaven, but left well alone. They began to move into the house, Chris attempting to find his rhythm on the concrete path, and Simon carrying his holdall from the car.

'Welcome home, darling,' Helena said as he reached the door. 'It's good to see you back.'

'Thanks, Helena.' The effort of just getting to the back door had clearly told on Chris, and Stella could see the beads of sweat on his brow. She kept her distance, but when he glanced at her, she smiled.

'Welcome home,' she echoed, feeling ever more superfluous.

'Thanks.'

Helena, clearly sensing tension, gestured to the tea table. 'Well, whenever you're ready, we've made you some easy things to eat, and a good, strong cuppa. But before you sit down, we've got a bit of a surprise for you.'

Stella caught the look that passed between Simon and Chris as Helena spoke, and she knew, instantly, that Simon had spilled the beans on the drive home. Suppressing a flare of irritation that Simon couldn't even keep his mouth shut for the half hour it took from the hospital, she interjected.

'We hope you don't mind, but we were worried about you coming home to, er, less than ideal circumstances, so we've done a bit of work to make things a bit easier for you.'

Chris looked at her, straight in the eye. 'I see.' Even she couldn't ignore the flatness of his tone. 'And what, exactly, have you done to my house?'

'Come and see!' Gabe, who couldn't keep quiet any longer, and forgetting that his dad's hands were both occupied with crutches, pulled on Chris's right hand.

'Steady on, old chap,' Simon admonished, and got a glare from Chris in response.

'I'm fine.'

'Course you are,' Simon tried to correct his mistake, 'but we don't really want to be driving you back to hospital when they've just got rid of you, do we?'

Stella watched Chris's back stiffen and realised immediately that Chris didn't want to feel beholden to Simon in any way. She wanted to interject, but didn't have a clue what to say, to either of them.

Chris was silent again as Gabe led him out of the kitchen and down the long back hallway, where the newly decorated sitting room, bathroom and bedrooms were. She took a deep breath as

Gabe showed Chris each one, telling his father about the things they'd done, and pointing out some of the new additions, such as the second settee from Helena's bungalow in the new sitting room, and the cleaned up tiling in the bathroom, which still had the same, rather dated avocado suite but had been repainted and perked up with the addition of a new shower curtain and towel rail.

Finally, they got to Chris's new, temporary bedroom, and as Gabe opened the door, Stella watched Chris swallow hard as he caught sight of the bed from the first-floor guest suite, and the unearthed William Morris curtains. Then, to her sudden, desperate worry, she saw that one of the decorators, clearly thinking the framed photo of Olivia, Chris and Gabe from the photoshoot had been intended to be hung, had done the honours on the wall opposite the bed, so that the late afternoon sunlight was pouring in and flooding it with radiance.

'Where did that come from?' Chris said hoarsely.

Stella could see, instantly, how blindsided he was by the photograph, and realised that she should have given it straight to Helena when she'd found it.

'It was in with the curtains,' Stella said gently. 'When I hung those, it fell out of the box. I meant to put it somewhere else, but in the rush to get everything finished I must have forgotten.'

Chris, seeming not to have heard her, hobbled over to the photograph on the wall and just stared. 'I'd completely forgotten about that one,' he said, so quietly that even Stella, who was a couple of feet behind him, could barely hear. When he turned back to face them, his face was drained of all colour. 'It was the shoot we did the month before she... before she...' He trailed off, swallowing deeply, and Stella felt her heart shatter. She took a step towards him, but he reflexively stepped back, shaking his head.

'Look,' he said, once he'd regained a little more control. 'It's kind of you all to be here, but do you think you could leave me alone?'

'If that's what you want,' Simon said dubiously. 'We were just trying to help.'

'Well, I didn't ask you to, all right?' Chris snapped back at Simon, meeting his gaze with a sudden defiance. 'This is my house, and I just need some space.'

Stella saw Helena take a step back, stung by his words, and wrap a protective arm around Gabe, as if to spare him from his father's unsteady emotional state. Stella realised, like a bolt from the blue, what seeing that picture placed so baldly on the wall like that, so unexpectedly, must have done to Helena, too. She looked pale, tired, and as if the careful façade of calm was about to give way.

'Come on, everyone,' Helena said, eventually. 'Gabe, let's go and have some tea in the kitchen. There's plenty there if you'd like to stay, Stella.'

But Stella had lost her appetite. 'Thanks, but I'd best give Fitz a walk. He's been a bit short-changed these past few days, while I've been... well...' She trailed off and glanced at Chris, who seemed turned to stone, standing in his newly painted bedroom.

'I'd best get off, too,' Simon said, dropping Chris's holdall onto the foot of the bed. 'Come on, Stella, let's call it a day.'

As Stella hurried out of the room in Simon's wake, she felt a sharp sting of frustration and irritation. Why could Chris not see that they'd spent all of this time doing this for him? Why was he just so fucking ungrateful, or at least, incapable of showing his gratitude to the people who loved him the most? And why did she feel so incredibly hurt because it felt as though he'd rejected her twice?

48

Chris collapsed onto the bed the moment everyone had left the room, and heard his crutches drop onto the newly varnished wooden floors with a clatter. He dimly remembered the crappy patterned aged Axminster that had covered the boards the last time he'd been in the room and, amidst his emotional turmoil, began to realise just what miracles Simon, Helena, Gabe and Stella had worked in such a short time. But that didn't quite counter the feelings of rage and shame, mostly directed at himself, that were bubbling under the surface. If he was such a fucking useless lost cause, what was the point of carrying on? He might as well hand the rest of the house over to them now.

Putting his head in his hands, he wondered if he wouldn't be feeling so blindsided if that photograph hadn't thrown him off balance. Would he have been quite so quick to show his ingratitude to the people who knew him best? Would he have reacted any differently? In his current broken state, he just didn't know.

Waiting for the rage to subside, he was completely unprepared for Simon's return as he crashed back through the door, still in control enough to close it behind him.

'What the fuck is wrong with you?' Simon didn't bother to lower his voice as he strode across the room and rounded on Chris, who was struggling to his feet in an attempt to show that he didn't need any of the oh-so careful preparations for his home-coming. 'Stella's been working her backside off for days to make sure that you and your ungrateful arse would be comfortable when you got back to this house, and you chuck it right back in her face?'

'Get out,' Chris retorted. 'I didn't ask Stella or any of you to do any of this. I just want to be left alone. Is that too much to ask?'

'Right,' Simon said, putting a firm hand on Chris's shoulder and gently, but firmly, pushing him back down to sit on the bed. 'This has gone on long enough. Time you heard a few home truths.' He began to pace up and down the bedroom.

'Home truths?' Chris replied, the sarcasm heavy in his voice. 'What could you possibly know about home truths? You've spent your whole fucking life in denial about the real world, where actual people live.' Long dormant resentments about Olivia's affection for Simon were bubbling to the surface, even though Chris knew he was being unreasonable.

'We're not talking about me,' Simon replied brutally. 'And frankly, it's about time you got real yourself.'

'Oh, fucking spare me,' Chris shot back.

Simon stopped pacing, but his fists were still clenched at his side. He took a deep breath, obviously trying to steady himself. 'Jesus, mate... when are you going to open your eyes and realise that you're pushing everyone away? Is that what you really want? If Helena wasn't living next door, she'd have buggered off, too. It's only the fact that she loves Gabe so much that she's still here.'

'Do you think I don't know that?' Chris's voice rose. 'I get up every day and have to live with the knowledge that Helena's daugh-ter, my wife, is dead, and that I—' he stopped himself just in time.

Chris saw Simon stop dead in his tracks, and felt that familiar, creeping sense of guilt and panic. 'You were saying?' he said quietly.

'Nothing. And I don't want to hear anything more from you, either, so just bugger off.' Chris slumped, the effort of trying not to break down becoming altogether too much. He was tired, and in pain, and, despite all outward appearances, overwhelmed by the kindness that Stella, Simon and Helena had shown in getting the rooms ready for his return to Halstead. So why couldn't he just be thankful? But every time he tried to feel positive, his guilt ate away at him, and turned everything else into ashes in his mouth. What did he have to do to get away from all this?

Simon hesitated, then moved back towards Chris, laying a gentle hand on his shoulder. 'We're here for you, that's all,' he said softly. 'Nothing more, nothing less. We care, Chris. I know that photograph was a shock, but it wasn't intended to hurt or upset you. It was a genuine mistake.'

Chris shook his head. 'It's not really about the photograph, Simon. You know that. It's about so much more than that.' For a terrible moment, he felt as though he wanted to unburden himself to Simon, to share the dreadful guilt he'd carried with him since the night of Olivia's death, but he couldn't. Not to him, not to his dead wife's best friend. He could no more confide in Simon than he could levitate through the hole in the attic floor.

'I can't do this right now, Simon. But I am sorry.'

'Tell that to Stella, Helena and Gabe,' Simon replied bleakly. 'They need to hear it more than I do.' He removed his hand and walked back out of the bedroom door.

Watching him leave, Chris put his head in his hands again. Simon was right – Stella and Helena had achieved more at Halstead in a week than he had in nearly two years; they'd focused on one aspect of it, and made a difference, rather than seeing the project as a large, messy, out of control behemoth. One step at a time, he thought, recalling something that the grief counsellor had told him. That was shortly before Chris had chucked in the sessions. But maybe the counsellor had been right? Maybe the small victories were the important ones.

But, no matter how hard he tried, he still couldn't get past the *what if* scenario that kept replaying itself in his brain. What if he hadn't rowed with Olivia that night? What if he'd agreed to her plans to convert the outbuilding, even though he knew it was out of their reach financially? Or what if he hadn't just lost his rag, and let the idea wash over him, knowing that she'd have changed her mind when she'd thought about it properly? Would he be sitting here now, ribs aching, ankle throbbing, the beginnings of a headache coming, feeling completely broken by the project, but also touched beyond belief by the consideration and patience Helena, Stella and Simon had shown? And would he be more able to accept that kindness, rather than reacting with anger and defensiveness?

Gradually, he became aware of another presence in the doorway. Raising his eyes, he saw Helena standing there, for once waiting for permission to enter his space. She looked painfully uncertain, and he could see the hurt in her eyes. It made him angrier with himself, and he struggled to swallow down that anger, desperately trying not to direct it outwards towards her.

'Was there something that you wanted, Helena?' he said, keeping his voice as calm as he could.

Helena just looked at him for a long moment, until he felt the frustration starting to bubble under the surface. 'Please,' he said. 'I can't do this right now.'

'Funny,' Helena said carefully. 'That's the response I've had from you pretty much every time we've tried to discuss anything more significant than whether or not you need my help with Gabe. Don't you think it's about time you started *doing* things?'

Chris felt the cut of her words, even though they weren't

entirely unexpected. She'd been so careful not to burden him, these past two years. She'd kept her grief apart from his, kept her own counsel, in an attempt, he realised, to allow him to manage his own. But now, he knew that was wearing thin. He'd crossed a line by being so awful about the work they'd all done, simply to help him, and the full force of her recrimination was about to come raining down.

'I'm trying, Helena,' he muttered.

'Are you? Only, from where I'm standing, it looks as though you've all but given up.'

'I fell through a ceiling!' Chris snapped back. 'What do you want me to do?'

'I want...' Helena trailed off and stepped forward to grip the foot board of the bed with two white knuckled hands. She shook her head, and Chris could see just how hard she was trying to keep a lid on her own emotions. Eventually, she raised her eyes to his again.

'I want you to forgive yourself, Chris. Forgive yourself for what you think you did to Olivia.'

'Wh-what?' Chris, blindsided, felt his throat closing and his eyes filling with tears. 'I don't get what you mean.'

'Yes, you do,' Helena said wearily. She moved a little closer, but kept one hand on the table. Chris could see the other hand shaking. 'I don't know what happened between you that night, the night she died, but her death wasn't your fault. It was a horrible, horrible thing, but no one caused it. It could have happened at any time.'

'How can I believe that?' Chris whispered brokenly. 'And how can you?'

'Because it's the truth, darling,' Helena replied. 'And you must forgive yourself.' Tentatively, she reached out and took one of his hands in hers. 'I know you blame yourself. You mustn't.'

'What did Stella tell you?' Chris said, suddenly jerking his hand away. He felt as though he was going under, and he was fighting for breath.

'She didn't tell me anything,' Helena said. 'She didn't have to. I've always known, from the way you've been, that you thought, if you'd done something differently, said something different, she might still be here. And, darling, that's simply not the case. You must believe that, deep down.'

'I should have let her do what she wanted,' Chris said, distraught now, the tears falling. 'I shouldn't have rowed with her that night. If I'd just agreed with her, let it go...'

'You always knew best how to reason with her,' Helena said. 'And losing her after a row, if that's what happened, was a terrible twist of fate – but that's all it was. It wasn't your fault. But it's time to let it go. I can't bear to see you spending the rest of your life like this, angry, guilty, loathing yourself for something that wasn't your doing. Olivia's gone – live *your* life now. That's what she would have wanted.' Helena sat down gingerly on the bed next to Chris, and drew him to her, and although he felt his ribs grumbling in protest, he let her.

'I don't know how to do that,' he whispered into her shoulder. 'I just don't know.'

'You'll work it out, if you try,' Helena whispered back. 'But it's time, Christopher. You just need to try.'

And there, sitting next to Helena, Chris knew, finally, that she was right. If this was Ground Zero, the only way was out. Feeling the release of the guilt he'd carried for so long, knowing that Helena didn't blame him, perhaps now, finally, he could let go.

49

That night, mortified by Chris's negative response to their efforts, Stella tossed and turned in her bed at the gatehouse, to which she'd retreated, although she wasn't quite certain if it was dry enough yet. The low hum of the dehumidifier from down in the kitchen had been somewhat reduced by closing the bedroom door, but at least the noise gave her something other to focus on other than the cacophony of her own thoughts and emotions.

What had been the point of it all, she wondered, again and again? She, Simon, Helena, Gabe and others had worked their backsides off to give Chris a decent homecoming, and he'd thrown it straight back in their faces. His anger, bitterness and disdain for their efforts had been obvious. And while she knew that a lot of his reaction had been because of his own internalised guilt, it didn't make her feel any better. Maybe he was just an angry prick who didn't deserve any of it, she found herself thinking. Maybe, more frustratingly, she just had a thing for lost causes.

And maybe it was time she took a proper break. Morwenna had been nagging her to fly over to France for a few days, to see how the wellness retreat project was progressing; perhaps she'd spend the rest of her leave there. Bugger Chris and his stupid, irrational head. She grabbed her phone, but the battery had died, so she resolved to text Morwenna in the morning instead. For now, all she could do was sleep. She'd been flat out for days trying to make things as nice as they could be for Chris, and she felt absolutely wiped out now she'd stopped.

Don't worry about him, Simon had texted her shortly after she'd left Halstead House. *He's in a lot of pain. When he realises just how hard we've worked, he'll come round.* God, how she wished it was Simon she'd developed feelings for. Although Simon would have come with his own baggage, of course, and she wasn't sure anyone was up to the task of taking on Roseford Hall, the British Heritage Fund and Simon himself. But there was no point in thinking in either direction; Chris had made himself clear, and she and Simon were just friends.

Soon, hopefully, it would be France, a few days of drinking wine and catching up with her mother and trying to forget all this had happened. At least she was back in the gatehouse and didn't have to endure being under the same roof as Chris. She couldn't imagine ever wanting to be in the same space as him again, the way they'd left things.

The moon was rising, cold and steady outside her bedroom window, peering gradually in through the gap in her curtains and casting its silver-white light over her bed. She wondered, against her better judgement, what Chris was doing now. Was he comfortable in his new bedroom that they'd worked so hard to make pleasant for him? Was he lying in bed watching the same moon rise?

A noise from downstairs made Fitz, who was, most uncharacteristically for him, sleeping at the foot of the bed, prick up his ears. He gave a short, irritable bark, disturbed from dreams about squirrels and juicy bones. Stella sat up in bed, also on the alert. There was another creak. The gatehouse was old, and prone to stretching its beams and boards like a dowager countess loosening her stays, especially as the summer nights cooled, but Stella sensed that this was something different. Fitz, obviously feeling the same, jumped down from the bed and padded across the bedroom floor, then whined at the door to be let out.

'All right, all right,' Stella said. 'I'm sure it's nothing, but let's go and take a look.' She swung her legs over the side of the bed, grabbed her black cardigan that she'd hooked over the bedpost and went to open the door. Fitz trotted down the stairs and Stella followed in his wake.

As Fitz skittered down the hallway, nose in the air, sniffing for all he was worth, Stella trailed behind, suddenly nervous. What if she was going to be confronted by an intruder on her doorstep? Fitz might talk a good game, but she doubted he'd stand up to someone intent on robbing the place. But Fitz gave one short bark, and then started to squeak. She headed to the back door, where Fitz had skittered and was now standing, tail wagging ten to the dozen in the dim light that was radiating from the security light outside the door. As she saw who was outside, she breathed out.

There, standing on the kitchen doorstep, still in the T-shirt and shorts he'd come home from hospital in that afternoon, and supporting himself on his crutches, was Chris.

'What are you doing here?' Stella asked. 'It's really late, and you told me to bugger off, remember?'

Chris smiled briefly. 'I know. And I know this is a very stupid thing to do, but I needed to see you.'

'At one in the morning?' Stella retorted. 'Are you completely insane?' His presence, standing there, bold as brass, with the dull roar of the dehumidifier in the kitchen counterpointing the tone of their conversation, was both unsettling and irritating. She was tired, she was still angry with him and she was also wondering how the hell he'd got all the way down the drive without doing himself another injury.

'It couldn't wait.' Chris braced himself on his crutches and took a step towards her. 'May I come in?'

'What, was there something else you wanted to hurl at me? Something else you thought I'd interfered in that you failed to mention this afternoon? Something that couldn't wait until round two in the daylight?' Stella's anger was being exacerbated by her exhaustion. The twin emotions of hurt and frustration, not only from this afternoon, but from his rejection of her after their night together, were bubbling under her skin, waiting to erupt.

'Stella...' Chris closed his eyes. 'I didn't come here to continue that stupid argument I started this afternoon. I came here to say I'm sorry. For everything.' He looked back at her, and she could see his eyes glistening in the moonlight. 'I had no right to attack you, Simon and Helena for trying to help me.' He shook his head. 'I've been such an idiot, Stella.'

'I can't disagree with that,' Stella replied, determined not to give him an inch. She'd buried everything, as usual, in work and other stuff, but standing there in the dead of night with the bloke who'd been responsible for much of her recent frustration was making her patience wear even thinner.

'What can I do to make things right?' Chris asked.

'Oh, I don't know,' Stella retorted. 'How about not knocking on my door in the middle of the night, waking my dog up and then expecting me to accept your apology?' She took a deep breath, but she was on a roll. 'Simon, Helena, Gabe and I... we all worked our backsides off to give you a decent homecoming, to make your life just that little bit easier when you got home, and you chucked it all back in our faces. And you think that turning up now is going to fix that?'

Chris looked shocked, momentarily, at her outburst, but soon recovered his wits. 'Of course not,' he said softly. 'I know it's going to take a lot more than that. But it just felt as though I was, yet again, being trumped by Simon and his bloody *noblesse oblige*. There he is, swanning in from the big house, fixing things I never asked him to fix, bestowing his favours on the plebs just because he can. And expecting me to be grateful.'

'Simon helped out because I asked him to!' Stella retorted, thoroughly fed up of the pissing contest that appeared, still, to be occurring between Chris and Simon. 'He knew you'd be cautious about involving him, but I convinced him it would be a good thing to build bridges, to help, maybe, to bring the two of you back together. And, yes, I know that wasn't my place, but I was also desperate for the help. Helena and I couldn't have done the work on the ground floor on our own in the time – he had a couple of decorators who got the job done, at virtually no cost, quickly and efficiently, and just to help you after you took that stupid tumble through the ceiling.'

'And do you know why I was up there in the first place?' Chris shot back, shifting his weight on the crutches. 'To get another dehumidifier down for the gatehouse, so you could get back home a bit quicker.'

'What, you didn't want me in your house a minute longer than I had to be?' Stella retorted. 'How kind of you.'

Chris's mouth dropped open. 'Of course not,' he said more gently. 'You know I'd have been happy for you to stay for as long as you'd wanted to. I just thought that, after, er, you know, you might want your own space back. I was honestly only trying to help.'

'As were we,' Stella said quietly. 'That's all we wanted to do, Chris. Why can't you just accept that people care about you? Why do you find that so hard to believe?' She purposely ignored his assertion about needing her own space; the part of her brain that still screamed to close the gap between them, even now, just couldn't be trusted to allow her to speak rationally.

'I don't know.' Chris dropped his gaze to his feet and his shoulders sagged. 'Probably because I keep acting like this.' He gave a hollow laugh. 'And don't assume I've just been like this since I lost Olivia... I've always been a bit of an emotionally illiterate twat, really, unable to accept people's good intentions as just that. Losing Olivia just proved, even more, how unworthy of affection I really am.'

Stella let out a long sigh. 'Chris, it's one o'clock in the morning and we're both tired. I can't believe you've hobbled all this way to have this out with me on the night you got out of hospital. Don't you think we should discuss this in daylight?'

'What can I say?' Chris looked back up at her and gave her a crooked smile. 'I'm an emotionally illiterate twat.'

Stella let out a short, choked laugh. 'That level of self-awareness means I won't give you a slap. At least, not tonight.'

'Glad to hear it,' Chris replied, then added, 'does that mean you accept my apology?'

There was a pause between them that felt as though it meant something more than just two desperately wounded people coming to a vague agreement in the darkness, but Stella was too tired to look any deeper. 'Yes,' she sighed. 'Now would you mind letting me get back to sleep?'

'Of course.' Chris took a deep breath and shook his head. 'Why do I feel like getting back up the drive is going to be harder than getting down here?'

Stella was torn between irritation and laughter. 'Would you like me to walk with you?'

Chris, looking sheepish, nodded. 'It seemed like a terrible idea to come down here at this time, anyway, and now it just seems like beyond idiotic.'

'I'd offer you a lift on my bike, but we'd probably both end up breaking more bones,' Stella replied. 'Just wait a sec while I get some trainers on.'

As Stella went to get her shoes, she tried to process what had just happened. How on earth did Chris think that turning up in the middle of the night to apologise would make that apology any easier? Wondering if he'd taken too many of the painkillers the hospital had sent him home with, she laced her trainers and prepared to help him back to his house.

50

The moonlight shone brightly overhead as they made their slow and careful way back up the driveway to Halstead House. Stella, despite her irritation with Chris, was mindful that each movement was an effort for him, and the sheen on his brow as they approached the house gave away his discomfort, despite the painkillers he must still be taking. Just as they were approaching the slight step up to the kitchen, he stumbled. Instinctively, Stella reached out to steady him, and as their bodies touched, and she felt the warmth of him under his T-shirt, and breathed in his scent, she closed her eyes briefly.

She couldn't *just* be friends with him – that much was painfully clear.

'Thanks,' he panted, righting himself with an effort.

'I can't do this,' Stella said, suddenly, in her frustration, feeling close to tears.

Chris looked at her, his eyes searching hers in the moonlight. 'I know,' he said softly. 'I don't think I can, either. Stella...' He trailed off, looking adorably uncertain.

But Stella had heard enough for one night. 'I'm going away for a

few days,' she said, before he could say something they would probably both regret. 'I think it's best if we have some breathing space,
don't you?'

Chris drew in a sharp breath, and then tried to compose his
features into something more neutral. 'Yes,' he said softly. 'Perhaps
it is.'

'Well... goodnight, then,' Stella said, hesitating for the briefest
moment on the doorstep. 'I'll see you around.'

Chris, steadying himself on his crutches, leaned forward and
placed a gentle kiss on her cheek, and her face grew warm with the
contact. 'See you soon,' he murmured as he broke away again.

As she headed back to the gatehouse, Stella let out a long sigh.
Perhaps a few days in France would allow her the space she needed
to get her relationship with Chris into some kind of perspective. At
least having the English Channel between them would mean he
wasn't likely to rock up at her house in the middle of the night
again, she figured. She just hoped that, somehow, getting away from
it all would make it hurt a little less.

* * *

The next morning, Stella rang Morwenna, who was thrilled that
she was intending to visit.

'I've missed you, darling,' she said. 'And the food and wine here
are divine. You'll love it.'

'I've missed you, too,' Stella said, realising that she meant it.
Shortly after she ended the call, she booked her flights, and seven
wonderful days in France were sorted out. Helena was going to have
Fitz, and Gabe had promised to muck in and walk him, so she felt
secure in the knowledge that he'd be well looked after. Helena had
already bought in some pigs' ears for him, so he would be more
than happy with the arrangement. As she handed him over, and

said goodbye to them all, she tried to focus on the days ahead, rather than the fact that, weirdly, having booked the time away, the last thing she now wanted to do was leave.

Simon was giving her a lift to the airport, and he arrived promptly, as she knew he would.

'So your mum's meeting you at the other end, then?' he said as they travelled to Bristol for the flight.

'Yup, or her, er, partner.'

'Do you get on well with him?'

Stella grimaced. 'Kind of. I used to worry that he was only with her for the money, but he's stuck around. And he seems to make her happy.' She paused. 'It's nice to see, really.'

Simon sighed. 'If there's something I've learned over the past few years, it's to seize those moments of happiness while you can. You just never know when they're going to disappear.' He shook his head. 'Sorry. Doing the project for Chris really brought everything back to me.' He swallowed. 'Olivia was my best friend. She'd be horrified if she knew how things have fallen apart between me and Chris. And what her death's done to him.'

Stella shook her head. 'Everyone makes choices, Simon, about how to react to things that hurt us. Do we sink, or do we swim? And, most importantly, if we choose to swim, is there something worth saving ourselves for? It seems to me that Chris isn't quite sure about any of that yet.'

'Well, he bloody well should be!' Simon said vehemently. 'He has a roof over his head and a son and friends who love him. He needs to stop being such a prick about everything and realise what he's got.' He banged the steering wheel in frustration. 'He's going to drive everyone away if he doesn't start living his life again, and thinking of someone other than himself.'

'He fell through the attic floor because he was looking for a dehumidifier for the gatehouse,' Stella said softly. 'He said he was thinking of me.'

'Well, that's progress of a sort, I suppose,' Simon conceded. 'But he's got a long way to go before he rejoins the rest of the human race.'

As they said goodbye at the airport drop off, Stella pondered on Simon's frustration. It was so easy, she thought, to offer advice from the sidelines, but far more difficult to act on that advice when you were the one who needed to.

51

Knowing Stella was gone for a week didn't stop Chris from repeatedly trying to catch a glimpse of her every time he passed the kitchen window, which looked directly down the drive to the deserted gatehouse. After he'd caught himself doing it for the fifteenth time in one morning, he growled out loud and pulled down the blind.

'Everything all right?' Helena, like some benevolent but annoying guardian angel, poked her head through the kitchen door. 'Do you need some more painkillers?'

Only for my heart, Chris thought, unguardedly. Out loud, he simply replied, 'I'm fine.'

'Well, I'm sure you'll be pleased to know that Stella texted me earlier to ask how Fitz was, and she's enjoying her time away. Her mother's place is well on the way to being renovated; I was thinking of booking in there myself next summer for a break.'

'I'm sure you'd have a lovely time,' Chris replied. 'Was there something you wanted?'

'Only to see if *you* needed anything,' Helena said. 'I was going to head out to the supermarket.'

'I'm good, thanks.' Chris forced a smile. 'You and Stella clearly thought Gabe and I wouldn't be capable of doing more than shoving things into a microwave for a while, so there's plenty to choose from in the freezer.'

Helena looked thoughtful. 'You know,' she said softly. 'When David died, I worried for a long time about what would happen if I ever felt myself having... feelings for someone else. What would my friends think? What would Olivia, God rest her, have thought? What, really, would I think of myself? Would I ever not hate myself for falling for another man?'

Chris shook his head. 'I don't know what you're getting at, Helena.'

'Then you're even more dense than I made allowances for,' Helena said briskly. 'So can I suggest you, er, as the Americans might say, get with the programme, or, as Gabe might put it, stop mucking about?' She pulled out a chair and sat down at one end of the kitchen table.

So this is happening, Chris thought. He sighed. 'Tea?'

'Yes, thank you, darling.' Helena regarded him as he poured two cups, and she was clearly itching to help him, but didn't. Chris thought there was a metaphor for his life in there, somewhere.

'So,' Helena began again, once Chris had settled himself at the table, too. 'If you were, perhaps worrying about what certain people in your life might think or feel if you were to, say, decide to begin something new with someone new... I don't think you need to worry.'

Chris shook his head. 'Helena, it's not that simple.'

'Isn't it?' Helena regarded him levelly. 'It seems to me that if Olivia's death could teach you and me anything, it's that we can't take anything for granted. Isn't that a good enough reason to be courageous, to put yourself out there again?'

'Helena,' Chris replied. 'I don't think it's quite right that I should be taking advice about my love life from the mother of my dead wife. You'll forgive me if I don't enter into this conversation?'

'I can forgive you for a lot of things,' Helena said gently. 'But what I won't forgive you for is Olivia's death.' She held up a hand to silence him as he tried to speak. 'Because, darling, it wasn't your fault. And until you learn to forgive yourself, you'll never be able to move on.'

'And who says I want to move on?' Chris retorted, the pain that Helena's words evoked rising to the surface of his skin. 'I'm not ready. For any of this.'

'Then why are you looking down the driveway every five minutes for someone you know isn't coming back until next week?' Helena replied. 'And why did you order a squeaky bone for her dog in your last Amazon delivery if you couldn't care less? And why were you rooting around in the attic for something to help her dry her house out when you knew how dangerous it was up there?'

'Circumstantial evidence, at best,' Chris said, but there was a wryly impressed tone in his voice at Helena's observational skills.

'That's as may be, but you've got some time now to have a good think about what you *really* want. And when she gets back, I suggest you both sit down and talk about it.'

Chris shook his head. 'You're incorrigible.'

'Always.' Helena's eyes twinkled. 'But think about what I've said. Stella could be your second chance. Don't just dismiss her out of hand.'

'I'm scared to death, Helena,' Chris said, his mood changing swiftly from hope to despair. He put it down to the painkillers. 'How can I trust that I won't lose her, too?'

'You can't,' Helena said more gently. 'But isn't the possibility of happiness worth the risk? Sometimes, you just have to take that leap. If that's what you want, of course.'

She took a sip of her tea and grimaced. 'And it wouldn't hurt you to learn how to make a proper cup of tea, either. This is like dishwater, darling.' Standing up, she put her still full mug in the sink. 'Let me know if you do decide you need anything.'

'I will.' Although, with a blinding flash of insight, Chris knew immediately what it was that he really wanted. And it wasn't anything that Helena could buy in Waitrose.

52

After four days in France, Stella was feeling a whole lot calmer about the stalemate with Chris. Her mother and Damon had made her very welcome, and several nights of excellent food and wine had restored her spirits, and her perspective.

She was pleasantly surprised by the transformation Damon and Morwenna had wrought upon the old farmhouse that they'd initially come out to France merely to recce. Over the time she'd been staying with them, she'd seen Damon's devotion both to the house and her mother, and was beginning to see that he truly was committed to both. Gradually, her reservations about him had been broken down.

On the fourth evening, she was sitting out on the patio, a rather rustic construction, but one that had stunning views out to the surrounding countryside, when Morwenna brought her out an early glass of the local rosé wine.

'It's so stunning here.' Stella sighed. 'I can see why you love it.'

Morwenna smiled. 'I have to admit, it makes a nice change from London.' She paused. 'We're hoping to open the retreat properly next year, once we've got the spa facilities installed and had the gardens landscaped.'

'Sounds expensive,' Stella said. Faint alarm bells began to ring. 'Can you afford it?'

'We can if I sell the London house,' Morwenna replied. 'But that's kind of up to you, darling.'

'Why me?' Stella replied. 'The house is yours. You can do what you want with it.'

'Well, yes,' Morwenna conceded, 'but you know I'd never sell without making sure you were provided for. Daddy would turn in his grave if I sold the place from under you.'

Stella smiled. 'Mum, I'm nearly twenty-nine years old. It's sweet that you're thinking about me, but I *can* stand on my own two feet these days, you know.'

'That's not all,' Morwenna said. She paused, regarding Stella speculatively. 'Your residency ends at the end of June next year, right?'

'Yeah,' Stella replied, taking a sip of her wine. She didn't really want to think about it, but when she'd signed up, she knew the post was only for a year.

'We'll be ready to open by then; in fact, we're taking bookings for next summer already.' Morwenna paused, looking out across the garden to the countryside beyond. 'How would you feel about coming to work out here, when your current residency finishes? I'd love to offer some kind of creative courses, be they writing, or painting, and since you've had the experience at Roseford this year, I thought you might like to give this place a trial run when that ends?'

Stella swallowed down the lump that was suddenly forming in her throat. Her mother had undertaken a lot of hare-brained projects over the years, but this time in France really seemed to have grounded her. She had a peace and a calmness that Stella hadn't ever seen before. She wondered if it was France, Damon or a combination of the two that had done it. Whatever it was, it was lovely to see.

'Mum, that's so sweet of you,' she said gruffly. 'And of course I'm happy for you to sell the London house to make the retreat really happen. To be honest, I can't see myself going back to that life anytime soon.'

'So what are your plans for when the residency ends, then?' Morwenna asked. 'I know you've got a while yet, but it's never too early to think about it.'

'This, from the woman who thought nothing of pulling me out of school at a moment's notice and dragging me to obscure places whenever the mood took her?' Stella said wryly.

'Well, I'm getting old,' Morwenna replied, grinning. 'Although Damon makes me feel half my age...'

'TMI, Mum.' Stella rolled her eyes. Her thoughts drifted back to Roseford, Chris, Helena and Gabe, and the friends she'd made since she'd been there. Like Morwenna, until recently, she'd really felt as though she was putting down some roots. If she hadn't been able to stay on at the gatehouse, she'd felt certain, until last week and the set-to with Chris, that she was going to stay in the village, no matter what. Now, she wasn't so sure.

'Can I think about it?' Stella asked. 'It's a lovely offer, Mum, and this place is wonderful. But I need some time to decide.'

'Of course, darling,' Morwenna replied, topping up both of their glasses. 'There's no rush. But from what you've told me, there might not be a lot to stay for once your residency ends. And the weather's far better over here.'

Stella gave a small smile. She'd given Morwenna the broad strokes of what had happened at Halstead, and Morwenna had reacted with predictable disgust, despite Stella's attempt to add a little nuance, to make her understand why Chris had behaved in the way he had.

'Well, whatever happens with this place, Daddy wouldn't want you to be left without a home,' Morwenna was saying, as Stella tuned back into the conversation. 'So even if you don't come out to work here, I'm going to make sure you get some of the proceeds.'

'You don't have to do that, Mum,' Stella replied. 'I'm fine. I'll be fine.'

'That's as may be, but it's only right,' Morwenna said. 'And then you can, at least, put it towards a home of your own, wherever it might be.'

As Morwenna went inside to check on how Damon was doing with dinner, Stella's mind raced. *A home of her own*. The thought both comforted and terrified her.

53

'Are you quite sure about this?' Simon asked, a few days later, as he helped Chris settle himself in the passenger seat of the Range Rover. 'I mean, far be it from me to judge, but you didn't exactly part on the best of terms, did you?'

'Nope,' Chris replied. 'But let's just say I had a flea put quite forcefully in my ear by Helena and for once, I have to concede, she's absolutely right. So, if you wouldn't mind putting the brakes on any *I told you sos* and *we were right all alongs*, that would help a lot.'

'Fair enough,' Simon said, but he glanced at Chris as he got into the car. 'Although is bringing Fitz strictly necessary? Don't get me wrong, I love him, but if he leaves hair all over my boot, you're cleaning it out.'

'What, the lord of the manor getting car proud?' Chris snorted. 'I thought dog hair and dead pheasants were par for the course for your lot.'

'Oh, get that bloody chip off your shoulder, will you?' Simon snapped. 'It never sat well with Olivia and it sits even less well with me.' He gunned the engine as he turned out of Halstead's driveway, his irritation with Chris communicating itself from the way he was driving.

'Well, you'd know,' Chris retorted. 'I mean, Olivia told you pretty much everything, didn't she? Probably more than she told me.'

'Oh, don't be so daft,' Simon scoffed. 'She was my best friend, but she *loved* you. More than anything. And one thing she did tell me was that, if she ever wasn't around to do it herself, she was relying on me to give you a talking to if you needed it.'

'Oh, and I suppose you're more than happy to do that now?' Chris retorted. 'Well... go on, then. Let me have it.'

Simon slowed down and pulled into a lay-by. Switching the engine off, he turned towards Chris. 'I loved Olivia,' he said quietly. 'And if she'd chosen to settle down with me, I think I could have made her happy.' He held up a hand as Chris started to interrupt. 'But the minute I saw her with you, I knew that you could give her true happiness, because she loved you so much more. I made peace with that, and was happy to see her become your wife, and then a mother to Gabe.'

'That's big of you,' Chris snapped back, to hide his shock. Simon had never admitted to him just how deeply he'd felt for Olivia, and how much her death must, too, have hurt him.

'Let me finish, please.' Simon drew a deep breath. 'Stella can never replace Olivia. No one could. But it's clear to everyone that she could make you and Gabe happy again, if you'd allow her. And you, despite her better judgement, I'm sure, could make her happy, if she's prepared to allow you to.'

'Why do you think I'm getting my backside to the airport to meet her?' Chris growled. 'The pep talk's a bit late, Simon.'

'Then take it as my blessing,' Simon said, after a pause. 'I know you and I have never really seen eye to eye; that you tolerated me because I was Olivia's best friend. And perhaps, at times, I did try to undermine you because I felt jealous. But if losing her has taught me anything, it's that friends matter. Even if you and I wouldn't have chosen to be friends, perhaps that's what we've ended up being, despite everything.' He shook his head. 'And friends want their friends to be happy, don't they?'

Chris opened his mouth, realised he couldn't actually speak for the lump in his throat, and closed it again. Swallowing, taking a moment to compose himself, he looked back at Simon, who was, himself, staring steadfastly at the steering wheel.

'I appreciate that, Simon,' Chris said eventually. 'And yes, despite everything, I do consider you a friend. I'm sorry I've not acknowledged that over the past couple of years.'

'I'll let you off, under the circumstances.' Simon gave a hoarse laugh. 'Now, shall we get on? Stella's plane's coming in soon, and it would be good to be there to meet her.'

* * *

Stella looked out of the small, slightly misty window of the EasyJet plane as it began its descent into Bristol and let out a deep breath. She wasn't keen on flying and would have preferred to go by ferry, but hadn't fancied the long trek back from Poole or Portsmouth, so needs must. Her mother had given her a lot to think about, and as the runway came into view, she was no closer to deciding what to do.

Morwenna's proposal had been an attractive one; become the Writer in Residence for her wellness retreat after the Roseford post had ended, and start a new life in France with them. For all of Stella's doubts that Morwenna and Damon would make a go of it, the retreat was a wonderful place, and now they were going to sell the London house, their own future seemed assured. But where did that leave her? She'd have her fair share of whatever money was made from the house sale, but she'd still need to think about what happened after the Roseford Hall residency ended. Did she want to go and live with Morwenna again? Would it be a step backwards after the joy and freedom of this year? Or would it be another new beginning, in the south of France, with new opportunities galore? And what would she be leaving behind?

Despite herself, her mind drifted back to Chris. He'd been so reluctant to take things any further with her, even though she knew he felt the attraction between them. She couldn't keep pining after someone she couldn't have for the rest of her life. She wasn't going to fall into the trap of romanticising their situation, just because she also loved his son, his mother-in-law and his house. Not when he couldn't give her what she needed him to. Shaking her head, running a hand irritably over her eyes, she tried to focus on the sensations of descent into Bristol, seeing the patchwork fields and cotton wool sheep coming more sharply into focus, crossing the liquorice laces of the M5 motorway and the cars, no bigger than a Scalextric set, threading along its lanes. She might love the English countryside now she was in it, but was it enough?

Thankful she'd only packed a small carry-on bag for her break, getting through Passport Control in Bristol was a breeze, and as she went through the doors into the Arrivals hall, she looked for Simon, who she'd called when she knew what time she was coming in. Scanning the people waiting, she couldn't see him, and reached down for her phone to give him another call, just in case he'd got caught in traffic or was having trouble parking. As she was finding his number, she jumped as a wet black nose was thrust into her hand, nearly causing her to drop the phone.

'Fitz!' she exclaimed as she immediately recognised her beloved dog. 'What are you doing here? I'm pretty sure they don't allow dogs at the airport, unless they're sniffing out drugs.'

'I told them he was my support dog,' a gruff voice replied from off to her left. 'They took one look at my crutches and decided I must be telling the truth.'

This time, Stella did drop her phone, and Fitz glanced down at the floor, a quizzical look on his face.

'What are *you* doing here?' Stella asked.

Chris drew a little closer. 'I hitched a lift with Simon. He's just parking that vast Range Rover somewhere.'

'Why?' Stella asked.

'Well, drop off's limited to ten minutes, so—'

'No.' Stella shook her head. 'You know that's not what I meant. Why are you here?'

Chris looked, for a moment, endearingly uncertain, but Stella couldn't help noticing that something had changed about him. The haunted look in his eyes seemed to have been replaced with something softer, something more settled, despite his visible nerves at seeing her.

'Fitz has missed you this week,' he said softly. 'And so have I.' He drew a little closer to her, mindful of the people hurrying past, and reached forward to take her hand. 'I've been so scared, Stella. Scared to admit how I feel about you, and scared that if I do, something will happen to take you away. I know I don't deserve it after the way I've treated you, but I'd like a second chance, if you're willing to give it.'

Stella looked down at their joined hands, and then up into Chris's eyes, which were filled with tenderness. 'I don't know what to say,' she said softly. 'This is absolutely the last thing you said you wanted, and now you've come to meet me and suddenly you want another chance?' She shook her head. 'What if you wake up tomorrow morning and you've changed your mind again? I don't want to keep being messed around, Chris.'

Pain flared behind Chris's eyes, but it was gone again in an instant. He took another step closer to her. 'I promise you,' he said, his voice husky. 'I mean it. Simon, Helena and Gabe have made me see what a total dick I've been to you, in pushing away what might make me happiest in the world. I don't want to keep doing that out of some misplaced sense of duty to Olivia. She'll always be in my heart, but it's time to move on.'

Stella smiled briefly. 'Simon's given you a talking to? And you didn't punch him in the face, I hope?'

'We came to an understanding,' Chris replied wryly. 'And although there's a way to go, we thrashed out some things that have been festering for a while. But I don't want to talk about Simon.' He let go of her hand and raised his own to her cheek, and Stella, despite her doubts, leaned into the caress. She'd missed him too. Suddenly, she wondered whether she did want to go and live with Morwenna and Damon again, no matter how gorgeous the place was in France, or whether she wanted to stay in Roseford; be a part of Chris's life and village life. Even if that meant taking a non-writing job after the residency had finished, perhaps Roseford was where she really wanted to be.

'What do you want to talk about, then?' Stella said softly.

'Us,' Chris replied. 'You and me. The future.' He shook his head. 'For the first time in a long time, I can see things so clearly now, Stella. I know what I need to do. And I want you there, by my side, to be a part of that, if you want to be.'

Stella drew a deep breath. 'I'd like that. But do you think we can go somewhere a little quieter to work out exactly what that means? Security seem to be getting suspicious that Fitz might not be a support dog!'

Sure enough, there were two airport attendants heading their way, so, gathering up Fitz's lead, which Chris had dropped when he'd taken Stella's hand, they headed quickly out of the terminal and towards the car park.

A sharp toot from a car horn drew their attention, and there was Simon, grinning from his Range Rover.

'All sorted, then?' he asked as he pulled up next to them.

Stella glanced at Chris. 'To a point,' she said, giving him a quick smile. 'But let's get home, shall we?'

As they hurried to strap themselves into the Range Rover, once Fitz was safely ensconced in the boot, Stella smiled as Chris got into the back with her and slid a warm hand into hers. There was a *lot* to talk about, she knew, but perhaps this was the start of something that, eventually, they could call a new beginning. Feeling her heart flutter as he raised her hand to his lips and kissed it, and seeing Simon's knowing glance in the rear-view mirror, she hoped with all of her heart that it would be.

EPILOGUE
THE FOLLOWING SUMMER

'Are we all set? The first guests will be here in an hour,' Stella called down the Rogues' Dining Room to Gabe, who was putting the finishing touches on the series of desks and easels that had been strategically placed around the space, but could easily be manoeuvred if the writers and artists wished to work in different places during their stay. This truly was a project that had taken its sweet time to come to fruition, and now that Halstead House Artists' and Authors' Retreat was about to open its doors, Stella felt a sense of excitement, but also trepidation.

'Everything all right up here?' Chris wandered up the corridor, having appeared from the newly restored staircase, whose rods shone honey gold in the early summer sunshine. 'Is there anything else that needs sorting out?'

'We're all good, thanks,' Stella replied. 'Has Niall delivered the fresh bread for lunch, and the other deli stuff?'

'Yup,' Chris said. 'He sent his new apprentice, Carmen, with everything in the van about an hour ago. I've just got to make it look presentable in the dining room when the time comes.'

Stella reached for Chris as he drew closer, and she marvelled, yet again, at the transformation, not just of the house, but of the man who owned it, in just under a year. He'd put on a few pounds, and now looked healthy and rested, and as if some great, immovable weight had been miraculously lifted from his shoulders. In all senses, it really had. His face and arms were tanned from working so hard with the landscape gardener on the grounds during the spring, which were also looking spectacular, and back to their former Victorian glory. A dark blue and white checked shirt, rolled to just below his elbows, complemented his colouring, and smart dark blue jeans and trainers completed the look.

'I think we're all ready,' Stella murmured, tilting her face upwards for a kiss. As their lips met, Gabe, who'd finished checking over the desks and easels, made vomit noises from behind them.

'Give it a rest, squirt,' Chris replied good-naturedly. 'We're allowed a quick snog before the guests arrive.'

'Yeah, but do you *have* to do it when I'm here?' Gabe replied. 'I mean, I'm at school all day. Can't you just do it then?'

Now that the house was pretty much sorted out, Gabe had moved schools to the excellent state secondary on the outskirts of Roseford. It had been the right time to move, and Gabe was very happy there. It also meant that he could walk to school, and he'd made some friends who lived nearby, so he was often to be found hanging out in the local park with them after school, rather than spending nights far from home. Both Chris and Gabe far preferred this arrangement and Helena, too, was glad to see more of her grandson during the week.

Stella reached out her other arm to Gabe, who allowed her to pull him in close for quick hug before wriggling away again, muttering 'gross' under his breath, and running back down the Rogues' Dining Room, with a grin.

'What time does your mother get here?' Chris asked.

'Six o'clock tonight.' Stella grimaced. 'I tried to put her off, on opening day, but she was quite insistent. She said it's the only week she can get away, as her own retreat is fully booked from next week until early October.'

'It'll be fine,' Chris soothed. 'Helena's primed to ply her with booze if she interferes too much and, frankly, if it keeps Helena out of the way, then all the better.'

'Ssh!' Stella chided. 'You know we couldn't have done this without her.'

'I do know that.' Chris looked down at her and smiled. 'And I couldn't have done this without you.' He placed a gentle kiss on her lips, which made her smile even broader.

'It's been a team effort,' Stella replied, easing back slightly, in case Gabe returned. 'And it's everything we could have wanted.' She paused. 'I think Olivia would have approved, too.'

Chris smiled. 'I think she would.'

Stella had got to know Olivia well in the year she'd been working with Chris to bring the retreat to life. The revelations Chris had made to her during their first night together had, in the end, been a kind of catalyst for him to come to terms with her death, and his own new life. Little touches around the house alluded to Olivia; from the small silver-framed photos on the mantelpiece in the drawing room to the cushions in the master guest suite that had been made from fabrics in her favourite colours. Each guest room had its very own framed canvas of one of her works, hopefully to inspire the artists and writers who stayed there in the future. Coming to terms with her loss, celebrating her life and her talent, were things that helped Chris and Gabe to move on, but also allowed Stella to process her own role in their lives.

The renovations over the past year, with help from Stella's share of the proceeds from the house in London, had really turned Halstead House into the perfect retreat. Halstead had been restored to its former glory, making it a family home and securing its future as a business. Olivia's vision had merged with Stella's to make it a wonderful, inspiring place for writers and artists to explore their creativity, and the moment the bookings had gone live on their brand-new website, they'd been inundated. The Rogues' Dining Room was the centrepiece in a beautiful restoration, and Stella was looking forward to leading the first groups who were coming to stay. A local artist from the next village was going to be on hand for extra guidance, and it was set to be a memorable time for all of them.

Stella and Chris, as they had done many, many times on this long, complicated journey of theirs, turned and looked out of the tall windows that overlooked the gardens, the valley, and stretched to the hills beyond.

'It's all about finding home, in the end, isn't it?' Stella murmured.

'And finding the people you want to share that home with,' Chris replied. 'I think you can say, definitely, that we've both done that.'

Fitz, from his basket in the corner of the Rogues' Dining Room, put his head on his paws and sighed in contentment.

ACKNOWLEDGMENTS

My excitement at starting a new series of novels is only equalled by my trepidation. Will I be able to create a world that readers will love? Will my characters be able to pull those readers into their stories? And will the new place nestle into my heart as much as my previously invented worlds? Well, in Roseford, I hope the answer is yes! I've drawn on several places to create Roseford, including the wonderful villages of Montacute and Lacock, and the ramshackle elegance of Tyntesfield, all of which are owned by the National Trust. If you've visited these places, or if you intend to visit them, I hope you will notice some of the details I've borrowed to bring Roseford to life. The Long Gallery, for example, is Montacute House's most wonderful feature, and one I couldn't help borrowing for this novel.

Likewise I drew on the real life inspiration of Kildare House, in my home village, to paint the picture of Halstead House, and I hope, like Halstead, Kildare will once again have the chance to shine, restored to its former glory in the near future.

As ever, writing a novel is a team effort, and I'm so grateful to my wonderful agent, Sara Keane, my fabulous editor, Sarah Ritherdon, and the amazing team at Boldwood Books, whose continued support as I embark on this new series of novels has been second to none.

Also, to the friends and family who tolerate my authorial tunnel vision when I'm embedded in a project, thank you. If writing this book in particular has taught me anything, it's how lucky I am to have you all. A special shout out to Carly and Rob Kilby, whose gorgeous dog, Dyce, provided the inspiration for Fitz.

Finally, to you, my wonderful readers, thank you so much for embarking on this new journey with me. I hope you've loved your introduction to Roseford as much as I've loved writing it, and I hope you'll stay with me for the next novels, too!

MORE FROM FAY KEENAN

We hope you enjoyed reading *New Beginnings at Roseford Hall*. If you did, please leave a review.

If you'd like to gift a copy, this book is also available as an ebook, digital audio download and audiobook CD.

Sign up to Fay Keenan's mailing list for news, competitions and updates on future books.

http://bit.ly/FayKeenanNewsletter

A Place To Call Home, another heart-warming read from Fay Keenan, is available to buy now.

ABOUT THE AUTHOR

Fay Keenan is the author of the bestselling *Little Somerby* series of novels. She has led writing workshops with Bristol University and has been a visiting speaker in schools. She is a full-time teacher and lives in Somerset.

Visit Fay's website: https://faykeenan.com/

Follow Fay on social media:

facebook.com/faykeenanauthor

twitter.com/faykeenan

instagram.com/faykeenan

bookbub.com/authors/fay-keenan

ABOUT BOLDWOOD BOOKS

Boldwood Books is a fiction publishing company seeking out the best stories from around the world.

Find out more at www.boldwoodbooks.com

Sign up to the Book and Tonic newsletter for news, offers and competitions from Boldwood Books!

http://www.bit.ly/bookandtonic

We'd love to hear from you, follow us on social media:

facebook.com/BookandTonic

twitter.com/BoldwoodBooks

instagram.com/BookandTonic

.

Printed in Great Britain
by Amazon

79626040R00183